SWORDS, SORCERY, & SELF-RESCUING DAMSELS

Published by Clockwork Dragon, LLC
www.clockworkdragon.net

First printing, April 2019

Swords, Sorcery, & Self-Rescuing Damsels is a work of fiction. People, places, and incidents are either products of the authors' mind(s) or used fictitiously. No endorsement of any kind should be inferred by existing locations or organizations within it.

No men were harmed in the making of this book.

ISBN: 978-1-944334-26-0

SWORDS, SORCERY, & SELF-RESCUING DAMSELS

EDITED BY

LEE FRENCH & SARAH CRAFT

Clockwork
Dragon
Books

EDITOR'S NOTE

The term "damsel in distress" originated in the late 17th century. The generally accepted meaning is a person (usually a woman) in some form of peril who requires an outside party to rescue them. Such renderings often reduce women to one or two dimensions, characterizing them as weak and useful as nothing more than a prize for defeating the enemy.

This depiction sucks.

Heroism is more than brute force, luck, or a dashing smile. Strength comes from many places other than muscles. I'd like to hope that my son recognizes this simple fact, and stories are an amazing way to help make that dream come true.

Within these pages, ladies display cleverness, determination, compassion, curiosity, and more. They may need help, but they require no rescue.

—Lee French

TABLE OF CONTENTS

Jody Lynn Nye lists her main career activity as "spoiling cats." She lives near Chicago with three feline overlords, Athena, Minx, and Marmalade; and her husband, Bill. She has published more than 50 books, including collaborations with Anne McCaffrey and Robert Asprin, and over 165 short stories. Her latest books are *Rhythm of the Imperium* (Baen), *Moon Tracks* (with Travis S. Taylor, Baen), and *Myth-Fits* (Ace). She teaches the annual DragonCon Two-Day Writers Workshop, is a judge for the Writers of the Future Contest, and writes book reviews for Galaxy's Edge magazine.

FALCON'S APPRENTICE

JODY LYNN NYE

"**M**arie-Jeanne!" Father called.

Marie-Jeanne bound the last cord around her soft boot top and tied a firm knot, then rushed out of the door of the mews into the cold spring air. Her brown braids danced on the shoulders of her gray woolen smock.

Father looked impatient, his thinning black hair even more disarrayed than usual. He leaned on his crutch for strength. The Comte de Velay, a bulky man who would have made two of Father and Marie-Jeanne combined, loomed over the much shorter falconer. His broad, bearded face was set in a grimace. On his wrist, killer talons gripping the leather gauntlet, stood Mistinguette, the valuable young kestrel on which both Father and Marie-Jeanne had been lavishing endless attention and care. The huge white bird turned its head toward the sound of her flapping footsteps. Her fierce eyes were covered by the embroidered blue leather hood.

It seemed that the blindfolding had not been enough to keep the kestrel from striking. Blood ran down the side of the Comte's face. A gouge the shape of Mistinguette's beak almost beside the liege lord's eye told the tale. Marie-Jeanne ran for the box of clean lint and the earthenware jar of Frere Benedict's salve that they kept in a chest just inside the door.

"You told me she would be ready by today! Why is she not enchanted for obedience?" the Comte demanded, as Marie-Jeanne stretched her meager height up to wipe away the blood and dab the green paste on the wound. He hissed at its contact, but the pain would subside in moments, as the holy salve healed swiftly. Nothing would be left but a tiny scar.

"As I have explained, my lord, to instill obedience in a hawk is to damage its natural instincts toward hunting," Father said, bobbing his head humbly. No matter how many times he had told the lord that, it did not remain in de Velay's memory. "It must keep its wild tendencies. If it becomes too tame, it sees prey animals as its equal, not its inferiors. She is ready, I swear to the good God."

The Comte thrust the bird back toward Father. "If it bites me again, I shall strangle it, whether it is worth two hundred livres or not!"

"Perhaps, then, it should not go out today," Father said, gently touching the kestrel on the backs of her legs to make her step up onto his gauntlet. "I will get your goshawk Remy ready for you."

"No! His grace the Bishop of Mende joins me on the field today. He brings his own falconer and his white gyrfalcon. I want to show him I have as fine a bird as he. The kestrel comes."

"Yes, my lord," Father said, in resignation. He thrust Mistinguette toward his daughter.

Marie-Jeanne accepted the bird on her unprotected arm and withdrew well away from the Comte's reach. She cooed calming words in the kestrel's ear and stroked her soft, speckled breast feathers. Mistinguette's wings bated slightly, then settled into place. The hawk liked her, though its way of showing it did was kind of painful. Marie-Jeanne tried not to cringe at the sharp talons' grip poking pinpoint holes in her skin through her woolen sleeve. She didn't dare cry out, or the Comte might decide the hunting bird wasn't worth his time after all. Father was the one who knew all the enchantments to communicate with and guide his charges, not she. He and the journeymen were vague when she asked them what the training entailed. Someday she would learn all of the secrets of falconry, but she had not yet!

"Prepare it to depart," the Comte said, grandly. "That and the minor birds for my sons and the ladies. We leave at first light. Coneys are running wild across the barley meadows. It should be a good day's hunting."

"Yes, my lord," Father said, his head keeping time with his words. "I am not yet fit after my fall during the last outing, my lord. Er, may we not await my son Emile's return? He ought to be back today after bringing your kindly gift of the white merlin to the Bishop's palace at Chartres?"

"You have other apprentices," the Comte said, dismissively, without a care for Father's injury, though Marie-Jeanne knew that his carelessness was the reason for it. "Send one of them."

Father hesitated. He and Marie-Jeanne knew that though they had been trained in the spells and cantrips of falconry, none of the young men in his employ dared get near Mistinguette.

"My daughter will go," Father said, projecting an assurance that Marie-Jeanne was sure he didn't feel. "She will do well."

"That girl?" the noble asked, his disdainful gaze searching her from her thick brown braids down the heavy woolen smock and hose to the soles of her worn leather shoes. Like Father, she was small-boned, and looked years younger than her fourteen summers. "I have seen her running in the fields like a wild animal herself. Has she ever aided on a hunt? There are dangerous creatures out there that also hunt rabbits."

"She will do well," Father said again. "Only wait here a moment while I kit her up."

Limping on his crutch, he dragged Marie-Jeanne into the mews. "Shoes tied? Yes," he said, pulling bags and boxes down from shelves on the wall opposite the falcons' perches. "You'll need a hat for the sun and a bag for the kills. You're strong. You can carry plenty of coneys and small game birds. Let the men take on anything larger. Wear a heavy cloak. It looks as if it might rain. Draw the hawk under cover with you. Her temper will fray if she gets wet."

"Why me?" Marie-Jeanne asked, although she took her cloak down from the wooden peg on the wall. "The day is fine. I could gather strawberries for Mother. Or mushrooms. I know where there are morels."

"I need you to go. Today is not a day to run free. Do your duty!"

"Send Simeon or Pierre. They have experience."

"Mistinguette will not behave for them," Father said simply.

"Father, this is the season of La Bête!" Marie-Jeanne protested. Stories of the terrifying shaggy, fanged beast that was part boar, part wolf, who tore apart the unwary and unholy, had kept her up at night after many a bonfire party. "I heard that she was spotted again in Gévaudan, and left a body torn apart, but with no blood in it."

"You know the comte does not believe in such legends," Father said. "Perhaps the bishop's prayers will keep the monster away." He shook his head and ran a knobby knuckle down Mistinguette's feathery breast. "The best defense you have is here. Follow her lead. She will guard your life."

3

"So, have you heard the latest rumors, my lord?" the comte asked his honored guest as they trotted along together. "La Bête has struck again, it seems."

"Pah!" the clergyman said, waving a gorgeously gloved hand. Clean-shaven, the bishop had a long, narrow face with high cheekbones and a thin, pointed nose with arching nostrils that made him look disapproving even when he smiled. "The court of inquiry is already looking into it. The man who was killed was unpopular and rumored to have cheated many of his customers. You will see, it will turn out to be one of those. No supernatural beasts stalk here!"

"But, my lord bishop," put in Comtesse de Velay, "there have been many incidents of brutal killings, including innocent children, all torn apart as if by a beast."

The bishop crossed himself. The rest of the party followed suit immediately.

"We fear the wolf and the boar for a good reason, my lady," he said. "One does not have to look to Satan. Those poor children might have fallen afoul of a real beast. And we are far from Gévaudan."

The nobles' huntsmen and servants shook their heads, careful to keep their skepticism out of sight of their lords. The bishop might be anointed by God and protected by divine hands, but the rest of them feared what Satan might have set loose on Earth for the rest of them.

Marie-Jeanne had no time to tremble or look around for the fabled man-killing monster. In the trail of the nobles on their great horses, she sat astride a donkey saddled with nothing more than a couple of flour sacks padded with straw. She had to admit how fine her lord looked in his red hat and surcote, astride the steady chestnut stallion that was almost as red. The horse's saddle looked large enough to sail on and glinted with silver. The saddlecloths were embroidered with the crook and sword symbol of Velay. The bishop had the wheatsheaf of Languedoc on his garments and his dark bay horse's trappings, but in gold and surrounded by a shield to show his status as the overlord of the province. The ladies and gentlemen all looked so impressive in their silks and fur-lined cloaks. Servants leading or riding beasts of burden carried baskets of food and jugs of wine for an open-air feast when the sun reached its height. A pack of fine hounds milled around them, yelping to one another in excitement. Marie-Jeanne was both honored and terrified to be in their number.

With every bounce on the rough road, Mistinguette's claws tightened on Marie-Jeanne's wrist. Even the thick gauntlet she now wore to protect herself from the kestrel's talons only blunted the points, not the fierce grip. She would have bruises, she knew it. The thought of punishment by her father and the hope of a gift of money and a share of the kills from the Comte or the Bishop were all that kept her from slowing down so that the hunting party would disappear out of sight. On her back flapped the enormous leather bag to hold prey. At her hip, she had a small creel containing the lure that would attract Mistinguette back should she stray after being flown. It was baited with pieces of pigeon, which were beginning to stink in the growing warmth of the day. The kestrel could smell the meat and tried to climb down from Marie-Jeanne's glove to get at them. Only the hanging jesses in the girl's fist kept her from getting away.

Spring in the Languedoc came earlier than it did to most of France. Tiny, yellow-green leaves festooned the dark brown branches of beech trees. The oaks still stood proudly naked, their shaggy, gray-brown bark silver in the slips of sunlight that penetrated through the thick forest. They were making for the barley fields, where the growing grain had already attracted pests. While the hunt would cut down on the number of rabbits, it would also trample a good portion of the crop. Father's friends grumbled, saying they did not know which was worse. Flies swarmed to her sweating flesh. With one hand for the reins and one for the hawk, she had to ignore the itchy bites.

"Ho!" called the hunt master. Marie-Jeanne kicked the donkey to hurry it to join the rest of the group. As soon as she could stop, she scratched her bites. The donkey lashed his tail to rid himself of the flies.

They had paused on the outskirts of a field, next to a small house. The farmer and his family bowed and scraped apprehensively. The farmer's wife offered small beer to the hunters to refresh them after their ride. The Comte made a face, but he didn't spit it out. If the bishop had not been nearby, he surely would have. It was too early in the year for new wine, and peasant beer often tasted bitter.

True to the report, brown rabbits ran to and fro among the bright shoots of barley. The Comte grinned.

"My lord bishop, would you care to make the first strike?" he asked.

The bishop bared his big white teeth. They made him look rather like a hare himself.

"I shall. Robert! Bring me Matilde!"

The bishop's falconer sprang off his small brown horse and presented himself at his master's saddlebow. He held up the shimmering white gyrfalcon to his lord. Before the Comte could make a similar cry, Marie-Jeanne clambered awkwardly from the donkey's back and dragged it behind her as she hurried to present Mistinguette to his gauntleted wrist. With a quick swipe, she removed the kestrel's hood. She got a grudging glance of approval for her pains. So far, so good. All she wanted from the day was not to disgrace herself or her father.

"Smooth and easy, my lord," she said. "She's had as much jostling as she can take."

"I know, I know!" the comte grumbled.

The bishop lifted his hand to the sky. The gyrfalcon needed no more urging. She opened her great wings and rose up like an angel toward the blue heavens.

All the smaller birds in the field scattered like ashes in the wind. The rabbits continued their frolicking, unaware of death hovering above. The white falcon held in the sky for a moment as if she was painted there, then dove straight for the biggest, plumpest coney. An audible crack sounded as the hawk broke its prey's neck. The huntsman jumped down from his horse to retrieve the dead rabbit and present it to the bishop.

At the shock of the feathered killer, the rest of the herd scrambled for safety. Little was to be found as the rest of the party released their hawks in pursuit. Smoothly, the Comte raised his arm and loosed Mistinguette into the air. She floated away like a leaf. Lady de Velay sent a kiss after her favorite merlin. The tiny bird arrowed after the lead rabbit, veering off just as the beast leaped into a hole at the field's edge. A dozen of its kin followed it, vanishing like drops of water down a drain.

At once, the dogs went after it, digging at the dirt and warbling like out of tune choristers. Marie-Jeanne smiled. The rabbits would be miles away in a minute, vanished along the endless corridors of their warren.

"Heel, sirrah! Heel!" The huntsman called in the dogs, who had caught nothing. But Mistinguette fluttered her pale wings on the air, and dove into the barley, halfway across the field. She didn't come up again.

"A strike, by Jesu!" the Comte said, with a laugh. "Go get it, girl."

"Yes, my lord!" Marie-Jeanne said. With a look for apology at the farmer, she sidled into the young grain.

It didn't do to charge in upon a hawk with its kill. One had to approach the bird carefully. Marie-Jeanne neared the row where she heard the sound of satisfied peeping. She parted the stalks of grain. Mistinguette looked up at her with fierce eyes, standing on the belly of the rabbit she was disemboweling.

"Now, now, my chick," Marie-Jeanne said in the most soothing voice she could. Father always said that hawk magic began with eyes, hands, and voice. She began to stoop low and eased a gloved hand toward her charge. "Come to me, then. You'll get your treat. Let me have the rabbit." She felt in the lure pouch and brought out a chunk of pigeon flesh. "Look here! This is for you."

She extended the gobbet of meat toward the fierce beak. Mistinguette snatched it from her gloved fingers, leaving a gouge in the leather. Marie-Jeanne took the kestrel onto her wrist and hastily stuffed the rabbit into her bag. Flowing blood was said to attract La Bête. She glided out of the barley field and presented the hawk to the Comte.

"A fine catch," the bishop praised him, as Marie-Jeanne displayed the dead coney. "A bit smaller than mine, though." The huntsman took charge of the prey, handing it off to one of his apprentices. Marie-Jeanne curtseyed and drew back.

The Comte smiled, showing his teeth through his beard. "The day is young." He hefted the falcon so that her wings flipped. "She will catch many more fat rabbits for me today."

Mistinguette shrieked in protest at the mistreatment.

"Hand to her strings, my lord!" Marie-Jeanne cried, alarmed. "She's going to bolt!"

Her warning came too late. Before the comte could grab for the jesses, the kestrel shot away from him and flew into the nearest treetop.

"Come back here!" he bellowed. "I swear, I will kill that hawk! Get her, girl!"

Marie-Jeanne pressed her lips together. No word of criticism must escape them, but he knew how flighty the kestrel was! Keeping Mistinguette in plain sight, she went out into the open and took the lure from her bag. On a twelve-foot cord, the leather bag had been made to resemble a flying dove, but years of being stooped upon by countless birds of prey had torn it into a figure more like a blackened hedgehog. Still, the hawks recognized it and came to it, most of the time. Marie-Jeanne played out the cord and began to swing the lure in a wide circle. Mistinguette's head went up. She saw it, of course she did, but the stubborn kestrel hunkered down again, clinging to her branch. Marie-Jeanne sighed. If only she knew the chants and spells that would bring the hawk to her wrist!

A keening wail rose from the forest behind them. All the horses and donkeys bucked or danced at the sound. The huntsman plowed in among his dogs, cuffing them to make them stop howling at the mournful noise. Marie-Jeanne froze. The lure dropped to the ground.

"What in hell was that?" the comte demanded.

"Some poor beast being torn by a wolf," the bishop said, with an expression of disapproval at the noble's blasphemy. "Nothing to do with hell at all, my good comte."

"Very well, then," de Velay said, sulkily. He did not like to be corrected, even by Holy Mother Church. "Let us go on with our hunt."

But the cry had alarmed Mistinguette. She lifted from the branch and fluttered into the woods. The bishop laughed.

"Curse it, let her go!" the comte barked. "She's of no further use to me. I have better birds."

Marie-Jeanne knew better. Once out of sight of his illustrious company, he would demand that Father reimburse him the price of the costly falcon, meaning that the family would work for years with catastrophically reduced pay. It would be a horrible way to reward Father for sending her on her first hunt.

"I will find her, my lord," she said, gathering up the lure. De Velay waved her away impatiently. Marie-Jeanne marked the direction that the kestrel had flown, and ran after her, hoping to spot a glimpse of her white feathers against the dark trees.

The lure was of no use among the undergrowth of the forest. Mistinguette had not yet learned to come to her name. Without Father's cantrips for finding and trapping, all Marie-Jeanne could hope was to find the kestrel on a low branch and coax her back onto the glove.

The forest was usually alive with the sounds of birds and small animals, but it was eerily silent that day. Marie-Jeanne could not help but think that the terrifying cry had silenced them all with fear. Her own heart beat hard against her ribs. What if La Bête was real? What if it came upon her in the woods all alone? Would anything be left of her to tell her grieving parents what had become of her? Her blood ran like ice in her veins.

Behind her, the rest of the hunting party had carried on. The nobles shouted encouragement at their birds as they flew after rabbits and pheasants that the dogs flushed from cover. Soon, their voices died away in the distance. Marie-Jeanne crossed herself, hoping that she would not become lost. She had scavenged in the forests for mushrooms and nuts all her life, but usually in the company of friends or siblings, one at least who knew the way home.

A reassuring peep sounded from far ahead.

"Mistinguette!" Marie-Jeanne called. "Come back, chick!"

Another peep, as if in answer, gave the girl a direction, at least. A well-worn deer path led her that way. She pushed aside branches, scaring a squirrel up the nearest tree, where it scolded her as she passed. More peeps made her turn left, then right, then right again, stepping over humped roots and avoiding the piles of scut left by animals.

"I'm coming, chick!" At last, the plaintive sound seemed to come from above her. Marie-Jeanne looked up. Mistinguette clung to a branch high over her head. The girl held up her wrist and the lure.

"Come down to me, chick!" she called, keeping her voice soothing.

The kestrel rose a handspan, then dropped back, scrambling to clutch at the branch. She tried again, swung upside down, and flapped hard to right herself. Marie-Jeanne realized with horror that the hawk's jesses were caught. If she struggled too hard, she could break her neck.

The thought of Father shamed and impoverished struck Marie-Jeanne with shame. She had no choice. Fastening the big leather pouch tight to her back, she found a handhold and pulled herself up against the stout bole. She felt for a toehold and boosted herself up another foot. The first big branch was still over her head. One long stretch with her right arm, and she managed to hook a hand over it. The gloves kept her from skinning her palms on the rough bark.

Mistinguette's flapping and calling became more frantic. One long feather, dislodged by her struggles, floated down past Marie-Jeanne's head.

"Don't struggle, dear one!" the girl pleaded. The hawk could do herself a mischief, perhaps even break a wing! "Oh, how I wish I could tell you – all you need to do is sit calm!" That was unlikely. Mistinguette would probably tear her face in her hysteria. What would Father or one of the boys do? She had seen Henri, the eldest journeyman, soothe an eagle from insane fits to cooing affection with a few soft words. Not that the bird was tamed, far from it, but she had never understood how he had done it. When she asked, the boys put her off. Did they seem…embarrassed as to how they had learned to communicate with the hawks? In all the years since Father had let her begin to handle the birds, she had been bitten, screamed at, battered by wings, soiled upon, scratched, and coldly ignored by them. What more could they possibly do?

It didn't matter. Her duty was clear: save the bird then go back to face whatever punishment the comte chose to subject her to for not controlling it. He was not a bad man, only impatient. If she was successful, he would calm down. She'd receive no money, but at least Father would not be the loser on the day.

A warm stream rained down on her unprotected head. Marie-Jeanne touched the liquid and looked at it. White and pasty. She groaned. The bird had soiled on her hair! Stifling her resentment, she gritted her teeth and felt for the next handhold, and the next. Mistinguette was upset. She understood. Suddenly, a mad golden eye glared at her. Marie-Jeanne recoiled just in time from a strike by the deadly beak.

"There you are!" she said, in the same tone Mother used to talk with babies. "Hold on, my chick. I'm here. I'll help you."

Mistinguette couldn't understand her or didn't believe her. The kestrel swung upside down, bating and flapping helplessly. Marie-Jeanne pulled herself up to the branch above the falcon, and gently drew her up by the tangled jesses. The kestrel shrieked, a sound that penetrated the girl's ears like a spike.

Mistinguette fought hard. She beat her powerful wings, trying to take off through the treetops. Marie-Jeanne held on, keeping up the stream of calm nonsense words, all the while desperately hoping she wouldn't tumble off the narrow branch.

"There, there, my chick. You're fine now. Look at what you've done to your feathers! So untidy. You don't want anyone to see you like that, do you? No, of course not. Let me smooth them down. You'll feel much better when you're neat."

As she spoke, she gathered the wild kestrel into her lap, petting and petting at the skewed feathers, patting them down into place. Mistinguette panted, her beak half open. Marie-Jeanne closed the heavy cloak about them both, enveloping them in a tent of wool. It smelled familiar and comforting to her. She hoped the hawk found it so.

Gradually, the kestrel stopped struggling. Marie-Jeanne's hands found her crouched in her lap, in the hollow formed by her smock's skirts. Mistinguette scratched with one foot after the other, making herself comfortable. She fixed the girl with a searching look, then very deliberately hunched down, her tail feathers held high.

She's going to soil again, Marie-Jeanne thought, in despair. *Mother will make me wash all my clothes in the brook.*

But no white stream issued from the hawk's backside. Instead, Marie-Jeanne felt a warm spot in the bottom of her skirt. When Mistinguette rose, a small white sphere lay where she had been crouching. An egg!

"Well, aren't you the clever girl?" Marie-Jeanne exclaimed. Father would be pleased. The kestrel was old enough to produce eggs! They would have to find her a mate. She reached for it to put it in the lure bag. The shell was still soft. It deformed slightly against the glove leather.

The kestrel jumped up on her wrist and nudged at the egg.

"You don't want me to take it? Why not?"

Mistinguette looked up at her, then rolled the egg toward Marie-Jeanne.

"You...want me to have it?"

The kestrel shrieked. She bent down with her beak open, then looked up at the girl again. Her meaning was clear. Marie-Jeanne gasped.

"You want me to *eat* it? Father would be furious!"

Mistinguette nudged the egg again. Marie-Jeanne raised it to her mouth.

"No, I ca—"

She had no time to finish her protest. The falcon shoved the small sphere into her open mouth with its hard, little head. Marie-Jeanne almost vomited. The shell tasted bitter and salty. It was very small, though, about two inches long. She might be able to swallow it whole. But, ugh, the shell collapsed and broke on her tongue! The slimy insides, all still hot from the falcon's body, filled her mouth. She gagged, ready to spit, then she caught Mistinguette's eye. For once, it was patient, waiting and watching.

Suppressing her disgust, Marie-Jeanne swallowed once, twice, and the mouthful of slime and shards went down.

"There," she said. Her voice sounded weak in her own ears. "Happy? Now, may I take you down so that the comte does not wring both of our necks?"

Mistinguette peeped like a new-hatched chick and climbed up from the woolen skirts to take a post on Marie-Jeanne's right shoulder.

The girl could not believe her eyes. The kestrel understood her!

It peeped at her again, as if to tell her to hurry. Marie-Jeanne didn't hesitate. She tied the hanging leather jesses to the neck of her cloak and turned to face the trunk. Slowly, she felt her way down. It seemed years before her foot crunched onto the fallen leaves and twigs at the base of the tree. Marie-Jeanne sighed and dusted her gloves together.

Then, she winced.

"I don't know which way is home," she said. "I followed your calls. I turned this way and that, and I can't really see where the sun lies. We could be lost in here for days!"

Mistinguette almost chuckled as she trod on Marie-Jeanne's shoulder. She took hold of a lock of the girl's hair in her beak and tugged.

"What, you want me to go that way?"

Another tug.

Marie-Jeanne trembled at the notion that a miracle was occurring. A beast that could understand the speech of men? Or...was this the secret that the falconer's apprentices refused to share? Had they eaten an egg that made them bird-kin? She must ask Father, but first, she must return home safe and alive.

She turned in the directions the kestrel indicated. To and fro, to and fro, Mistinguette guided her, not even protesting or crying out when Marie-Jeanne tripped on a root or raised her arm to swat at biting flies.

The forest was still quiet, but it was a waiting silence. The animals sensed some kind of danger. Could it be La Bête? Marie-Jeanne drew her belt knife. She walked faster through a small clearing, feeling eyes on her back. The villagers complained of wolves in the woods. Had she rescued the falcon only to be eaten by a beast?

Snuffling noises broke the silence. Marie-Jeanne heard them off to her left and diverted to avoid the source. A musky odor filled the air. It could be her imagination, but her senses seemed keener than before. Every leaf had a sharper edge. Every smell had intensified so much she might have had her nose pressed to everything she passed. Sounds, too, reached deeper into her ears, creating a landscape in her mind. This was magic, then. Marie-Jeanne felt the sort of awe she experienced during mass, of something so great that her poor small brain could sense but a dust mote of a distant mountain.

A sudden burst of sound and smell erupted before her. Marie-Jeanne stumbled backward and fell against a tree, moments before a great gray boar hurtled into the clearing, no more than twenty feet away from her. Its tiny eyes had a mad glint. It saw her and bared its teeth. The sharp, pointed tusks at the sides of its mouth gleamed. It pawed the ground like a bull. She couldn't fend it off with only a knife. If only she knew some of Father's protective spells!

"Jesu preserve me," she prayed, clasping her hands together. "Oh, God, I will be dutiful!"

The boar lowered its huge head and charged toward her. She was doomed.

An earsplitting cry erupted in her right ear, rising higher and higher until she feared her skull would split. Marie-Jeanne dropped to her knees. The boar, whose approach threw clods of earth up on both sides, stopped so suddenly its front legs buckled. Mistinguette shrieked her hunting cry again, louder than ever. The boar charged at them, but a yard from Marie-Jeanne, it rebounded as though it hit a stone wall. Marie-Jeanne gasped. The boar scrambled up, bellowing angrily, but it hurtled out of the clearing, avoiding them in a wide arc.

She stared at the kestrel. Mistinguette tilted her head and chuckled again, as though to say, "It was nothing, really. You could have done it yourself."

Marie-Jeanne shook her head. Magic. The world was full of wonders. She had so much to learn.

In between steering her toward home, Mistinguette let out her hunting cry any time an animal approached them. Marie-Jeanne tried to imitate the sound, but the kestrel sounded as if it laughed at her efforts.

"You must give me a chance to learn," she told the bird, sternly. "No one has ever told me what it was really like to be falcon's kin!"

They emerged from the forest by the barley field. The farmer and his workers were doing their best to repair the damage done by the hunting party. By the position of the sun, more than two hours had passed since the falcon had flown away. Marie-Jeanne sighed. She could discover no sign of the comte and his guests but footsteps and hoofprints. If she was lucky, perhaps they had stopped to dine, and she could retrieve her donkey. Otherwise, it would be a long and a disgraceful walk home. She wished for some of that promised feast, even a crust of bread and a sip of watered wine.

"A raw egg is hardly a meal," she pointed out to the kestrel. "Too bad I didn't keep the coney. I could have cooked it for us." Mistinguette peeped in reply.

At least the path was dry. Marie-Jeanne trudged up a gentle hill, following the broken branches left by the party. She hoped they weren't far ahead.

A distant murmur met her enhanced hearing. That was the comte and comtesse, and the bishop! She had found them!

With an apology to Mistinguette, she began to trot down the hill. A strange smell met her nostrils. So strong it made her eyes water, she knew it wasn't dog, horse, or human.

As she looked down the road, she saw it: a beast the size of a large man, but on all fours, with thin black fur over gray skin. It could have been a boar bred with a she-wolf. Marie-Jeanne's heart wrenched. La Bête! It held the entire hunting party at bay.

"Spread out, men," the comte said, his voice amazingly calm. He had his arms out to his sides, his sword in one hand and a dagger in the other. Two men lay on the ground. At first, Marie-Jeanne thought they were asleep, but one of them had no head. "Keep it from charging the ladies. Madame," he said to his wife, "ride hell for leather. Go home and summon all the men-at-arms!"

The comtesse turned her horse this way and that, looking for a way around. Any time she moved, La Bête growled at her, making as if to charge. With a wrench of the poor beast's head, the lady kicked her steed. It leaped into a gallop. La Bête sped after her. It was fast as lightning.

A page in red livery sprang into its path.

"You shall not harm my lady!" he cried. The horrible beast cannoned into him. With one bite, it severed his head then plunged its jaws into his heart. The men charged at it with their hunting weapons. Like a whirlwind, La Bête tossed one after another onto the ground. The comte brought his sword down on its spine. The blade bounced off as if it had been a stick. La Bête jumped onto his chest and opened its jaws.

"No!" Marie-Jeanne screamed. But instead of the word emerging, a deep-throated scream came from her lungs, rising higher and higher into the sky. Mistinguette added her shriek.

In a heartbeat, the beast sprang off the comte's body and hurtled toward the girl. Marie-Jeanne didn't know where the courage came from, but she found herself running at the monster, her arms wide as if they were wings. She screamed and screamed, feeling herself fill with power. The kestrel kept up her cries as well, creating a veritable wall of sound into which La Bête hurtled. And fell.

It rose to its feet, looking shaken but angry. Marie-Jeanne saw its face clearly for the first time. Its teeth were as long as her fingers, and its tiny eyes gleamed with evil.

"You monster!" Marie-Jeanne shrilled. "Foul beast of Satan! Die! I will break your neck! Die!"

La Bête charged her again and again and again. It could not penetrate the kestrel's spell. Marie-Jeanne faced an impasse. If she stopped screaming, it would devour her, and destroy the comte and the others. She glanced at Mistinguette. The kestrel kept up her cry, keeping her safe, keeping them all safe, but for how long?

By now, all the hawks had joined their voices to Marie-Jeanne's. Seeing hope, the comte rallied the hunting party. They mustered all their weapons.

"I'm sorry, girl!" the comte called. He dropped his hand, and the huntsmen loosed quarrel after quarrel at the monster. The arrows bounced off the invisible wall, but also from La Bête's hide.

"It is an unholy monstrosity," the bishop declared, regaining his wits at last. "Robert! Bring me Matilde!"

With a puzzled look, his huntsman ran to him, bearing the crying gyrfalcon. From a saddle pack, the bishop took a small bottle. He uncorked it and put it into Matilde's talons. The gyrfalcon looked as confused as the hunter, until Mistinguette raised a call higher and shriller than ever before. Matilde lifted from the bishop's wrist and flew over La Bête. It dropped the bottle on the beast's head.

Holy water poured down the black-furred creature's body. Where it touched, it left red runnels like fire. La Bête leaped in the air, trying to catch the gyrfalcon, then it rolled on the ground, keening in pain.

"At it, men!" the comte shouted. He led the charge at the monster, with all the men, horses, and dogs behind him.

Despite its agony, La Bête sprang up. With one final snarl at Marie-Jeanne, it galloped into the undergrowth. Cracking branches and threshing footsteps disappeared in the distance.

Marie-Jeanne dropped to her knees and let her voice die away. Mistinguette leaned over and chucked her in the cheek with her head, as if to say, "Well done."

"Well, then," the comte said, swinging out of his saddle and striding to her. Unlike his usual bluff self, he looked abashed. "It seems that not only the falcon, but the falconer is full of surprises. I apologize for doubting your father when he said you would do well. You have done more than well, child." He held out a hand to help her up.

"Thank you, my lord." Marie-Jeanne discovered that her voice was no more than a hoarse croak. Mistinguette peeped.

The comte smiled.

"Say no more," he told her. "I think we've all heard enough from both of you for today. I see why I cannot control your falcon. I'm not enough of a wild creature. But it seems it takes one wild spirit to defeat another. You and your kestrel shall ride with me again. I have more to learn from you."

"And I from her," Marie-Jeanne said, stroking Mistinguette's soft speckled breast. "So much more."

L ee French lives in Olympia, WA with two kids, two bicycles, and too much stuff. She writes across a variety of F/SF subgenres, including epic fantasy, space opera, and cyberpunk. An active member of SFWA, she is best known for her young adult urban fantasy series, Spirit Knights. Her stories appear in numerous anthologies, including the award-winning *Merely This and Nothing More: Poe Goes Punk*. Her work can be found online at www.authorleefrench.com.

SHE REMEMBERED

LEE FRENCH

Twin streams created by unrelenting rain funneled in the wagon ruts of the packed earth road. A chestnut mare trotted down the center, her hooves splattering thin mud in every direction, including upward. The horse's exhausted rider had lost track of time in the constant gloom, and couldn't guess if they'd reach Cork by dark or not.

Aife stared at the leather-wrapped hilt of the sword strapped to her saddle, still dazed by the reason she carried one. Fifteen years ago, she'd set aside the mercenary life to bear a daughter. She hadn't intended for the break to last so long. Whether she remembered how to swing a blade or not, though, she had to try. For Moira's life, she would kill a monster or die trying.

The horse slowed and whickered. Aife checked the road. Ahead, a stopped wagon with an odd shape in the back blocked the way forward. One lone figure stood at the rear, working on the left wheel. Hairs on the back of Aife's neck stood at attention. No matter how soft she'd let herself become, she knew a classic ambush setup when she saw one.

If Keric had come with her, she wouldn't have worried. Even the most audacious brigands didn't bother a pair of armed riders. One woman of her age with a sword, though, wouldn't give such criminals much pause.

She scanned everywhere except the wagon. On the right, low grasses and wildflowers covered a gentle slope upward with scattered shrubs and small trees. Yellow, her husband's favorite color, dominated the blooms. No one save a skilled mage could hide there. Skilled mages didn't debase themselves with banditry.

On the left, a line of giant cedars marked the western edge of a sizable forest. An entire army could lurk within it. Aife saw no arrow tips or other weapons, but doubted she would in the rain.

Expecting attack, she gripped the sword hilt. The moment she saw or heard anything, she could slide off the horse's side and use it as a shield. If they let her reach the wagon, she'd have to contend with the unknown figure, but she could hide behind it.

As the horse neared the wagon, Aife tensed. The horse tensed. Even the air and rain tensed, holding its collective breath in anticipation.

She discovered the odd shape came from a sheet of canvas pitched over the back with a peak in the middle like a tent. Hitched to the front, a fat pony stood with its head down. The unidentified person paused in their work and waved a hand high at Aife.

Aife snapped her head to the trees and leaned to the side.

Nothing happened.

"Excuse me," the figure said. The woman sounded as exhausted as Aife felt. "Can you help, please?"

Bandits and highwaymen frequently used women as lures, but seldom did those poor souls seem so worn and used.

"What's the trouble?"

"The wheel is stuck in the mud, and the damned horse won't move when I tell it to."

Still watching the trees and still holding her sword's hilt, Aife reined in the horse beside the woman. "Where are you headed?"

"Cork. You?"

"The same."

Someone in the wagon giggled.

Aife drew her sword and pointed it at the wagon. "Who's inside?"

The woman raised her hands in surrender and sucked in a breath. "My daughter. Please don't hurt us."

Her reaction drew Aife's gaze. Damp wool swathed the woman from head to toe, as a scarf, skirt, and jacket. She seemed young, with no more than twenty summers behind her. Her open face and earnest brown eyes reminded Aife of herself half a lifetime ago.

The child giggled again with the same voice as Moira.

"Gemma, come here," the woman said. She delivered the command with firm, clear voice. Aife used that same tone with her own daughter.

The canvas rustled, then a little girl with brilliant blue eyes and a mop of blonde curls poked her head out. Aife guessed her age as two years.

"Ma ma ma ma ma."

Aife blinked at the girl who sounded too much like Moira. Shaken, she sheathed her sword. "My apologies," she mumbled, unable to tear her gaze from the child.

20

"No, I understand. Can't be too safe out here." The woman lowered her hands. She took a step to her daughter, kissed the girl's forehead, and shooed her inside again. "Gemma play."

"Pwa pwa pwa pwa pwa." The girl disappeared and giggled again.

"Pardon my Gemma. She's…" The woman sighed and shook her head. "Something's wrong with her."

Not sure what to say, Aife climbed off her horse. "You handle your beast. I'll push."

"Thank you. I'm Delaney."

"Aife. Nice to meet you."

Delaney hurried to the front of the wagon. Aife strained her muscles to rock the wagon back and forth. She gave up after the fourth try and tied a line to her horse for extra power. Between the added horse and Aife's efforts, they slid the wagon wheel out of a sucking mud puddle.

All the while, Gemma's giggles burst from the wagon in random clusters.

As Aife untied her horse's lead, Delaney checked her pony's feet.

"I can't think you enough. We would've been stuck here forever if you hadn't come along. My husband didn't want me making this trip. Maybe I should've listened."

"Why are you making it?"

Delaney sighed. "To see a mage. There's something wrong with Gemma and I know it. The other little kids in our village can talk. They can dance and sing and learn games and all kinds of things. Gemma understands a few words, but that's all. She's simple. Which I could live with, I suppose, if her father hadn't been such a capable mage. This seems wrong to me." She set down the last hoof. "I just have to know for sure if there's something a mage can fix. Even if there isn't and it's a waste of my money."

Aife covered her mouth. Moira had been the same as a toddler. She'd asked her husband for money to take the girl to a mage for the same reason. He'd refused.

"It's good your husband was willing to pay for that, but—"

Delaney barked a sour laugh. "Oh, no, he thinks I'm overreacting and doesn't know I'm doing this. She's just a bit behind, you know." She climbed into the driver's seat and picked up the reins. "Every child is different, after all. Sometimes, their little heads just need to cook longer."

"That's what my husband said." Aife remembered the first time she'd asked. He'd used the same words. Bewildered, she climbed onto her horse and urged the mare to keep pace as the wagon rolled forward. "It's exactly what he said. Their little heads need to cook longer."

"That's an odd turn of phrase for two different men to use. I wonder if they know each other? What's his name?"

"Breasal Cuinn of Cork."

Delaney blinked at her. "That's…that's my husband's name."

Aife frowned at her horse. "Didn't you say Gemma's father is a mage? Breasal isn't a mage."

"Breasal isn't Gemma's father. I married him when I was already pregnant. Her father was a breeze-through-town adventurer-type I was stupid enough to believe. Goddess bless, this is a shock. How could one man marry two women? Why would he even do it?"

Pieces of a bewildering puzzle clicked into place for Aife. She had to explain everything to Delaney. She had to save Gemma's life with Moira's.

"About sixteen years ago, I was one of those adventurer-types. My partner was a mage, Keric. I got pregnant with his child. He kept working to build savings for us, so we could live comfortably for a few years. The second time he left, he never came home, and I assumed he was dead."

She remembered that last kiss. He'd brushed a hand over her rounded belly and promised to return long before the birth.

"We had little. I knew no one. I panicked. Breasal swooped in and promised to take care of us."

She remembered his warmth and gentle touch. He hadn't demanded much of her. At the time, she'd thought him kind and generous.

"My daughter, Moira, is like Gemma. She didn't talk until she was five, and since then, she's never gotten better than simple statements of fact or want. She understands more than she can explain, but not much. Giggles at strange times."

She remembered tears. For both Keric and Moira. Years ago, Aife had surrendered to the inevitable fate of caring for her daughter for the rest of her life. She'd mourned the loss and moved on. Aside from her purpose on this ride, the past few hours without Moira had been a guilty pleasure, a terrible joy.

"This morning, Keric returned." The moment had turned her world upside-down. "I learned he'd been under a magical geas and unable to leave where he was, or even send a message." All that time, she'd thought him dead. She'd cried in his arms for an hour or more. Fierce love still glowed between them, and she should've felt it. Somehow, she should've known to go looking for him. So much time had frittered past, wasted by what she didn't do.

"One look at our daughter, and he knew something was wrong, so he examined her. Moira is under a curse. Vile magic has been draining away her life force since she was born. It's stolen her mind and soul, leaving her with only enough to survive."

Recounting Keric's report made her eyes burn. If only she'd defied Breasal's wish to not take Moira to a mage, like Delaney had mustered the will to do. If only Delaney had been the first, perhaps there wouldn't have been a second.

"Since she started her courses a few months ago, Moira has suffered illness after illness, her health declining with each passing day. She's bedridden now. Keric says the dark magic is killing her, probably because she's no longer a child. He tried to remove the affliction, but it was too powerful for him. What he could do was discover its source."

"Breasal," Delaney whispered. "It's Breasal, isn't it?"

Aife nodded. The rage that had put her hand on a sword hilt again after so long roiled in her gut, pushing aside her weariness from the morning's turmoil. "I don't know what he is, but I do know he's killing my daughter. I also know he's in Cork. I'm going there to stop him and save my daughter." Keric would've come, but he didn't think Moira would last much longer. He'd stayed behind to do everything in his power to keep the girl alive as long as possible.

Delaney stopped her pony. Aife halted her horse. Though the rain had lessened to a fine, misty drizzle, the sky had darkened.

"Night's falling," Delaney said. "I knew we should've started earlier in the day, but after lunch was when I managed to get up the gumption. Would you mind camping with us tonight? Safety in numbers."

"I should've left earlier too." Aife nodded. The time in Keric's arms had been a glorious luxury she shouldn't have afforded herself.

The two women tended the horses, the quiet broken only by

Gemma's errant giggles. Inside the wagon-tent, they prepared a small, cold meal from Delaney's supplies and compared their experiences with Breasal by candlelight. In both cases, he'd demanded little in exchange for providing much. He'd found delight in the girls and never acted improperly toward them.

"Two days a month on a schedule like clockwork," Delaney agreed. "That's how often we see him. I didn't realize it was so little until I sat down and added it up. Once I figured that out, I decided I should go, because he'd been to visit last week."

Aife had noticed the same many years ago. Like a fool, she'd never given it much consideration. He traveled for business, so of course he rarely stayed at home. "What does he do for the rest of the month? You know, I don't ever remember discussing his business. He always wants to talk about Moira or me, or the household, expenses, anything and everything except himself." That tendency had endeared him to her, of course. He seemed so selfless.

Delaney blinked. "Goodness, you're right. I have no idea what he does. Some sort of merchanting something or other." She frowned and passed Gemma a cracker to make her stop giggling. "Four days out of every month, maybe two more for travel. That's twenty-two days left to account for. What if— What if there are other women with other children? If he's in Cork right now, what if he's got one there? And another five or more in other villages?"

"All those children, and all those mothers," Aife whispered.

"And we never meet each other because we're too tired to ever get out. Even if we weren't, no one wants to talk about a child like this." Delaney rummaged through a lumpy sack and retrieved a small leather pouch. She offered it to Aife. "This is the money I planned to pay the mage to look at Gemma. You take it, and you use it to get at that bastard. He's ruined a lot of lives. If he's been doing this for a long time, he's ruined a whole lot more than we'll ever know."

Aife held out a hand to push away the coin purse. For a farm girl, the number of coins offered had to represent years of scrimping and saving. "I can't take that."

"Yes, you can." Delaney dropped it at Aife's feet. The coins inside clunked. "This all stinks of magic. I'm no warrior or mage. I can't fight Breasal and hope to win, especially not with Gemma to look after. You can. And you need support. This is what I can do for you."

Picking up the pouch, Aife didn't know what she'd do with the money. She didn't need anything and couldn't stomach the idea of using it to pay for a room or food in Cork.

"Don't you dare 'accidentally' leave it behind come morning." Delaney snuffed the candle and settled with Gemma.

If she didn't use it, Aife decided, she'd find Delaney and return it. With that thought, she settled under a blanket and fell asleep.

Gemma woke them in the morning. Aife helped Delaney turn around the wagon, then urged her horse onward. Within an hour, she crested a low hill.

Aife hadn't visited Cork in sixteen years, yet little had changed. Villages dotted the three roads leading to the massive, singular gate in the high stone walls around the city. Stone buildings marched to the ocean, where ships bobbed with the waves at the deep-water port. Horses, oxen, wagons, carts, and walkers clogged the area near the gate.

As she neared the city, a chilly breeze brought the stench of too many creatures in too small a space. Dogs barked, donkeys brayed, children shrieked, people chattered. Guards stood at attention and watched people pass through the open gate without stopping anyone.

She didn't know where in Cork to find Breasal. Once upon a time, she would've plunged into the seedy underbelly and knocked heads together until someone pointed her in the right direction. That approach took skills she hadn't practiced in a long time.

Since no one knew her anymore, she figured no one would treat her like a criminal or mercenary. She stopped her horse beside a guard.

"Excuse me. I'm supposed to find a man named Breasal Cuinn to deliver a package. Do you have any idea where he might be? Or know of a place to ask after him?"

The guard smiled at her. "Of course, ma'am. Master Cuinn's place is on the north side, along Crevard Row."

Aife blinked at him. "I…didn't expect you to know that."

He laughed. "I guess it's your lucky day. Master Cuinn passes through here all the time, and he's a frequent guest of the Duke. I sometimes escort him."

"Thank you." Aife moved on, eager to keep the guard and his colleagues from remembering her.

Three-story houses sharing side walls lined Crevard Row on both sides of the street. Every house looked the same as every other house except for the window boxes. Flowers in every color spilled from planters hanging off the facades.

Planters full of daffodils and yellow daylilies made her pause outside one house. As she reined in the horse, the front door opened, and a woman stepped out.

The woman, perhaps five or six years older than Delaney, wore a black wool dress with a white pinafore and a white bonnet covering her hair. Her shoulders sagged with weariness. Aife thought she recognized the droop of a young child's mother.

"Excuse me, miss? I'm looking for Breasal Cuinn. Do you happen to know where he lives?"

"This is his house," the woman said as she closed the door. "But he's not home. Come back after dark if you want to see him."

"Thank you." Aife watched the woman walk away. She didn't want to trouble anyone, but she needed to know.

Once the woman turned the corner, Aife urged her horse to follow. Two turns later, the woman disappeared around a corner. When Aife stopped to look for her, the woman stepped from behind a column, pointing an accusing finger at Aife.

"Why are you following me?"

Aife had hoped to speak with her under more private circumstances. She saw no other option than ignoring the passersby and asking the most direct question she could. "Do you have a young child who seems behind in speaking and learning? And their father was a mage?"

The woman narrowed her eyes. "Who are you?"

"One of Breasal's wives."

"What?"

"I know he has more than one, and I know we all have children who aren't right."

Her brow furrowed, the woman turned her back on Aife and strode several paces away. Then she turned around and marched back. She jabbed a finger at Aife again. For a heartbeat, Aife thought she meant to shout, then the woman closed her mouth and frowned.

Aife climbed down from her horse and touched the woman's arm. "I don't mean you or your child any harm. Please, hear me out. I can help you."

"I'm not his wife. I work for him as a maid. The cook and I, we both have little girls who need extra help. He takes care of us."

Using the horse as a screen against strangers, Aife told the maid everything she knew.

"I don't want to believe you." The maid sighed and rubbed her face. "He's so sweet to us."

"Because he doesn't want you to discover the truth. If he was wretched, you'd have a reason to question him."

The maid slumped her shoulders and nodded. "What will we do without my income?"

Aife thought she'd found a use for Delaney's coins. She dug out the purse and offered it. "I need to get inside that house without him knowing. Take this and show me the way so I can save our daughters."

The maid stared at the pouch. She lifted it from Aife's hand and poured half the coins into her pocket, then handed the pouch back to Aife. "Leave your horse stabled someplace. There's an alley that runs behind the houses, and they all have back doors. His is number five twenty-seven. That door is always unlocked during the day. Give the rest of the money to Iona, the cook. Tell her you're Breasal's wife, there to surprise him from out of town, and she should take the rest of the day off. He'll come in through the front door about half an hour after dusk."

Tucking the pouch into a pocket, Aife smiled at her. "Thank you. I hope we all notice the difference immediately."

They parted ways with a clasp of hands. Aife found a stable and left her horse behind. At the house, she climbed the fence as the maid had told her. Iona accepted both the coins and explanation without question.

With a few hours before dark, Aife drifted through the house until she found his office. She rifled through everything. His records showed he spent a lot of time paying attention to the movements of male mages, and possibly sponsored their exploits and conquests. A ledger revealed he kept ten wives at a time, each referenced by the name of her isolated village.

To her horror, she found documentation suggesting he'd managed all this for at least seven decades. Files held information about woman after woman, each with a daughter fathered by a mage. He'd financed funerals for dozens of girls aged twelve to sixteen.

She found Keric's name on a file. Her hands shaking, she opened the folder and read everything. According to Breasal's records, he'd approached Keric after Aife became pregnant. Keric had refused his offer, so Breasal had manipulated him into a job expected to kill him, or at least to keep him away from Aife long enough to swoop in and woo her. He'd planned to convince her to move if needed so Keric couldn't find her and Moira.

Aife clutched the file to her chest. She wanted to weep and scream at the same time. Fifteen years ago, she should've taken Moira and searched for Keric. Instead, she'd let a monster whisper honey into her weary ears. By the time she'd regained her strength from the difficult birthing, he'd owned her.

If Keric hadn't returned, she never would've known. Moira's death would've shattered her.

Dropping the file, she gripped her sword and stalked to the entry. There, she stood where the opening door would hide her. And she waited.

She remembered the soul-crushing despair when she could no longer ignore Moira's problems. She remembered wondering what she'd done wrong to doom Moira to such a terrible life. She remembered hating herself for wishing she'd never had Moira.

Every day, she woke to face the slow, building horror of what would happen to Moira as she aged.

Breasal had caused it. All of it. Even if destroying him didn't fix Moira or all the other girls, Aife would still do it to avenge all the stolen lives and to prevent him from stealing more.

Once upon a time, she'd fought for money. Though the causes she'd chosen had been good, never had she fought for this kind of true, pure justice.

The sun set, darkening the room. Aife held a hand ready to catch the door. She'd wait for him to close it, take a step, and thrust the blade through his body. No need for all the swordplay she'd forgotten or muscles she'd allowed to wither.

Too soon and not soon enough, the knob turned. The door opened. A silhouette stepped inside.

28

"Iona?" Breasal called.

He shut the door. Aife took a step and thrust her sword at the center of his back.

Breasal turned. Her blade slashed across his jacket. He sucked in a breath and sidestepped. She swore and raised her sword again.

"Who's there?" He darted to a shadow and disappeared.

"Your wife," Aife growled. The vile bastard had turned the darkness against her. She held her sword and focused on the blade. If the lights came on, she wanted to see. Otherwise, she needed to ignore the shadows and listen.

Breasal's voice echoed around the room as he chuckled. "Aife, I should've known it would be you who'd come for me."

"Why's that?"

"All your years as a swordswoman gave you strength. It took so much work to lure you at the beginning. Of course, now your daughter is at the end, I have no further need for you. It's fitting that you should die the same day as she, isn't it?"

Aife swallowed a surge of panicked grief. Keric had promised he'd keep her safe. She had to trust him. He'd said he could do it. He would do it.

"Not to worry, though. I've already found the next one. She's plump and ripe for the taking."

Shadows flickered on the edge of her vision to the right. Ignoring them let her hear his breathing. He had slipped to her left.

"Why do you do all this? Why all these children?"

"My dear Aife, no power is free. No matter what you want, someone always pays."

"And what did my daughter pay for?"

He laughed at her. She heard him slithering closer.

"What do you think? Immortality, of course. Youth. Strength. Riches."

The darkness writhed to her right and lunged toward her. Trusting herself, she slashed to the left.

Breasal squealed and hissed. Warmth spattered Aife's face and burned her flesh. His blood stank of corruption and death. Something solid hit the floor near her feet. She stomped it. Bones crunched.

She swiped her face with her sleeve.

"If you were still a pretty young thing, those burns would be a shame." Breasal sounded pained and tense.

She knew her age. A few wrinkles, extra pounds, and gray hairs made no difference to her heart or soul. His taunt didn't sting, only the acid in his veins did. "If you were a decent person, that lost arm would be a shame."

"I can make a new one," he snapped

The shadows lunged again, this time from the left. Aife didn't think he'd moved far enough to reach her from the right. She thrust her sword forward and felt the blade hit something.

Breasal gurgled. Though she knew it would hurt, Aife rushed him and shoved her sword deeper. More of his blood sizzled through her shirt and scored her skin. They crashed to the floor together. His acid blood splashed her hands. She screamed as she wrenched her sword to the side, cutting through him.

He whimpered. Tears sprang to Aife's eyes from the pain in her hands. She lurched to her feet, yanked out her sword, and staggered to find a light. He needed to die, and she needed to see him dead.

She bumped into a table and found an oil lamp. Pawing the surface, she discovered a sparker beside it. With a shaking hand, she scraped the sides together to produce a spark and lit the wick.

Light flared. Breasal lay on the ground in a puddle of black ooze, gasping for breath and staring at her in shock. She'd split open his side, and it oozed more slime. Gray crept over his flesh as if time rushed to claim him.

Aife would take no chances. She locked her gaze with the monster's and shoved her sword through his heart.

High-pitched wailing wheezed from his mouth. His body darkened and crumbled. The ground shook. Aife stumbled until she hit the wall and slid to the floor. Struggling to wipe her arms on her pants, she watched his form fall apart and her sword hit the floor. Pulses of darkness leaped from the rubble, turning white before winking out.

Everything stopped. He left behind a dark stain on the rug. Her sword lay unspoiled in the center, gleaming in the candlelight.

Raising her hands, she saw the ooze had vanished, leaving behind raw, numb burns. They would heal. Scars would remain, inside and out.

If she hurried, Aife could reach home before dawn. She'd collapse with weariness when she arrived, but she'd know Moira's fate. Iona and the maid would tend to the house and everything inside it. Aife had no doubt they would do whatever they could for the other women.

She rushed to pick up her sword and flee the house. The stablehand helped her saddle her horse swiftly. The ride through Cork passed in a blur, then the headlong rush through the countryside. Aife pushed the horse as hard as she dared.

The poor beast frothed at the mouth and heaved for breath when it reached home. Dim light glowed around the edges of the curtains covering her front window. She slid out of the saddle and ran through her wild front garden under starlight. Her heart pounded as she threw her body at the front door to heave it open.

Fire burned in the kitchen hearth. Steam roiled from a pot over it, filling the air with mint and rose musk. Keric and Moira sat at the round table, each holding a clay mug.

Both snapped their heads to see who'd burst inside. Moira's face lit up. She set aside her mug, leaped to her feet and rushed to hug Aife.

Her strong, sturdy arms squeezed like Moira had never suffered sickness. "Mama! Papa say you save me!"

Aife crumpled, delirious with joy and tears streaking down her cheeks. Even if Moira never caught up, never regained what Breasal had taken from her, she lived. Her little girl lived. They needed nothing more.

Award-winning and bestselling speculative fiction author Raven Oak is best known for Amaskan's Blood (2016 Ozma Fantasy Award Winner and Epic Awards Finalist), Class-M Exile, and the collection Joy to the Worlds: Mysterious Speculative Fiction for the Holidays (Foreword Reviews 2015 Book of the Year Finalist). Raven spent most of her K-12 education doodling stories and 500 page monstrosities that are forever locked away in a filing cabinet.

When she's not writing, she's getting her game on with tabletop and video games, indulging in cartography and art, or staring at the ocean. She lives in the Seattle area with her husband, and their three kitties who enjoy lounging across the keyboard when writing deadlines approach.

ALIVE

RAVEN OAK

Black hair, blue eyes, tall frame for a girl. Throat slit ear-to-ear. The newest victim could've been a younger version of me, a *much, much* younger version if I ignored the number of silver hairs on my forty-five-year-old head. As King Leon's *sepier*, gathering information was what I did best as an all-around spy and problem solver, but a string of deaths—all women—had pulled me back toward Justice and the town of Loughrie.

As I stood outside the Merc's Guild, my throat throbbed in response to the report in my hands. I could feel the knife against my throat all over again. Had these women known their attacker? Had they struggled, as I had, or had their lives been over in a single gasp? The report sent to the king stated the Merc's Guild had handled the burning of all four victims, though they hadn't bothered reporting the murderers to the crown. Curious that they'd covered up their burning, leaving someone else to report it. The decision left me wishing I was back in Alexander rather than staring down my past.

It couldn't be coincidence that this girl looked like me.

The change in Loughrie was obvious in the line of mercs outside. Not one of 'em a woman, and none of 'em young. I nodded to 'em before glancing over their heads at the newly posted jobs. Caravan guards. One call for an archer at the border. None of it complicated, and none of it local.

I passed through the open door into the Guild itself where a whip of a girl scurried over. "Welcome to the Mercenary Guild. Fair work for fair pay. Are you lost?"

The round man nearly attached to her elbow could've been her father by the look he gave her, and she disappeared behind a curtain before I'd done more than open my mouth. "My apologies," he said, and I sidestepped his attempt to grasp my forearm.

I'd been here before—twenty years ago, not that the man recognized me now—and little had changed. Master Alfred and his three brothers grew fatter on crowns and notches earned by negotiating poor deals for those willing to live by the sword.

"The Guild currently does not have any jobs available."

Master Alfred's frown deepened when I smiled. "The line of mercs outside at that new postin' says otherwise."

"Well, yes. There are those jobs, but it would not be appropriate for a...woman," he said.

"And why not?"

His gaze followed along the adornment that curled around my leather armor before finally resting on my polished sword. "A woman of your...age might be better suited to work in a castle or large manor rather than on the dangerous road."

My cheeks grew warm, but I bit my tongue, choosing instead to fetch the scrap of parchment I carried bearin' the Guild's crest. He recognized my mercenary name as his green eyes popped against his face's sudden flush, then his eyes noted the *sepier* star pinned near my collar bone. "Lady Ida, it's been a long time since you've visited the Guild. Far too long! I meant you no slight, only...."

"Only?"

"Last job you had, you abandoned. Word was you left a comfortable palace job, and well, the Guild has a reputation to uphold."

While tossing his ample rear across the room was my preference, I forced myself to smile. "Course ya do. But I'm not here about—"

He leaned close and whispered, "Besides, have you heard of the Merc Meister? It's not safe for women fighters—not in Loughrie anyway. My apologies, but I have nothing for you. Maybe you can check in one of the larger cities or Alesta itself."

It wasn't good enough. I wasn't leaving 'til I had a clear path to tread. "Tell me more about these murderers," I said.

His stiffened posture shifted as his hands thrust forward. Perhaps I'd gotten soft as a *sepier* or perhaps it was my old age. Either way, he'd shoved me out the door before I'd finished speaking. When the door closed in my face, I turned to find a line full of men shuffling their feet as they suppressed laughter. If I couldn't get answers from him, I'd get 'em elsewhere. "The nerve of him," I muttered, only half-way an act. Fools had no idea the dangers of being a *sepier*. All they saw was an old woman who'd gained a boon from the king. "As if I were some common merc. Damn fool."

I shoved my way through the crowd to stop before the board

where I pretended to study it. Ten minutes in, someone slipped some parchment into the palm I held against my back. I didn't open it 'til I wandered away. Another ten minutes saw me tucked into the west corner table at a tavern called *The Drunken Footsman* while I waited on whoever had taken my bait.

Shortly after sundown, a young man with shoulders nearly as broad as the table claimed the seat across from me. He inclined his bushy red beard in the direction of my almost empty cup, and I shook my head. His gaze flitted around the tavern while the din carried on around us. "Lady Ida hasn't visited Loughrie in over a decade. One might wonder what brings her out of her cushy retirement now," he murmured.

"Maybe she needs a little coin, is all."

Laughter erupted from the bar, and he glanced over his shoulder at a man attempting to juggle mugs while hopping from one leg to another. "Or maybe it's the Merc Meister," he said, and I shrugged. "What have you heard?"

"Four victims, all women. All died the same way."

When I didn't elaborate, he said, "Actually, there've been five victims so far. Guild only knows of four because the other one wasn't a merc." At my raised brow he added, "Commoner. Maybe she saw something."

It was plausible. If all of 'em had been mercs, that'd explain why the Guild covered their burning. And why it was set on keeping word quiet. "Why only women?" I asked.

"No one's sure…though I have some ideas." He pointed to my throat. "The way you fled the Guild for a King's a famous tale around here. So's that scar of yours. Though no one knows how you got it. I heard some Amaskan in Sadai gave it to you."

Bile tickled the back of my throat as my muscles tensed. Who was he to know so much?

Blue eyes, twin to my own starred down at me. His dagger was against my throat as he laughed. "Leave? No one leaves the Order of Amaska. Not even you, sister dear. No one leaves…not alive anyway." The pinprick, then a sting as sharp as my sword slit my neck from ear to ear.

"Lady Ida?"

I opened my eyes to find the merc's hand shaking me. "Sorry," I muttered and downed the last swallow of ale. My gaze sought his jaw line, but no tattoo marked it. "Where'd ya hear this?"

"Around. People talk if you pay. If you did get that scar from them, I don't blame you for being afraid. Amaskans are born to kill. They may think they're doing holy work by killing sinners, but my Da always said 'Bad depends on your point of view.' Nothing but rotten assassins, they are."

I nodded, but settled my hands in my lap to hide their trembling. "Why bring up my scar?"

"I think it's connected. This murderer's trying to find you. Think about it—all women with dark hair, mostly fighters, and all with their throat slit. Until I saw you outside the Guild today, I hadn't made the connection."

I swore under my breath. How many others were making the same connection? To him, I asked, "How do I know ya aren't the killer yourself?"

"You don't. Folks figure it's a merc though. The killer seems to know where we gather, how we move, and the weapons we use." He traced circles across the tabletop with his finger as he spoke. "Details like someone's been studying mercs for a while now. But if I was the killer, I'd have just killed you rather than meet with you."

A little laugh escaped me, and he smiled—a grin made more earnest by the way his bushy, red beard danced. Something about it felt familiar, though I couldn't place it. "Have we met before?" I asked.

"I'd have remembered the honor of meeting the great Lady Ida. It's not something I'd forget."

I flushed, though whether it'd been a compliment or insult, I couldn't tell. The tavern door opened to allow entrance to a disheveled man in a black cloak. A few called out greetings as he folded his tall frame into a chair at the bar's end. His hood shadowed all but a scruffy beard and lips that trembled.

"That's Marc Silversmith," the merc said, and I glanced at the bar a second time.

Last time I'd seen Marc, he'd been one of the wealthiest caravan guards this side of the mountains. He carried the right bumps and lumps to be well armed, but the way he'd moved through the door was like a man with one foot in this world and one foot into the next.

"Now *he's* the man you want to chat with."

"And why's that?" I asked.

"The first victim was his sister."

By the time I'd fetched another cup of ale, my informant had fled, leaving me alone with a stomach full of squirming vipers and the need of a few more cups to settle 'em. Rather than wallow in my fear, I elbowed the juggler out of his seat beside Marc Silversmith. It hadn't been all that hard considering the mixed scent of sour ale and sweat coming off my old friend. I breathed through my mouth and said, "It's been a long time, Marc."

At first, he didn't move—he kept his gaze on the bit of ale that ran down the side of his cup—but the moment I swiveled toward him, Marc fumbled for the bulge at his hip. My hand reached his dirk first, which I pressed deeper into its scabbard.

"Easy," I whispered into his ear. "It's Ida. Remember me?"

His brows furrowed as he blinked, and like someone clearing away sleep, his gaze focused on my face. "Lady Ida?" His hand went limp against mine. "You can le-go. Surprised me is all."

I released his dirk and waited another heartbeat before sliding into my seat. "I'm sorry about your sister, Dorine," I said.

"Yeah, ain't everyone."

"Can I ask ya about…what happened?" When he reached for his cup, I slid it out of reach. "You've had enough, friend. Answer a few questions for me, and I'll let ya get back to it."

"Always were a royal pain," he said with a sad little smile. "Don't know what good it'll do, but ask away."

"Where was she before the attack?"

Marc swung his arm wide. "Here. Where she always is…was. Working the bar."

"Were ya here?" Those soft, brown ovals hardened at the question, and I asked, "Did she leave with anyone? Say anythin' off or unusual?"

"No. Wish she had."

"Was she friends with any mercs in town?"

"All of them. Since you left, all she ever wanted was to be was a merc like you. Even after…"

I winced, and when I pushed the cup back at Marc, he drank like a man trapped in the swirling sands of Sadai. I set a few coins on the bar before leaving him to it. What little conversation there was lulled as I passed.

Loughrie wasn't the merc's town I remembered. Not anymore.

The pounding on my door lasted a good few minutes after I'd opened my eyes and another two minutes past my shout to go away.

"Please, there's been another death," the innkeeper shouted.

Red-beard had me spooked, and I'd been all set to leave Loughrie in the past where it belonged, but another dead woman? I dragged myself out of the sad excuse for a bed with a sigh.

"Be down in a moment," I said before pulling on a linen shirt and breeches. I stuffed my feet into my boots, buckled myself into my leather armor, and was down the tavern stairs at a pace that left my old joints complaining. A man wearing the King's Army uniform chatted with the inn keep, the latter of which shoved a cup of ale and small plate of food in my direction. "I hear we have another body?" I asked and bit off a chunk of cheese.

"Lieutenant Colby," the man in blue said as he nodded at me. "Word is I'm supposed to report...to you?"

So this was the Lieutenant who'd sent word to the King. "Thanks for the reports on the victims. They were quite helpful." As helpful as too much ale the night before.

"I was expecting someone—"

I slid the coin from my pouch and held it up to stop him talking. If he'd finished that sentence, I might've had to kill him. Etched into the coin was a silver star marking me as *sepier*. When he opened his mouth, I shook my head to silence him.

"Um, yes, if you'll follow me," he said.

At least this fool knew who and what I was. I trailed along as he led me out of the inn and towards a lean-to held together by little more than luck and a prayer. Inside, a soldier with a lantern stood guard over a body. When the lantern light reflected off his face, I closed my eyes. Marc's disheveled black cloak was gathered around him like a shroud, but his throat wasn't slit. The place reeked of sour wine, and a quick glance about left me wondering about the last time he'd been home as dust gathered on everything. "When was he found?" I asked.

"Landlord was around this morning to collect rent. Found him passed out. Thought him drunk until he turned him over. You think it's related to the others?" the lieutenant asked.

I ignored him as I searched Marc's pockets. His registration with the Guild was wadded up in his pant's pocket along with a lock of hair. Probably his sister's. I set both aside and checked the pouch at his waist. A few coins but nothing else. I nudged his head with my boot. "Bring the lantern here," I said as I leaned closer. Something discolored his jaw near the ear, and I grabbed the throwing knife from the top of my boot.

"What are you doing?" the lieutenant hissed, and I brushed aside his outstretched hand.

"There's somethin' on his jaw." I held his beard hair taut and gently pulled the knife-edge across the hairs, cutting 'em a bit to get a better look at his skin. My insides shook as the hair fell away.

It wasn't the Amaskan tattoo I'd been dreading, but it was an intentional mark all the same. Someone had scratched three slanted lines into his skin.

"Looks like he scratched himse—"

My glare silenced the lieutenant. "The marks are evenly spaced and even in length. No one scratches themselves that cleanly. It's recent, too."

"Then what's it mean?"

I shook my head. No need to tell him. There wasn't anything he could do to stop what was coming or what was already here. Only an Amaskan would use that symbol. Marc had been spotted talking to me, and they'd silenced him—marked him an oath-breaker. He wasn't one, but it was a symbol I'd recognize. One meant to silence me.

The red-bearded merc had been right. The Amaskans *were* here, and from the looks of it, they were looking for me. My hands trembled as I returned my knife to its sheath.

"Burn the body immediately. Tell anyone who asks that Marc drank himself to death."

The lieutenant saluted me as I left the lean-to, my steps a lot less sure than they'd been before. It'd been twenty-five years since my brother'd left me for dead. Why would Bredych choose now to hunt for a dead woman?

I rubbed my jaw. The puffy scar marred it, but if I pressed against it, the tattoo was still there under the scar tissue. Like a curse.

A light drizzle left the morning chilly and gray as I set out for the Merc's Guild. Somewhere in this town was a red-bearded man who'd asked all the right questions. Maybe he knew more than he was letting on. Either way, I needed to find him before anyone else died.

Or before he did.

Several hours and a parched throat later, the red-bearded merc was nowhere to be found, though I'd had several folks tell me he'd last been seen at the tavern in the company of some lady merc. As afternoon rolled in with a storm, I settled into the tavern's back corner with a glass of wine and a hearty meal, though I only picked at it. Once done torturing myself with the idea of food, I tossed up my cloak's hood and retreated to the shadows.

When he walked into the tavern, the merc who I'd since dubbed Red-Beard glanced around at the dozen occupants before settling at the bar. Every time the door opened, his fingers squeezed his mug, but he otherwise kept his gaze straight ahead. A candlemark passed before he gave up waiting for me, assuming that was his goal, and left. I followed a few heartbeats behind and winced when I opened the door to the downpour.

The rain would disguise the sound of my footfalls, but it'd be harder to track him in all the shadows, which he hugged like a mistress. I used an empty wagon to reach the tavern's roof and ignored the groan in my right hip as the old injury reminded me how young I wasn't. Jumpy as Red-Beard was, I needed every advantage, and lucky for me, the buildings in Loughrie lay close together.

He was good, but not *that* good. Which meant he couldn't be Amaskan. Or if he was, he'd have to be new. Like the rest of Loughrie, he'd underestimated me, and I grinned as I followed along from the rooftops. While he meandered in the rain for a few minutes, he eventually circled around to the road leading out of town. I used the shutters on a house to climb down, careful of where I placed my feet when I landed. A light flickered in a barn up ahead as the door opened, and he stepped inside.

I spent the next few minutes dodging puddles as I prayed to the Thirteen that the storm would hide my approach. The barn was a smart choice—no real windows and two doors, three if ya counted the hay door in the rafters. My hip ached as I peered up at the hay door. It was reachable…with some inventive maneuvering I'd pay for in the morning.

Thunder rolled overhead, and I used the opportunity to walk around the barn's side. The wood siding was too slick to scale in the rain, but luck was with me. In the rear, a ladder leaned against the barn. Perfect.

A moment later, I'd climbed in through the open hay door and sat dripping in the rafters. Below me, three voices, including Red-Beard, murmured, and I crept forward 'til I'd reached the railing. Two of the men sprawled across hay stacks while Red-Beard approached. "She wasn't there," he said.

"Do you think she's on to you?"

The man who asked this slid forward off the hay, giving me a good look at his clothing. Black from head-to-toe, the fabric was fitted at the joints and waist, yet stretchable elsewhere. Cloth shoes covered his feet and when his hood fell back, his bald head shined in the lantern light.

Amaskan.

I didn't need the tattoo to confirm it, though I caught sight of the circle on his clean jaw when he turned his head my way. I held my breath, but the darkness hid me.

The face was older, the lines and wrinkles deeper, but it was the scar across his nose that confirmed it. The man pacing before Red-Beard was none other than Ilan, my brother's second-in-command. He'd been like a brother to me growing up in the Order of Amaska, and bile burned the back of my throat.

Watching him, the urge to flee was overwhelming. It'd be what he'd expect too. Always playing it safe—that was how he probably remembered me.

Red-Beard flinched as Ilan leaned close and whispered something in his ear. Red-Beard nodded, then left the barn. Fleeing was exactly my plan, but Ilan chose that moment to look up into the rafters. Behind me, the open hay-door swung in the wind and tapped against the siding.

"Got to close that door. Storm's getting worse," he said to the other guy, who shrugged in response.

I crept back as slowly as I dared and didn't turn around 'til my feet touched the ground outside. Long after I'd dried off in the warmth of the tavern, my body shivered and my skin crawled. I could've sworn his eyes still watched me. I took a long swallow of ale and waited for Red-Beard's return.

Desperation usually drove people to stupidity, but also to the familiar, and Red-Beard was no exception. Not long after I'd nursed my third glass of wine, he stumbled into the tavern, his cheeks flushed and his beard a dripping mess. When he spotted me, he grinned and made straight for my corner. "I've been looking for you," he said, and I nodded to the empty chair in front of me.

"We seem to have spent most the day looking for each other then."

He frowned at this. "Seems odd we couldn't find one another in a town this small, but we've found each other now. I have a proposal for you."

"Indeed? A job?"

"I…I know you've been looking into the murders, but I could see it in your eyes last time we talked."

"And what did ya see?"

"Fear. When I mentioned the Amaskans, you froze. Maybe you need a good job to forget the past. My employer's looking for those who're good at talking to people. He's looking to set up his business here in Loughrie, but the townsfolk might not be keen on the competition."

"What's he do? Your employer?" I asked.

Red-Beard pointed at my glass. "In Sadai he runs a very successful vineyard, but he's looking to expand here as the weather's more hospitable to growing grapes."

I took a sip of wine to cover my laughter. The Amaskans used both horses and wine to fund the Order. Whether he knew it or not, he'd tipped his hand with that story.

"If I decide to take your employer up on this offer, what'd I be doin'? Guardin' the wine?"

"Some, though mostly just making sure the good people of Loughrie let him make his wine in peace. Maybe some negotiating with the locals."

The tavern door opened and Red-Beard's friend, a tall man whose name I hadn't deciphered, walked in. His hood covered his bald head, but it didn't matter. From the way he slid through the space to his awareness of everyone in the room, his very movement screamed Amaskan. He tucked himself into a table alone, but his eyes flickered once in our direction.

"I'm interested, though I need to let the Guild know I've found work." While Red-Beard pretended to think it over, I studied his face. Only a few inches long, the red, wet locks of his beard curled around his face, almost hiding the tattoo on his jaw below his ear. Dry, the beard had covered the tattoo completely, but now, the barest hint of a circle was there if I stared hard enough. When he nodded agreement, I said, "I can meet your employer in the mornin'. Does he already have a spot in mind, or would ya like to meet here? Usual table?"

"You know the old barn at the edge of town? Has a big tree out front?"

"Used to be a sheep farm, right?"

Red-Beard nodded. "Now it's a vineyard. Or it will be come this time next year. Locals aren't too pleased with him for buying the land, so that's where you come in. We can meet there around noon."

"Noon sounds fine. Say, never did catch your name. I figure if we're goin' to be workin' together, I might want to call ya somethin' other than 'Red-Beard.'"

He laughed and held out his arm, which I grasped by the forearm and shook. "The name's Morei," he said.

"Nice to meet ya, Morei. I'll be seein' ya tomorrow then." Or sooner if all goes well.

I stood up first and left the tavern knowing full well that both Amaskans watched me. Once outside, the downpour continued, and I sighed as I rounded the corner to the alley. I grabbed a few rocks, which I tucked into my pouch, then grabbed a handful of mud. I smeared the thick stuff across my face 'til it was mostly covered. Hopefully between the darkness and mud, I'd blend into the shadows. I climbed into an empty wagon, unsheathed my sword, and removed my cloak, tossing the latter over me like a tarpaulin.

It didn't take five minutes for someone to exit the tavern, and Morei stopped a few feet in front of my hiding spot. He glanced about, and seeing nothing in the dim light, swore. I took one of the stones from my pouch and tossed it down the alleyway, a good twenty feet away.

Morei peered into the alley as thunder rattled the buildings around us. I tossed a second stone, which bounced off a stone wall before landing in a puddle, and he stepped into the alley. I held my breath as he passed by the wagon but almost laughed aloud when a rat scurried in front of him and he flinched.

Stepping from the wagon would've made all sorts of sounds but the Thirteen must've been on my side as a bolt of lightning hit a nearby tree and set the air a-buzz. The reverberating thunder covered most of the noise. Morei spun on his heel and turned into my blade as I drove it into his gut.

"It *is* you," he muttered as he stumbled back, hand clutching his innards.

"Ya couldn't let the past stay buried anymore than my brother could. I'm sorry, Red-Beard, but ya left me no choice. I wanted to run—probably should've—but I can't let 'em die for me. I'm sworn to protect these people, which I can't do if I'm dead."

Morei dropped to his knees and held out his hand. Clutched in his fingers was a silver ring. "B-belonged to Marc's sis-sister," he said. I took it from him, and he smiled. "Sorry, Lady Ida."

Damn him. I hadn't wanted to kill him. Why couldn't he have left it alone? Why join the Amaskans?

He exposed his throat. "Make it q-quick."

Before my blade moved, another blade sliced through his flesh from behind, nearly taking his head clean off. "Don't be sorry. Be Amaskan," the man muttered as he continued his forward momentum until I stood face-to-face with the third, unnamed Amaskan from the barn. He grinned and as lightning struck, he was on me, moving faster than I thought possible in the muddy mess. I brought my sword up in time to parry, but my feet slid backward in the mud. I fell to one knee, and his next blow knocked my sword from my muddy hands.

A miracle had saved me back then, but there wasn't one to save me now. His feral gaze left me shivering in the mud, and I thanked the Thirteen he wasn't my brother. If he had been, I'd already be dead.

"Ilan wanted the honor of killing the mighty Ida, King Leon's *sepier* and whore, but he'll have to forgive me this," he said.

I let him step into my space as he blathered and I slid my fingers into my boot cuff. As thunder rattled overhead, I shoved my knife into his heart. He grunted with surprise, then fell to the ground.

The rain pelted me, washing off the mud and blood as I stood, chest heaving in the cold. My hip throbbed, the scar at my neck pricked a million pins, and my stomach churned. As much as I wanted a strong ale and good, long nap, both would have to wait. Unlike his new recruits, Ilan wasn't stupid. Too long without checking in, and he'd know something was up, so I left the bodies in the alley and set off for the barn at the town's edge.

And prayed to the gods that I wasn't about to get myself killed.

The hay door still flapped in the wind, though a little less now that the rain was easing up. Ilan. He'd been my best friend and the first man I'd ever loved. He was family. Or had been 'til he'd held me down while my brother slit my throat.

Could I kill him as casually as I'd killed the two Amaskans in the alley?

From the rafters, I could kill him with one throw of my knives. It'd be done. And the past could stay in the past—where it belonged. Leon never need know about who I had been or how I'd gotten my scar.

But was that the Amaskan in me talking? The killer in me? Or was I more than that now?

I shook my head, and a few pieces of hair that had escaped my thick braid in the fight stuck to my neck. The front door slid open without much effort, and Ilan grinned when I stepped inside. He held no visible weapons, but I wasn't foolish enough to think him unarmed. No Amaskan ever was.

"It's been a long time, Shendra…or should I say Ida?"

"Shendra died when her brother slit her throat," I said. His authentic smile caught me off guard, and I asked, "Does he know?"

"Who?"

"Bredych."

"Aren't you curious how I found you?" he asked as he pulled out a piece of parchment bearing King Leon's seal. "It was a beautiful thing. A King choosing his lover for his *sepier*. A woman who'd saved so many at the Little War of Three only to rise through the ranks to Captain of the Royal Guard. It's unusual for a woman to make it that far, so when the rumors reached me, I was curious, as I'm sure you understand. And my plan worked! Kill a few women, and you come running. You never were good at staying dead."

He was curious. *He* killed the women. Not my brother, Bredych.

I rushed him, sword before me. It was a risky move—one knife and he could end me—but he'd be expecting me to play it safe. To be the same Shendra he'd known before.

And he'd be wrong.

He was still talking when my sword plunged into him. Ilan's eyes widened as his mouth moved soundlessly for a moment. "Ya always had to gloat, didn't ya?" I said as he dropped off my blade and fell into the hay.

Unlike Red-Beard, there was no apology. No remorse to make his death easier to bear. Just the same smirk he'd worn when he'd held me down and betrayed me twenty-five years ago.

"Itova be merciful," I whispered as I closed his eyes. "But not *that* merciful."

Five murdered women had forced me to face my past. What would these three dead Amaskans do to me?

My hip, which had stopped aching somewhere in the fight, reminded me that for the moment, I was alive. I left the barn and walked into the night.

And into my future, whatever that would be.

Connie J. Jasperson is a published poet and the author of nine fantasy novels, including the Tower of Bones series, set in the world of Neveyah. Her work has appeared in numerous anthologies. A founding member of Myrddin Publishing Group, she can be found blogging regularly on both the craft of writing and art history at Life in the Realm of Fantasy (http://conniejjasperson.com/). She and her husband share five children, numerous grandchildren, and a love of good food and music.

THORN GIRL

CONNIE J. JASPERSON

When Piers Arnesson was brought here yesterday, I was summoned to the dungeon. It was afternoon, which is unusual, and my master was in a frenzy. Lork opened the cell door, his eyes wild, forcing a bag containing several pots of healing salve into my hands. "They roughed him up, but he belongs to the Highest. Make him presentable. I'll question him when you've finished."

When I entered the room, a tremor of shock rolled through me. I found myself gazing at a priest of Aeos. All her priests are mages, and the yellow lightning bolt tattooed on his cheek proclaimed his element of lighting. He was about thirty-five, handsome, and defiant.

"I'm Piers Arnesson. And you are?"

I knew he wouldn't understand the hand language, so I gestured to my mouth.

He nodded. "And you are Silent. I'm so sorry for what you must have suffered." Rage passed through his eyes, belying the crooked smile on his lips, "They dosed me with silf. If I still had my abilities, I would get us both away from here."

I took care of him as well as I was able. He showed no fear or any sign he felt pain as I tended his wounds. After I finished, he thanked me.

I returned to my alcove but couldn't get him, or my situation, out of my mind.

A slave has no choices in life, a fact that was made clear to me the day the slavers came. When they cut out my tongue, they left enough so I could learn to swallow again once the scar had formed. I still taste and enjoy some flavors, but food holds little interest for me, save it fills the emptiness in my stomach. They took me through the portal to the Bull God's world, Serende, so different, so hot and dry—so full of minotaurs.

I was trained to be a lady's maid, but when my lady died I was inherited by her son, a priest of the Bull God. Fortunately for him, Tauron's priesthood, those minotaurs with the ability for magic, had been decimated by the plague. That allowed my master to rise to a rank he would never have gained had those with more intelligence survived. For a time, all went well, until Lork was assigned to a high position in the personal household of Baron D'Mal, the highest priest and absolute ruler of the Bull God's worlds.

The servants remained in Serende, except for me. Because Neveyah is a colder world than Serende, I was issued new garments and heavy boots, and a thick cloak for the journey. I found myself and all the rest of the baggage belonging to the House of Lork tightly crammed into wagons and riding back through the portal to the world of Neveyah.

This time I was taken to the wilderness and brought to the ancestral home of Tauron's highest priest.

Life in this empty, haunted place, is a test of my endurance. Most of the time, I sit in the vacant servants' hall mending my master's garments, listening to the guards nattering in the mess hall next door.

They whisper that the Baron remains in Serende but forges a mental link with Lork through a magical artifact hidden within the Keep, ensuring his fist is closed around his lands in both worlds. I can't imagine what relic could enable this or why this link between the worlds is possible. I only know that Lork's strange connection to the Baron increasingly affects his sanity.

Nightly, he paces his rooms, raving, drinking himself senseless. Lork believes he's the Baron's chosen successor and will rule both worlds. I believe he is less than a slave, an empty vessel for the Mad Baron and the dread Bull God to use in their evil rites.

This place is rife with shadows, even in the well-lit corridors. I know why the guards call this keep the Shadow Castle—the shadows are as thick as fog, and at times they surround me. It's whispered that the shadows are the souls of the dead king and his family.

Each prisoner in the upper tier of the dungeon is housed as a cherished guest. The cell is beautifully furnished, and the food is prepared by the Baron's two personal servants. They only cook—Lork is supposed to handle the rest of the prisoners' needs. But I'm Lork's property and he requires me to serve these pitiful creatures in his place.

Every morning, I make sure I am out of the dungeon and well away before the Baron occupies Lork's body. I suspect he has never examined Lork's conscious mind, despite his use of my master's body. Possibly it's beneath him, or he doesn't want to know. Regardless, Tauron's highest priest has no idea that his special prisoners are being cared for by a slave, a woman who remains a child of the Goddess Aeos.

Today is the second afternoon of Piers Arnesson's captivity. Before Piers, I tended to two men held in that cell. When they went to the altar, they never returned. Unlike the others, Piers has a strength of will as strong as any priest of Tauron.

When I enter his cell, I want to weep. His weapons and armor have been left lying there, deliberately arranged to taunt him. He appears free to move, but is bound by a magic geas, unable to touch them.

Piers is raving and weeping, so battered he's nearly unrecognizable. Blood trickles from his right ear, and I fear he will lose one eye. Livid stripes on the soles of his feet and the backs of his legs and buttocks vie with deep purple contusions on his naked body, clearly the marks of both lash and fist. He begs his lover's forgiveness, weeps for the loss of his magic. He appears broken physically and emotionally, yet he's still unbroken—I don't know how else to describe it. They cut him off from his magic, but whatever it is that binds him to the goddess Aeos hasn't been severed. I do what I can, bathing him and applying balm to his wounds.

When I have finished tending his injuries, Lork enters the cell with the drugged tea and sits beside the prisoner. I still have work to do to finish changing the man's bed and cleaning the room, but my master directs me to wait outside the door.

Piers has calmed and remains silent while Lork uses twisted logic and guile in his attempt to convert him to Tauron. But Piers remains steadfast, even knowing that what he has already suffered over the last two days will be nothing to what lies in store for him tomorrow. His lips are swollen, but his words are clear. "I didn't offer you my body. You used me against my will."

"Not I. Only the Highest can perform such a sacred ritual. To partake in the holy sacrament of the joining is a privilege granted to few—how fortunate you are to be so chosen! Only through pleasure and pain can we see the true nature of Heaven. Only through pain and sacrifice can we be deemed worthy of pleasure." Lork repeatedly swears that he didn't wield the whips although his hand held them, that he isn't in his body when the high priest and the dark god perform the ritual.

My thoughts halt as I process what Lork is saying. I can hardly breathe as my master attempts to reconcile rape and torture as a religious experience. It must have been a secret closely held by the priesthood, and under normal circumstances, a mere slave wouldn't have knowledge of any part of their sacred rites.

But I know, now, and despise my master for his cowardice and dishonesty.

To Lork's platitudes, Piers only replies, "You will break my body, but I will die unbroken."

Lork has finished and orders me to complete my tasks. He departs, intent on finding his wine bottle. I can no longer look at him, but he, being who he is, doesn't notice.

I am as gentle as I can be, and Piers seems grateful. I can't whisper comforting words to him, and even if I could, they would be hollow.

Something must have conveyed my horror and compassion to him. He allows me to hold his hand for a moment and then expresses sorrow for my plight as a slave.

I am shocked that this man considers me unfortunate when his final hours will be spent in unimaginable hell. He speaks of his life, of his lover, and his sadness for what he is leaving behind. Yet I sense he's at peace with his fate, feel the strength of his conviction that his soul will find a place at Aeos's Great Hearth. His only sorrow is for the loss of his bondmate.

As I prepare to leave, Piers begs a favor of me. "Please. Take my sword to Abbott Garran in Braden. He must be told what happened here." He stumbles over his next words, barely able to say his lover's name. "Tell…Moran…how much I love him. Tell him…loving him was the best part of my life. Tell him, please.

My first instinct is to shake my head and back away.

But I don't. Long ago, my first mistress told me that in every life a time will come when you arrive at a precipice. You must either leap the chasm or fall to your death.

I stand at that place now. A moment ago, I was a slave, an obedient woman of twenty-two who never had to fend for herself, never lacked for food or shelter.

But now? To attempt this is to seal my own fate. Yet, I have felt Piers's kindness, the way he cares about people, even one as lowly as me. I want to ease his pain in some small way.

I find myself nodding, agreeing to his request.

Piers weeps in relief, unaware that I have agreed not just for him, but because I am disturbed beyond explanation by the circumstances in which my master has placed *me*. Lork has made me an accomplice, and I can't live with the guilt.

I feel such terror, such trembling, as I pick up his black leather sword belt, finding it heavy and ungainly. A silver-handled blade rests in the black scabbard, and I have no idea why I am doing this.

Piers's thankfulness as I fumble, strapping the sword belt on, tells me I'm a coward. I retie my servant's belt over it, covering the blade with my apron.

As I leave his cell, I can't say if my dread is more for the decision I made impulsively or for this weapon I don't know how to use. Either way, I am committed. An oath of honor now binds me to go to a city many days away in a foreign country and give the blade to a man the legions call the Red Abbott, a man who terrifies them. Then I must tell Piers's lover what happened.

Two separate tasks I can't imagine completing.

The halls are empty as always, but the sensation of eyes on me makes me jittery as I scurry to my room in the empty servants' quarters. Not eyes…shadows, dark and swirling around me as if to conceal what I carry.

Such a fanciful thought. When he dies, will Piers become one of the shadows that haunt this house of horror? Perhaps, but maybe if I do this one favor for him, his soul will go instead to Aeos's Great Hearth.

It's winter and the nights are bitter in Neveyah. I spent all my years of servitude in a much warmer world but dress as warmly as a person who lives their entire life indoors can, putting on all three sets of my clothes, one layer after another. I wish for gloves but have none, so I'll have to keep my hands inside my cloak as much as possible.

Now I stand at the unguarded kitchen gate. Hesitating, I look out at the dark kamtara forest, the plant the minotaurs believe is holy. I see only league upon league of thorn bushes as tall as a man, some head high to a minotaur. Thorns are all that grows in this part of the valley, except along the streams, so I will have to follow the water.

No guards are ever posted at the outer doors here, and if I was seen leaving, no one follows me. Something important is kept in this fearsome place, a holy relic claimed by the deities of both worlds. Since Tauron now has possession of it, the perimeter and outside doors are left unguarded as a lure for the priests of Aeos, a trap that had ensnared Piers. The guards are stationed at various doors inside the main residence, areas I rarely had reason to be in.

Except for the unwieldy bar of steel that bangs against my leg as I walk, I am unarmed. The purse at my belt contains scissors, a sewing kit, and a comb—the tools of a lady's maid. I doubt they'll do much damage to the beasts who stalk the kamtara forest, but I can't part with them. They're all I have left of my dear, dear lady, who would be so mortified at what her son has lowered himself to.

I'm committed but still hesitate, fear filling my mouth with the remembered taste of iron. Other than the sword, I own nothing and have taken nothing. I have no provisions, only the garments and tool-purse of a slave, a sword I fear, and scant directions of how to get where I must go— "Follow the Escarpment south to the Gap." If I live to arrive at the Gap, the only way into or out of this valley, I should find a road that will lead me to the City of Braden.

Piers warned me that before he's allowed to die, he will be pressed hard and will eventually tell Lork what I am doing for him. He said he would try to hold out, to give me as much time as he was able. The look in his eyes...

But Lork is lazy and will see no reason to hunt me down. The guards say that the land is so hostile that none who escape the Keep survive. Certainly, a lady's maid won't last even a day in the wilderness. Water-sprites lurk in the weeds beside every stream, drenching the unwary with their water magic. Scorpions and soldier-wasps rule the kamtara forest. Other, more deadly beasts roam the wilderness, and I mustn't forget it.

Somehow, my feet carry me forward, as if they don't hear my mind screaming to turn back. Once through the kitchen gate, I enter the forest of thorns. I find what seems to be a path of some kind and begin walking.

I know a few edible plants from my childhood in a gentler part of the valley. The few yar blossoms and noe roots at the edge of the shallow creeks will keep me alive, but hunger is my companion. With my mutilation, I must chew carefully, chew and chew until they're soft enough to swallow without choking.

Squads patrol the wilderness, hunting for their meals and pretending they are too busy to return to Shadow Castle. The ground shakes with the rhythm of their marching as they tramp through the brush. Many times, I must hide beneath the thorns, watching as their heavily booted feet trudge past. Yet they can be silent when they choose to be, which makes me wary of blundering around blind corners.

It's nearly sunset, and a squad has just filed past me, the sound of their heavy steps dwindling. When I can no longer hear them, I crawl from my hiding place, but a sudden agonizing, burning pain assails my leg. I had forgotten the peril of wasps and for a moment I panic. With difficulty, I quell my terror and manage to get out of there with no further stings. I'm glad now I was bored enough to eavesdrop on the soldier's conversations as they discussed wild remedies and the healing properties of kamtara bark.

The thorns make getting the bark a dangerous chore, but once I learn the trick, I'm successful. I can sense the bark's healing properties. It's easily crushed between two rocks, and with water from the creek, it makes a decent poultice. This immediately lessens the swelling, but my leg is still painful. The kamtara scratches will heal, eventually.

I add the bark to my purse. When I've finished my scant breakfast, I began walking again. Bumping against my good leg with every step is the scabbard containing the sword, reminding me that I have nowhere else to go but to Braden. The city is centered in the gap at the southern end of the Escarpment, which is topped by the Mountains of the Moon, so I keep them to my right and continue walking.

The dawn of yet another day has arrived in this endless forest of thorns. I'm cold, hungry, and weary of being drenched by water-sprites every time I approach the bank of a creek to forage for roots. This time I'm as silent as I'm able in approaching the stream. I find the tender noe shoots and carefully pull them from the soft mud, separating them from their roots. I see no flash of silver, hear no chittering, and my hair remains dry.

Kneeling beside the water, I drink my fill and wash the roots, enjoying the heady rush of success. I stand, intending to slip back to my resting place.

A strange groaning sound halts me at the bank of the creek. Searching the small clearing, I see immense boots lying in the rushes, attached to strong legs clad in the leathers of Tauron's legions.

Against my better judgement, I look further and am appalled by what I see. A minotaur soldier lies beside the water, beaten and left for dead. His horns have been broken off, leaving gaping holes in his skull through which I can see what I fear is his brain. Blood is everywhere.

The people of Serende are born as humans and look much like us, although they breed taller and larger. At age fifteen, all males born on the soil of Serende are taken to the church where they must undergo the Ritual of Remaking. They are physically changed into minotaurs, given the head and neck of a bull. Some die in the process, and many are left unable to speak clearly but communicate with the hand language slaves use.

Only one priest of Tauron still remains visibly unchanged, the Highest. He was born a child of Aeos, and though not a minotaur to my eyes, he has been changed somehow. There is not one minotaur in either world who does not tremble and bow low when he passes, despite his small stature and lack of visible horns.

The wounded soldier is one of the silent ones, a lower minotaur, and his wordless moans are pathetic. But though his fingers can barely move, what he says captures my attention. *"Holy Aeos, have pity on your son. Take me to your Great Hearth."*

I'd heard rumors of a secret sect of minotaur warriors. At some great battle, the legions were nearly turned back by a great warrior in blue armor, a priest of Aeos they named the Blue Death. Followers of the Blue Death, these Minotaurs secretly worshipped the Goddess Aeos. It was only gossip, nothing proven, of course. But the evidence lies before me, dying of thirst within inches of water.

My hand shakes as I scoop a handful of water and trickle it into his mouth. His face has been severely beaten, but one swollen red eye opens, and his fingers move. "Thorn Girl...why do you wander in this wilderness?"

Thorn Girl. It's as fitting a name as any. I no longer need my slave name and barely remember that which my mother gave me. My own fingers move, saying the one thing he will understand. "Honor."

The soldier's eye drops to the sword at my side. He recognizes a Temple blade and gestures his understanding. His fingers are halting, but I understand him. "The wind in my head blows...my thoughts fly away." I can see the water brought him some relief. His moans have ceased, but as I watch, he falls unconscious.

Wounded creatures draw predators. I'm terrified to stay with him but can't abandon him. Against my better judgement, I gather enough kamtara bark to make a large quantity of poultice.

Then, using the scissors from my purse, I cut a wide strip off my outer skirt and spread the bark paste between layers. I carefully fold the dressing and bind his head, hoping the aromatics will help heal him. I pray to Aeos that covering the gaping holes will ease his pain. The remaking bestows the ability to withstand great pain and to heal quickly, so perhaps he will survive.

I need to eat, so I return to the creek to gather more roots and make cold compresses for the soldier's injuries. A flint and belt knife lay on the ground beside him. Most of my skirt is gone now, and it's cold, so very cold. I build a low fire, savoring the warmth and hoping it keeps predators away.

Fearful, and hungry even though I'd eaten several small noe roots, I keep watch, but despite my best efforts, I fall asleep. When I wake, I see him seated beside the fire. The dressing still securely covers his head, but his face is terribly swollen. "This fire was a mistake. But thank you. I'm Kerk. You?" His hands are bruised from the fight he lost, but the gestures are clear.

Determined to show no fear, I reply, "I left my name behind. You gave me a new one. I'm Thorn Girl now."

He nods, and his gaze falls on the Temple blade. "Where do you take your 'honor'?"

I can't be sure of his allegiance. Still, I opt for the truth. "To Braden. To the Red Abbott. I promised."

"You won't get there on this path. This is the Legion's trail and goes to the garrison at Balensfort. If they find you, that sword will be your death."

Horror clutches my belly—I stupidly built a fire alongside their road and camped here as if it were the safest place in the valley. My dismay must show, because Kerk adds, "I would repay my debt."

I cock my head but say nothing.

He sees my wariness. "After I've rested, I'll lead you on the forgotten trails. I must leave you there. I can't enter the city of the Red Abbott, not with the mark of the remaking still upon me."

I gesture to his head, and a grimace crosses his bovine features. "I should begin to heal in a day or two. In the meantime, we must leave here. Help me walk—everything spins." He must be in great pain, but if so, he doesn't show it.

I help him gather his few things as a cold mist sets in. We walk back the way I came. He's unsteady and sometimes leans heavily on me, but we manage. After we've gone some way, he points to a faint trail I hadn't seen before, and we take it. Perhaps half an hour later, we come to another creek. I sense Kerk is at the end of his strength. "Is this place safe?" My fingers feel frozen, and it's hard to form the words.

He looks around in a dazed way, but nods. I'm not sure how far behind us the legion's trail is and fear a fire would alert them. I see a sheltered place under the branches of a large willow on the bank above the stream. It's dry and warmer under there, and he immediately falls asleep. Once again, I gather yar blossoms and noe roots, along with some of the tender shoots, saving aside enough to make a small meal for my companion—a days' worth for me, but even a small minotaur eats a great deal at each sitting.

When he wakes just before twilight, I change the dressing on his head. The terrible wounds don't seem to be healing. Nevertheless, Kerk claims he feels better and thanks me for providing food. "I'll watch. You sleep."

Minotaur society is a strange mix of manners and barbarism. They're casually brutal with each other, but slaves go unharmed for the most part. Sport is everything to them, and there's no sport in maltreating someone who can't fight back. I don't fear he'll molest me and am more tired than I've ever been.

Just as I'm about to fall asleep, a squealing shriek carves through the evening, suddenly cut off. I sit up, seeing Kerk silhouetted in the dusk, wiping his knife on his trouser leg. "Rat-man." His knife points to a small form shaped like a human but with ratlike features. "They're attracted to blood. It's been stalking me." Wearily, he hefts the corpse into the stream, where it floats away. "Others will feast on his remains and leave us alone."

I say he should rest, but he replies, "You sleep." His fingers are slow, but I take him at his word.

The ground is hard, and the night is icy. I have only two skirts left for warmth and my cloak is torn and dirty, but it's all I have. I tuck my face inside and wrap my hands in the folds of what is left of my outer skirt. Although I don't know how I'll ever sleep again, I fall into a deep slumber, undisturbed by dreams or beasts.

Birdsong wakes me to gray daylight. I'm stiff from the cold, but still alive. Kerk sits leaning against the willow trunk, eyes closed. As soon as I move, he is awake. He passes a wide berchera leaf to me, upon which lies half a small perch, neatly fileted. His features are less swollen, and his hands speak more fluidly. "Sorry—only one fish came to breakfast. Perhaps tonight will be better."

I nod and thank him and accept the fish. I'm not sure if I like it raw or not, but it fills my belly.

We talk about the journey. "Five days if I was fit and could carry you, but now? Eight or more days before we get to Braden."

The fact his wounds aren't healing worries me. Minotaurs usually heal quickly, so they should be closing by now. Hopefully they will improve today. Still, he seems to have more strength, so once I've eaten, we resume our trek, keeping to the faint trails that follow the waterways.

We have been walking for nine days, all of which, other than Kerk's deteriorating health, passed quietly. I enjoy his company, and we talk about many things. He tells me of how his mates, those who also follow Aeos, traveled once beyond the invisible barrier that bars the Bull God's poisonous magic from leaving the valley, and told him what it was like. The land there sounds wonderful, but I can't imagine it's real.

The last few days have been difficult, as his wounds have turned septic. I've been foraging and tending him as well as I can. Four days ago, he developed a raging fever, and I can find no herb to ease it. I apply cold compresses, but they do little good.

He is deaf and nearly blind now, but intent on walking, telling me repeatedly that he wants to touch Aeos's untainted soil. I don't understand what he means, but it keeps him moving. I've had to support him most of the time, so we are going slowly.

This morning we crossed a shallow ford and into what can only be described as the pure land of Neveyah. It was then I understood what he meant. We must have passed through the barrier, because the soil, the air—everything is different, cleaner.

But now my companion is too ill to continue. "Tell me what you see, Thorn Girl. Tell me what this world looks like."

I get close to Kerk's eyes, so he can see me, and tell him everything— how colorful the birds are, how bright the yellow butterflies, how the deep blue sky is filled with song. I tell him how much I will miss him, and I talk until he can no longer see my words, and then I give him water and hold his hand. He tells me, "Keep walking to the west on this trail… see the walls tomorrow. You're strong enough… brave enough. You are Thorn Girl."

His last words are difficult for me to read because tears fill my eyes. Even though I would have been parted from him at Braden, losing him this way is unfair.

As the life leaves him, my fingers move in prayer, the ritual for the dead. Then I build a cairn from the river stones and camp beside his grave, unwilling to leave my only friend.

At dawn, I walk toward the west. The trail becomes an old, unused road, and after several hours I see the white walls of Braden in the distance, topped by a guard tower.

I've nearly finished my quest to take Piers's sword home. I dread having to tell his lover what happened to him, but I promised.

But after I've done my duty, then what? I don't know what my role will be. I have skills. I can read and write—I'll find work of some sort.

Three weeks ago, I was a slave, afraid of shadows. Now I am Thorn Girl, friend of minotaurs and mages.

Kerk was right. Inside of me is a woman who can do anything.

Robyn Bennis was born one day prior to the signing of the SALT II nuclear arms reduction treaty, a historic achievement she would later take full credit for. A biologist by training (and misfortune,) she has done research and development involving human gene expression, neural connectomics, cancer diagnostics, rapid flu testing, gene synthesis, genome sequencing, being so preoccupied with whether she could that she never stopped to think if she should, and systems integration.

She is the author of the Signal Airship Series from Tor Books and wrote her debut novel, *The Guns Above*, within sight of the historic Hangar One at Moffett Airfield.

Robyn currently lives in Madison, WI, where she has one cat, two careers, and an apartment full of dreams.

THE PRINCESS AND THE DRAGON

ROBYN BENNIS

Brave Sir Ramsay, by all appearances, was having trouble not only with the dragon, but with the very reality of the dragon. "It's a dragon!" he cried, diving under a jet of flame from the beast's mouth. He rolled, came to his feet, and added, "It's an actual dragon!"

In the highest chamber of the tower, Princess Purity Vesta Phantasos the Third did her best to look concerned, but only made it as far as annoyed. "'Tis! Woe is me, for the witch who locked me in this tower tasked yon dragon to guard it, just as the stories say!" She then added, in a voice too quiet to carry, "And as the scorched bones say, plus the warnings from the villagers, but details aren't exactly your strong suit, are they, Sir Raspy?"

"What?" the knight asked. While he was distracted, the dragon swept a great, clawed foot at him, throwing him a dozen paces. Brambles broke his fall but slowed his rise.

The dragon reared up and roared. On its hind legs, it was as tall as the tower, bearing tons of corded muscle covered in inky black scales. It came down hard enough to shake the ground, straddling him with its front paws.

Just as it seemed that he was doomed to be its supper, a lady's shoe hit the creature on the back of its angular head. The beast's slitted pupils widened, and it looked back. Sir Ramsay did not hesitate, but swept his longsword across the dragon's ear, slicing through a quarter of it. As the dragon keened and thrashed at the pain, he ran.

He stopped a hundred yards away and shouted something up to Princess Purity, though nothing he said could be heard at such a distance. Then he disappeared into the woods.

"Is he gone?"

"Yes, he's gone, Zeph," Purity said, stepping out of the tower window. She slumped into a nearby chair, across a table from a warty, old witch. "He'll be back, though." Just then, something hit her on the side of the head.

"There's yer bloody shoe back!" the dragon said, sticking her muzzle through the window. "If ya think yer daein' that agin, yer off yer heid. I nearly lost an ear, ya daft wee scunner."

"Sorry," Purity said, as she retrieved her shoe and put it back on. "But if one of those knights realizes it's all a front, they could expose the whole operation."

"Aye, an' if the dragon has ta' be doon one ear, so be it, eh?"

"Don't be a baby, Pam," Zeph said. "It's just a scratch." The witch fetched her sewing kit and began to suture the wound.

Princess Purity took the chance to slip downstairs and pick out some clothes for the evening. She returned wearing soft leather shoes, woven leggings, and a grey cloak that matched the color of the tower stones. In the meantime, Pam had been sewn up, and was now purring as the witch scratched her nose.

"No armor?" Zeph asked, when she saw what Purity was wearing. "They'll have crossbows, you know."

"I intend to armor myself by not being shot at."

"Are ye sure?" Pam asked. "We're lookin' at more guards than yah've dealt with a'fore. They'll gee yeh a right smart if yer not careful."

"Then I'll be careful," Purity said. "Can we go over the operation, please?"

The witch brought out the maps and plans and walked them through it. The operation was indeed a tricky one, but if successful, it would go a long way to ridding the Petty Kingdom of Camhaidan of its petty leadership. Tonight's theft of the privy council's account books would mark the culmination of a plan that was years in the making, started after her Uncle Dundas poisoned her father, took over as regent, and promptly drained the royal treasury.

"Accoutrements?" Purity asked, when Zeph had concluded her briefing.

The witch handed a chicken foot to Purity, who after years of doing this, knew enough not to turn her nose up. Zeph explained, "For opening locked windows from the outside. I've imbued it with an insubstantiality charm that should allow it to pass through glass, and a limiting cantrip to stop it going through your fingers or your backpack."

Pam sniffed the air. "What about to the rest a' the chicken? Is it here? Can I have it?"

Zeph shook her head. "I was going to cook it, but it must have caught the insubstantiality charm through sympathetic resonance, without catching the limiting cantrip. Damn thing fell straight through the table, and the floor too. Must be halfway to the Earth's core by now."

Shaking her head in commiseration with Pam, Zeph next handed over a skeleton key, which Purity was already quite acquainted with, having used it in several past operations.

"And what about this knockout bottle?" Purity indicated a little clay beer bottle with a wooden dowel where the cork would usually go.

"I've made several improvements since you last used one."

"I hope so. Last time, I woke up two days later, in a dank cell."

"Not this time. I've taken your advice and reduced the thaumaturgical charge, which should decrease the effective range to within three yards of the bottle. I've also weaved a minor cantrip into the sleep spell, so in addition to being knocked out, anyone effected will also crap themselves."

Pam let out a guffaw, but Purity only sighed. "Really? Why do you do these things?"

"To drain their morale."

"They'll be asleep!"

"Yeah but, for, you know, next time. Anyway, it's too late to take it out." Zeph scrunched up her lips and ran her eyes over her work table, looking for anything she'd missed. "Ah! Your new magic wand." She pushed a few scrolls aside and picked up the black, lacquered stick. "Mid-range thaumaturgical focus with a delivery like a brick through a stained glass window. And an underarm holster, for concealment."

"Does yer wee plan include time for a meal?" Pam asked. "'Cause, I don't know if yeh realize, but it takes a good lot a' energy to fly and breathe fire."

"We know!" Zeph said. "You know how we know?"

"I keep reminding yeh?" Pam said.

"Yes!" Purity and the witch said, together.

"Well, I remind yeh about half as much as mah stomach reminds me. Consider yourselves lucky."

"There should be time for you to grab a snack while I'm infiltrating the castle," Purity said. "Satisfied?"

Pam was not impressed. She eyed Purity, as if assessing her for caloric content. "Aye, we'll see."

Purity only rolled her eyes.

The moon set shortly after the sun, leaving the world below in near-darkness. The only lights were stars reflected off a stream here and there, and the occasional glow of a farmer's hearth fire. Purity could imagine those families now, snug and comfortable after a hard day of spring planting.

Imagining it was all she could do, for she was on the back of a dragon, whipped by freezing winds above her waist and baking from heat below. Pam's body was warm even at her coldest, but the exertion of flying kicked her internal temperature high enough to bake a scone.

Purity knew this to be a fact, because Zeph once tried it, "in the interest of natural philosophy." On that day, natural philosophy claimed three trees blown over by dragon force winds, and the wooden fence which Pam held onto by her claws. It netted two dozen perfectly cooked scones, one satisfied witch, and a dragon so amused by the absurdity that she giggled herself to sleep that night.

Tonight, however, Purity could tell from the way the muscles moved under her that the dragon was straining her last reserve, after the exertion of her afternoon stage combat. Luckily, the castle was up ahead, the torches on the battlements just becoming visible. Pam stiffened her wings, setting herself on a glide path.

Purity shouted over the slipstream, into the dragon's ear, "I need a distraction."

"Easily done, Lass." Just past the wall, Pam pulled her wings in tight, and they dropped like a stone. Fifty feet short of splattering them both onto the castle courtyard, Pam extended her wings. As she swooped low, she loosened a sputter of flame into hay bales stacked outside the stables, then rose into a climb.

By the time every guard and stable hand was looking at the fire, Pam was near the apex of her rise. Purity was ready. She had her harness unbuckled, and as Pam arced over the parapet, Purity jumped off and landed on her feet atop the wooden roof. Pam wasted no more energy, but nosed into another dive to pick up speed, and disappeared into the night.

The first thing Purity noticed, inside the castle, was that they'd scrubbed the walls in the time since she lived there. That was good, in the sense that cleanliness is important, but it was very, very bad in the sense that her cloak was too dark to let her blend in.

It occurred to her that she should have worn armor.

She skulked down the parapet stairs, looking like nothing so much as an intruder skulking down the parapet stairs, to find two guards at the bottom. She immediately noted that the guards no longer wore the face-obscuring helms she was expecting, and which would have allowed her to move freely if she stole their armor.

Worse yet, they were no longer arranged on either side of the door, facing out—an arrangement which allowed a silent intruder to approach within a yard without being spotted. They were standing on either side of the corridor, so that one could always see up the parapet steps.

Which he did. How could he not, when her uncle was so much better at security than her father had been, and she had come disguised as dirty masonry?

By more reflex than thought, she grabbed the knockout bottle from her belt, pushed the dowel down to prime it, and gave it a wild fling into the corridor. Half a second later, she felt a wave of drowsiness come over her. The feeling passed and was replaced with a brief but uncomfortable urgency.

The guards, on the other hand, caught the full effect. One of them clattered to the floor, so loud that it seemed every piece of his armor clanked against every other piece on the way down. The other slumped, but his cuirass locked into the steel fauld around his waist, and he remained in precarious balance, on his feet. Purity was nervous that he was only playing possum, but the blurping, bubbling sounds inside his armor indicated that the bottle had done its work.

As she snuck quietly around the corner, she could hear servants running to see what the noise was, and skidding to a halt when they hit the smell. "Good God," one of them said. "I didn't know a person could die of dysentery standing up."

She ducked into an unoccupied chamber and waited for the commotion to die down. Soon enough, the stricken guards were dragged off to the infirmary, but they were promptly replaced. The real problem, however, was the curiosity of others. Servants and courtesans trickled in from every corner of the castle to hear what happened. The first servants on the scene described what they'd found over and over, and their account of the smell became longer and more obscene with each retelling.

By the time the passageways were clear, all hope of using the now-extinguished stable fire as a distraction was gone. It was, however, still the middle of the night, in a castle exhausted by an unexplained fire and stories about pooping.

Most of the corridors were clear, and she knew them well. The records room was easily accessible, just off the council chambers, but said chambers were guarded at all hours. When she was near, she had to slip out a window and inch from stone to stone, gaining tenuous handhold on the rough, exterior bossage as she went.

It was not quite as harrowing as all that, however, as the council chambers were only on the second floor and there was a relatively soft, thatched eave projecting out from the first floor, just a few feet below. After many minutes of shuffling sideways, always looking over her shoulder to see if she'd been spotted from the courtyard, she was outside the deserted council chambers.

A quick peek inside confirmed that the exterior door was closed, and Zeph's semi-substantial chicken claw made short work of the window latch. It could not overcome the lack of oil on the window hinges, however. Opening the window made a creaking sound that, from Purity's vulnerable perspective, seemed the loudest noise the world had ever known. She didn't dare close the window once she was inside but went straight for the records room and shoved the skeleton key into its lock.

As soon as she had it open, she dashed inside and shut the door behind her. She huddled against it, holding onto the inner handle until she was positive that no one was coming to investigate the sound. Only then did she take out her wand and tap it to generate some light.

She began to go through the records and was shocked to find that there were thousands upon thousands of them. Where her father had operated with a few ledgers, her uncle seemed to be rebuilding the kingdom out of paperwork. There were entire shelves full of records, and more piled on the floor, whereas a single writing table had served her father's scribes and accountants. The writing table might still be there, but if so it was buried under stacks of record books and piles of parchment.

"Can nothing go right?"

No sooner had she said it, then she was answered by the door to the council chambers swinging open. She thought of quenching her wand, but if the light really was shining under the records room door, suddenly turning it off might draw more attention than leaving it on.

One man entered, then another, who chatted with the first, closed the window, and sat down himself. Three more came in over the next quarter of an hour, while she stood perfectly still. And finally, her uncle arrived. She could not make out his words, but she recognized his loud, arrogant voice through the door.

It was a council meeting. It was a goddamn council meeting, in the middle of the night. Then again, that was the traditional time for corrupt leaders to meet and plan their malfeasance, wasn't it?

Whatever embezzlement or misappropriation they were discussing, they seemed to be having a good time with it. There were frequent bouts of laughter, which Purity used as cover to thumb through records. She couldn't carry the entire room back to Zeph, but she only needed to find some critical documents to expose her uncle's corruption.

And though she was necessarily slowed by the need for stealth, she had plenty of time. The meeting must have lasted four hours or more before it finally broke up. By then, she had a stack of documents picked out that just barely fit into her backpack, and another stack that she could cradle in her elbow.

When she counted as many footsteps leaving as had come in and added an extra ten minutes' wait for good measure, she slipped her wand back into its holster, pushed the door open, and looked out.

Her uncle sat at the table exactly opposite her, pointing a crossbow at the records room door. "Ah, Purity," he said. "Glad you decided to join me. Come out. Come out. Drop those records, please. Hands where I can see them."

"Uncle Dundas," she said, quite politely. She let the papers in her arms drop to the floor. "Wasn't expecting to see you tonight."

"Nor I," he said, "until something about those dysenteric guards reminded me of the style of your friend. Zelaniah, is it?"

"Zeph."

"Yes, 'Zeph,'" he said, putting ironic emphasis on the shortened name. "Don't expect to see her again. After you've married my son, I'm sending you both to a remote outpost, up in the mountains."

"And you'll continue as regent, I suppose?"

"Better for everyone if I do. My son is an idiot."

Purity didn't answer. She only stood, trying to think of a way out of this. But even as she explored options in her mind, they evaporated in the line of pink light that appeared in the window. That was it, then. Pam wouldn't risk extracting her in daylight, so all hope of escape was gone.

"What are you looking at?" her uncle asked, wisely choosing to not take his eyes off her.

"Just the sunrise," she said, resigned to it.

His eyes narrowed. "What ruse is this? The sun doesn't come up for hours."

She frowned, but as the light continued to brighten outside, her lips curled into a grin. "Oh, nothing," she said.

Still, he didn't look back. Smart.

But outside, the fires were growing larger and more numerous. Pam must have gotten worried about how long it was taking and had decided to provide Purity with another distraction. That, or she was just bored.

A guard rushed into the room, and shouted, "Sire, the outbuildings are all aflame!"

"'Sire?'" Purity asked, putting her own ironic emphasis on the honorific address reserved for kings. "Really?"

Her uncle's eyes grew anxious. They whipped over to the guard, for the barest instant.

It was all Purity needed. She pulled her wand from its holster and fired in one fluid motion. Her uncle was not much slower and pulled the trigger on his crossbow. The bolt flew straight and true, right for her heart, but had only sailed a quarter of the way when it impacted the wand's magical energy. The deadly missile deflected and hit the ceiling, while the magical energy continued on, threw her uncle from his chair, and sent him flying out the window.

She dashed to the broken glass, glanced down, and found to her disappointment that he'd come to a soft landing on the thatch below. She waved for Pam, who swept in and plucked Purity from the window with one of her great claws, swift as lightning but gentle as a mother cat picking up her favorite kitten.

"That was'nee yer uncle, was it, Lass?" she asked, when Purity had gained her seat on Pam's back, and secured herself in the harness.

"It was," she answered, and grinned. "But we had a falling out."

The dragon giggled all the way home.

"If that guard hadn't been there, I could have grabbed the other papers," Purity said, as she paced in the highest chamber of the tower.

Zeph was hunched over the documents Purity had managed to recover, sliding an emerald reading stone across them to magnify the tiny columns of figures. "Mmm hmm," she said.

"Do you have anything yet?"

The witch sighed and looked up. "Nothing you're going to like."

Purity narrowed her eyes, in an expression more reminiscent of her uncle than she would ever admit.

"Everything I've read so far suggests that he's a very clever treasurer. Far superior to..." She noticed the tightening in Purity's eyes and seemed to think better of her next words. "Some previous kings."

"He *is not* king!"

"No, but he's astute. These initiatives are brilliant. He's obviously studied the economic works of Fan Li, and I thought I had the only copy of his writings in this hemisphere."

"But... but..." Purity searched through documents until she found the one she wanted and pointed to the bottom line. "He drained the royal treasury!"

"True, but he spent it on roads, a postal service, mercantile development, agricultural improvements. Did you realize that four fifths of farms in this kingdom were still using light turnplows? In soil as rocky as ours! Unbelievable! So, your uncle started a program to help them buy heavy plows."

"With borrowed money!"

"Yes, but, with usury rates as low as they are, it only makes sense. In the current slack mercantile climate, and with so much farmable land going unused for lack of proper tools, thrift will only reduce future grain levies. Whereas, the heavy plow project alone will boost levies by, I'm just estimating here, but something like a third over the next fifty years."

"But he's bankrupting us!"

"That's a common misconception. Kings will only go bankrupt if their usurers lose faith in the ability of future levies to match projected outlays." Zeph was about to go on, before she was interrupted by shouting outside the tower.

They went to the window, to find the valiant knight from the day before. He was not gleaming in the morning light, because he'd come back without his heavy armor, and had traded his sword for a long spear. "What?" Purity asked, cupping a hand to her ear. And then she said to Zeph, "Better wake Pam."

"She's not going to be happy. She just went to bed."

The knight came closer and shouted up, "As I love you, so will I set you free!"

"Are you sure you're in love with me, valiant sir knight?" Purity shouted back. "For lo, I worry you may only be in love with the idea of me."

He called back, "What?" But before he could get an answer, his eyes were drawn to Pam, coming around the side of the tower. She did not swoop up and over it, as she had the previous day, nor did she breathe fire as a demonstration of her power. She only walked—shuffled, really—out to meet the knight, yawning several times on the way.

She shot a look back at the tower—one that mixed molten grumpiness with a promise that, the next time this jackass showed up, Purity would have to entertain him by herself. She turned back just in time to dodge the knight's charging spear thrust, and just stopped herself from squashing him under her foot.

"I think we should cancel tonight's operation," the witch said, coming back up the stairs, out of breath.

"Pam needs the rest, yeah," Purity said.

"That and, well, maybe we ought to re-evaluate our entire plan to overthrow the regent?"

This was too much. Purity put her hands on her hips and looked hard at Zeph. "He killed my father!"

Outside, a paltry sputter of flame shot past the window.

"I know, I know. So… maybe we can lock him in a dungeon instead of whipping up a homicidal frenzy in the populous? That way we can, you know, still get his advice. From time to time." When she saw that Purity wasn't buying it, she added, "With the encouragement of a hot poker, if necessary."

"You mean, you want to torture him for economic policies?"

The witch shrugged. "Yeah?"

Purity considered it, while the sounds of battle floated in through the window—roars and grunts and stomps. Finally, Purity threw her arms in the air and said, "I'll think about it."

There was a great yelp, and they again ran to the window. Outside, Pam flopped around, legs flailing and wings kicking up gusts as she writhed on the ground. Twenty yards from her, the knight stood next to a ballista, concealed in the bushes.

Purity rushed downstairs. By the time she left the tower's hidden entrance, Pam was over on her side, breathing heavily, a ballista bolt in her chest. Purity leapt onto the dragon's ribs and wrapped her hands around the missile.

"Don't pull it out!" Zeph called, coming behind her. She carried the bag she used for midwifery and had a long strip of clean linen over her shoulder. She handed a glass bottle and the end of the linen to Purity. "Dump this on the wound, then wrap the opening up tight."

The knight ran to them, complete bafflement showing not just in his eyes, and on his face, but infused throughout this entire body. "What's going on here?"

By the time Purity stopped hitting him, Zeph was ready to take the bolt out. The knight only wobbled on his feet, bleeding from a broken nose and split lip. He was developing some pretty nasty bruises, what with being at a complete loss for how to stop a lady from punching him.

If Purity considered this unfair, then it only underlined the fact that he should have given up his antiquated views of womanhood *before* he shot her friend in the lung.

She took further advantage of the knight's confusion by tying him to a tree, then went to help Zeph. The bolt came out in an operation lasting two hours, but Pam didn't stir.

Evening was coming on, and they were lighting great bonfires to keep her warm, when Pam finally cracked open an eye and, in a wheezing voice, asked, "Is there anything tah' eat?"

Beneath Purity's relief, anger still boiled, as she stroked the dragon's nose and said, "Only what's in the pantry. Some bread, a little jerky. Do you want to eat him, instead?"

"She needs to eat if she's going to live," Zeph said, her eyes also on the knight.

He cleared his throat and said, "Perhaps we can start with my horse, which is tied up half a mile down the road."

Purity stared at him. "Might not be enough."

"If she's still hungry afterward, then she can have me." The knight drew a breath, eyes downcast. "Seems only fair."

Pam snorted. "Hush yeh. Yer too wiry. But a wee bit a' horse would really hit the spot."

Purity spent her evening in a rather unexpected way: slaughtering a horse and hand-feeding little cubes of its ragged, bloody flesh to Pam.

"If I may ask," the knight said, "why do you play this trick upon virtuous knights, and how have you come to tame a dragon?"

Pam started to laugh at that last question but had to stop when it caused a painful coughing fit. "These two, tame me? Laddy, yeh have it backwards."

"We just borrow the place from her. We didn't start the 'princess in distress' rumors, either. My Uncle Dundas did that. He poisoned my father and, when I fled here to keep from being married off, he spread that story in the hope some idiot knight would deliver me to him. We only play along because admitting the truth would raise too many questions."

"Uncle Dundas?" The knight blinked his swollen eyes several times. "Purity?"

She blinked right back. "Have we met?"

"When we were children. I'm your cousin."

"I don't have a cousin named Raspy."

"*Ramsay*. Sir Ramsay. Dundas is my father."

"Oh shit!" Purity said. "You're the little snot he wants to marry me to!"

Sir Ramsay slumped in his bonds. "He told me that if I rescued the 'princess in the tower' and brought her to him, I *wouldn't* have to marry you. I think he was hoping I'd fall in love with you, before I realize what was going on. He knows I'm kind of a romantic."

"What a right bastard," Pam said.

"Yet such a poet with numbers," the witch said, in far too admiring a tone for Purity's taste.

"Ugh," Purity said, as she cut Ramsay's bonds.

He stood and worked the feeling back into his limbs. While he was still rubbing his arms, he said, "Don't take this the wrong way, but... *would* you consider marrying me?"

"You're joking, right? I must have hit you harder than I thought."

"No, really. Think about it. My father was able to stifle your coronation when you were younger, but what can he do if you come back of age and already married to his own son? He's planning to have you sent away after the coronation, of course, but he expects to already have you in his custody. If we return free, with a witch, a dragon, the truth about your father's assassination, and his own son on your side, it will be a trivial matter to turn the tables on him. The castle guards like me better, anyway."

The witch nodded along with every point, as if she had been thinking this, herself.

"The thing about it," Purity said, "is I have no intention of ever sleeping in the same bed with you, or any other man, ever."

Sir Ramsay's eyes opened as wide as the swelling would allow. "Oh. I didn't know." He looked from her to the witch, and added, "So, you two are..."

Purity shook her head. "No. We were for a while, but we broke up a few years ago."

"Oh," he said again. "That must be awkward."

"It's fine. We're better friends now than ever." She flashed a sweet little smile at Zeph, who returned its mirror.

"So then," Sir Ramsay said, after some consideration, "what are your thoughts on sham marriages?"

As she was pondering it, the witch whispered, "It's a good compromise. Your uncle will be shamed and exposed, while the country will continue to prosper."

"Okay, then," Purity said. "But only if I get to torture him whenever I want. He killed my father, for heaven's sake."

"Then it's agreed." Sir Ramsay got down on one knee in front of Purity, retrieved a dazzling sapphire ring from a pouch at his waist, and said, "Princess Purity Vesta Phantasos, will you sham marry me?"

She patted him affectionately on the head and said, "I suppose so. Whatever. Sure."

Pam sniffed and made a show of wiping a nonexistent tear from her slitted eye. "It's like I always told yeh, Lass. Look long enough, and yeh'll find true happiness, forever after."

Robert J. McCarter is the author of six novels, three novellas, and dozens of short stories. He is a finalist for the *Writers of the Future* contest and his stories have appeared in *The Saturday Evening Post, Pulphouse Fiction Magazine, Andromeda Spaceways Inflight Magazine*, and numerous anthologies.

He has written a series of first person ghost novels (starting with *Shuffled Off: A Ghost's Memoir*) and a superhero / love story series (*Neutrinoman and Lightningirl: A Love Story*), as well as two short story collections. Next up is Woody and June versus the Apocalypse, a story of adventure and love and taking things (even the apocalypse) in stride.

Of his latest novel, *Seeing Forever*, Kirkus Reviews says, "Sci-fi as it should be: engaging, moving, and grand in scope."

He lives in the mountains of Arizona with his amazing wife and his ridiculously adorable dog. Find out more at RobertJMcCarter.com

ASHNA'S HEART

ROBERT J. MCCARTER

Kyla's cheeks flushed hot as Masters Oster and Wesfro laughed at her, the six other robed masters in their chairs of stone looking surprised or just looking away. The eight men sat in the large volcanic cavern that served as the council's chamber with Kyla standing before the semi-circle of elders. The forever-lights that hung from the cavern ceiling flickered now and then, a symbol of her people's waning grasp of magic.

"A woman like you got us into this predicament," Wesfro said once he had stopped laughing, his big hand smacking his thigh for emphasis.

"I am not Ria," Kyla said, clasping her hands tightly, hoping they did not see that she was quaking just like the volcano beneath them was beginning to. She felt responsible for Ria's treachery, but she didn't know why. She had her best red robe on and her curly black hair demurely pulled back, trying to look respectable and responsible.

"She trained you," Oster shot, his thin face angry. "She was your mistress. How can you, who are barely a woman, not even a priestess yet, stop her?"

The chamber was hot, not its usual warm and she felt sweat trickling down her back.

She was young, yes, and her power was not yet in its full blossom, but she remembered other lives when it had been, when the power of fire was hers to wield. She remembered the old days when the great fire mages could take on the form of a dragon.

In their contentment, her people had let magic slip from an everyday nomadic necessity to a rarity, left to the realm of the priestess. They believed less and less in magic and the old ways as she believed more and more.

She was so close, she could feel the ancient magic in her, she could feel her destiny calling, she could feel the dragon wanting to come out. That would be power enough to snatch Ashna's Heart back from Ria, return it to the heart of the volcano, and save her home.

She smelled the sulfurous breath of the volcano and wished she had worn lighter robes. "What have you to lose?" she asked. "All I need is a ship and a crew."

Master Oster shook his head, his hand going to his short grey hair. "No! We must leave this island, we need every ship. It will take years even if we devote all our resources to it."

And then the argument began. Wesfro saying they should trust in the remaining priestesses of Ashna to keep the volcano quiet, Oster saying that he was a fool and that they must leave. It was as if she wasn't there, as if she didn't count, as if she didn't have any magic at all.

Kyla knew the priestesses would eventually fail no matter how hard they tried. It took the power of Ashna's Heart to keep the volcano at bay. Ria, the greatest among them, had betrayed them when she stole it and thrown the remaining priestesses into disorder. Kyla had tried talking to them, but her training was not yet complete, her vows not yet taken, they didn't listen either.

As the council argued, there was no talk of going after Ria, of returning Ashna's Heart, and they gave no more thought to the apprentice priestess in front of them.

What could she do?

She felt the dragon within waking just as the volcano was. If only someone would believe her.

Her thoughts went to Li, the handsome foreigner she loved. He would believe in her. He would help her. He would be able to find a ship and lead the quest.

She slipped away while the argument raged.

From the stern of the ship, Kyla hugged her cloak close and stared back at her island home as it slowly slid towards the horizon. Jagno was dominated by a massive, green speckled cinder cone thrusting up from the Nuran Sea, the very top of it frosted in snow. The land flared out from the volcano to relative flatlands along the coast that were dotted with villages and cities.

The wind ruffled Kyla's wiry black hair and brought the scent of the sea tinged with smoke and sulfur. The black smoke was only a thin tendril as it rose up from the once extinct volcano. She couldn't be smelling it—maybe it was a memory from a long-ago life or still stuck in her nose from the council's chamber. The smoke warned of what was to come, the signal that sent her stealing forth with her beloved Li and their friends to find the only thing that could quiet the volcano. Ashna's Heart.

The dawn light made it clear that there was no pursuit. Li had secured this small ship, assembled the party, done everything she'd asked without questioning her. She felt unsure, no one had manifested the dragon in centuries, nor had she in any lifetime she could remember, but her heart told her it would be necessary, so she must find a way.

She heard the scuff of a boot on the wooden deck and Li was there, his strong arms around her.

"We will find it," he said, his words colored with his foreigner's accent.

She nodded but did not speak, leaning into his embrace. She felt guilty about that smoke, as if she were the cause, as if she had woken the volcano. The smell slid down her throat and tasted like ash.

She closed her eyes, trying to banish the scent by focusing on what she could hear. The waves against the hull of the ship, the cry of a seagull, the groan of taut ropes, the sharp snapping of sails. Behind her, she could hear the chatter of her companions. Anden going on about the paramour he had just left while Wicks thumped his hammer on the deck. Theanne and Ivan speaking softly of their love. And Shu, Li's sister, chanting, the soprano lilting of her prayer a comfort.

"I fear I will not see my home again with these eyes," Kyla whispered, looking at Li's face. His skin was light, his straight jet-black hair hanging around his face, the breeze playing with it like she wished she was. His brown eyes, though, were what always drew her in. They were kind, but with a wariness of one who has seen much. "I just found you." She looked back to the island and the smoke.

"We will find each other..." he began.

Kyla did not say her part. She did not have the heart to say, "No matter how many lifetimes it takes." She had the gift of life-knowing and could remember her soul's journey ten lives past and knew that her soul had been living for much longer, for millennia. But of all those lives, this was the first time she had found Li.

"We will catch Ria," he said, his voice fierce. "We will return the heart. We will save your...*our* people."

Kyla nodded.

"Your magic is strong. We have Anden's bow, Wicks's hammer, Ivan's sword, Theanne's sight, Shu's prayers. We will prevail."

She smiled at her beloved and nodded, although in her heart she did not believe it.

The months flew by like an old man's days—with speed, leaving little memory of them in their wake. Guided by Theanne's visions, they followed Ria from island to island, through the archipelago, ever to the north, always behind, Ashna's Heart just out of reach.

Eventually, they followed Ria to Untor, an island on the edge of the Nuran sea. It was dominated by Mount Denton, a huge, extinct volcano.

The party set out in the cool of spring on the bottom of the island and ascended into a fierce snowstorm.

"Tell me again," Anden said through gritted teeth as they walked up the narrow trail, the wind driving stinging snow into their faces. "I need to know why I'm doing this."

Kyla sighed, her hands pausing in their dance, the air suddenly becoming cold.

"Don't stop!" Anden said, his teeth chattering, his slim face peeking out from his grey cloak, his quiver peaking over his shoulder. He was reed thin, a creature of the sun, not the ice.

She chuckled, resumed her mudras, and the warmth returned, making the cold bearable. "Ashna lived thousands of years ago. She came to our little island when the volcano still erupted and fell in love with our nomadic people. She was a fire mage, the greatest that ever lived. She danced and quieted the mighty volcano and our land became verdant and prosperous. It is said that when she died, she followed hidden passages deep into the depths of the volcano and laid herself down. She summoned her mightiest spell, gave up any hope of future lifetimes, and became one with the volcano, forever calming it. When her attendants reached the cavern, they found a ruby-red heart where the woman had once been. It is said that it contains Ashna's power and her soul."

There was more to the legend, but she couldn't bring herself to speak it. The part about Ashna's jealous sister who cast a seed of doubt among the priestesses of Ashna, that seed having finally taken root in Ria and her theft of the heart.

Kyla stopped and looked up. Ages ago, part of the volcano had blown off, leaving a nearly sheer cliff thousands of feet tall. She was no seer like Theanne, but she could feel power. Ashna's Heart was close.

She quickened her steps, signaling to her tired companions to continue.

As she fell from the heights of Mount Denton, Kyla did not worry about dying, for she knew that her essence would return—even if it was as a humble bee or ant. She tried not focus on their quest and what it would mean to her people if she failed. She fought back the bitter thoughts of the ambush Ria had sprung on them at the top of Mount Denton's massive cliff. She tried not to grieve for Theanne and Ivan, fallen in the battle. And she swallowed down the bitter taste of spite knowing that Ria, once her mentor, was now her enemy and had so easily met Kyla's fire with water, sweeping Kyla off the cliff.

She did not have time for regret or doubt or weakness. She cultivated one thought, and one thought only.

I am now the dragon.

The wind whipped around her body, the sound of clashing arms having faded, her ears now filled with the noise of her flapping traveling cloak, her nose still filled with the iron scent of blood. She was wet, the air icy, and her cloak sodden, but she was not cold because of the fire that burned in her. She was mage and had mastered the element of fire lifetime after lifetime. She had been raised and trained by the priestesses of Ashna. She must not fail.

As the valley below rushed up, she chanted, her dancing hands forming the correct mudras, fighting back her doubts, her guilt, as her body tumbled, and her curly black hair whipped crazily around her. Only a dragon would do to save her life and defeat her enemies.

I am now the dragon.

Her power came from her center, from her heart, from the flame there that was so bright. First, it warmed her, and then she grew hot, steam rising from her clothing. The spell took hold and she began to change. Her limbs shortening into her elongating body, scales forming, an iridescent shade of red, her skull elongating and her teeth growing into the sharpest of fangs. Wings sprouted from her back, tearing through her clothes.

I am now the dragon.

But she was too late. She had the power, she had the knowledge, but not the time. Her half-woman, half-dragon body slammed into the ground. She died as the battle raged on far above.

In her last moment, she knew she had failed her people and took that pain with her into death.

The dragonfly was large for its kind, with a wingspan as wide as a man's hand is long. It was ruby-red and lived near a pond on the edge of the Ganden Forest on the island of Thenos. Its life had been unremarkable, first as a nymph in the brackish little pond eating and avoiding being eaten, and then as that lovely red dragonfly.

But something was different about this dragonfly. It was not just the need for food and the desire for survival that drove it. There was something else. It often left the pond and its abundant food supply to explore the surrounding forest and the road that humans with their horses and contraptions traveled on.

It was a beautiful place, an old forest filled with secrets, and the ruby-red dragonfly saw it all, ever seeking. Its tiny insect brain did not know what it sought, until one day she found it.

On that trail, through the dense forest came a group of humans riding horses. A tall, proud man with dark hair and prominent cheekbones rode in front, followed by two other male humans and one female.

She zoomed close, her four wings beating out a precise path until she was right in front the man, flying backwards.

She saw his dark, hooded eyes, a pink, still-healing scar on his cheek, his set jaw and tight lips. These things didn't mean all that much to her, as a dragonfly, but she felt something. She felt a longing she didn't understand and something else she had never felt in this life: guilt. She knew somehow, she had caused that hooded look on his face, she could have prevented that wound on his cheek, she was responsible for the missing humans that should have been in the company.

Then those eyes widened, and those lips moved, forming a word. The dragonfly could see magnificently in colors humans could only imagine, and all around her at once, but she had no sense of hearing. But still, a word snuck into her tiny mind. *Kyla.*

The face changed. A smile. Joy. As the human laughed, the dragonfly danced in the air for she had found what she sought. Another word entered in her mind, a word that was like joy itself. *Li.*

A dragonfly does not live long. Half a year at most, with much of that time as a nymph. Kyla the dragonfly spent most of her short adult life traveling with Li and his companions through the Forest of Ganden. They sought something. While Kyla-dragonfly didn't know what or why, she shared their desire and sense of urgency.

For the ruby-red dragonfly it was a joyous time. She would eat many bugs along the way—dragonflies are skilled and voracious hunters—and fly along with her human at other times. At night when the humans built their campfire and slept, Kyla-dragonfly would fly up into a tree and fall into a watchful slumber.

On a late summer's night with the air cool, when she felt they were close to finding what they sought the feel of magic woke her. She saw it creeping below, a tendril of warm air her amazing eyes could see. It wound its way around Li's body as he sat watching, his back against a tree. It slipped up his nostril and he fell asleep. Something was very wrong.

She took to flight, a bit unsteadily. While she could see into the infrared spectrum and could easily make out the approaching humans, she could not see her surroundings very well in the scant moonlight.

She flew slowly towards the first human. He was squatting down, with an arrow drawn back and aimed at Li.

Kyla-dragonfly's magic was still with her. Not the chanting and mudra type, but something much more primal. Her magic served her need and, suddenly, she could clearly see the human that was about to slay Li. She flew fast, down the shaft of the arrow, while her body changed. It became harder and longer, filled with the heat of her anger.

The human flinched, the bow jerking up and the arrow flying off into the night, but the dragonfly's wings compensated easily, and she met her mark.

For she was the arrow now and the attacker's eye her target. Kyla-dragonfly could not hear the man scream, but she somehow knew that her friends would awaken, they would have a chance.

This was comfort to her as the man's hand slapped down on her abdomen. She burrowed deeper, past the eye into the brain.

They died together.

The Draco lizard loved her wings. Not grey-green, like the rest of her skin, but a wonderful ruby-red with delicate black mottling. Flying was the most glorious thing.

Her wings were built on the scaffolding of very long and flexible ribs. They ran along her slim body from right past her front legs, down her back, joining with her back legs just above the knee. The lizard, not having a very large brain, did not reflect on her love of flying—gliding really, there was no flapping involved. She did not notice that for the rest of her kind it was no different than scurrying up a tree or munching on a fly. It was just part of life. But not for this lizard. Flying was joy.

She was different in other ways. She spurned males, having no desire to mate, and being large for her kind was able to parry their advances. She would puff up her dewlap—the pouch on her neck, which was also ruby-red—and the males would scurry away.

This Draco was restless, incomplete, ever seeking something as she wandered the tropical island of Canor.

Then one day she saw a tall human on horseback with three other humans riding behind. They were worn and disheveled, their heads down. She could feel their sadness, sense that they were missing something essential to complete their mission.

The lizard did not think, she leapt from her tree and glided to the man, landing on his shoulder, her claws digging into his worn leather jerkin.

His tired face swung around, a look of fear that quickly melted into a smile, his laughter ringing out.

"Kyla," he said to his companions, two human males and one female, who repeated the word and laughed.

She had found Li again. Her dewlap swelled with pride as Kyla the Draco lizard looked forward, perched on her human's shoulder, ready to continue their journey.

The journey across the sea was hard on Kyla-lizard. No trees. No forest. No flying. She learned to survive on cockroaches and to avoid the rats, staying with her human whenever she could, using his body heat to keep herself warm. When the boat would pitch in the stormy sea and Li would go out into the water and wind, Kyla-lizard would retreat to where the horses were kept and cling to the mane of the horse that carried Li.

She was glad when they came to land, although the island was hot with only a few palm trees along the shore and rolling sand dunes beyond.

They camped and rested for several days, giving Kyla-lizard the chance to climb trees and unfurl her red wings as she glided from one to another.

Soon the quest continued, and she hid from the sun behind the flowing white cloth that Li wrapped around his head. Weeks passed until the sand started to disappear, merging into rolling hills covered in the yellow straw of dead grass. A small mesa rose up out of this land and atop it stood a tower made of sandstone blocks, proud and tall, surrounded by a jumble of cut stones as if the castle and keep that used to be here had crumbled while the tower had remained.

Kyla-lizard sensed the magic and emerged from her hiding place, crawling off Li and onto the mane of the horse. This task was for her, she could feel it. She looked back to Li and then to the tower. He nodded, a grim smile on his lips.

He guided his horse around the back of the mesa and up the remains of an ancient road cut into its side. When they came to the jumble of stone blocks, Li stopped and looked at the lizard. She climbed onto his shoulder and then onto his hand. He understood what she wanted and stood up in the saddle to extend his arm up as far as it would go.

Kyla the Draco lizard unfurled her wings and flew across the downed sandstone blocks to reach the tower. She shouldn't have flown that far in the still, hot air, but her magic had aided her, a breeze lifting her at the last moment, so she did not have to touch the downed stones. She feared them. Some ancient force still lingered there.

Up the tower she scrambled, until she found a window looking south over the vast desert they had traveled back to the blue strip of sea on the horizon. Through the window, she saw a cobweb-covered skeleton sitting on a throne, looking towards the sea.

The window pulsed with magic. Magic that would stop a man, but not a lizard. Kyla-lizard carefully crept through and down the wall, across the dusty floor and up the skeleton to its hand.

On it was a ring of shiny gold with a large green stone, unworn as if time had no effect on it.

She used her claws and pulled on the ring, but it resisted, as if it was still tight around flesh that was long gone. She pulled harder to no avail. Instinct drove her as she brought her own magic to bear and pulled on the ring one last time. It flew off and clattered to the dusty floor, Kyla-lizard tumbling down after it.

She rose, shaking her head, and went to the ring, putting her forefoot on it so it stood, and slipped her head through it. The tower shook violently. She scurried across the floor and up the wall to the window. Outside, the whole world seemed to dance as the tower swayed, the sound of it a deafening roar.

But something was different. She could see far across the sea to a cloaked woman standing on a ship. The human held a large ruby-red stone that Kyla-lizard longed for. She knew this ring was what the humans needed to complete their mission, that it would guide them.

The vision faded, and she paused. The ring was too heavy—she would not be able to fly with it around her neck. But she would not get down the tower before it collapsed, either.

There was a deafening snapping sound, like the earth below her had broken, and the tower started to fall.

Kyla-lizard jumped and fell straight down, the sandstone blocks of the tower falling right above her. She would be buried along with the ring.

She unfurled her lovely red wings, her magic coming to her aid once again. The wings stretched in size and a breeze gave her lift. A stone block raked down her back, taking skin with it, but she was flying, farther than ever before, the joy of it filling her heart. She cleared the tumbling tower and the rest of the stones and crashed into the dirt beyond.

She was still too heavy and didn't land well, tumbling on the dirt, breaking the ribs of her wings, one of them piercing her body.

Through the pain she felt joy. She had succeeded. The ring would let them continue their quest. Li picked her up in his hand while the female human tried to save Kyla-lizard with her own magic. But it was too late.

The last thing Kyla the Draco lizard saw were droplets of water flowing down Li's face.

The large lizard, a Komodo dragon, basked in the sun on the southern edge of a small, unnamed island deep in the Sindu Sea. She weighed as much as a strong man, with long claws, sharp teeth, and a powerful tail.

This lizard had scales a deep shade of red around her eyes and down the top of her back and tail.

She was perched atop a cliff on black, volcanic rocks, watching the ocean as months slipped by. During the day, she left only to hunt or when the sun became too hot, and then moved to a nearby palm tree and watched from the shade.

One day a ship arrived, and a small boat made landfall. There was a strong human male with long black hair caught at the neck in red silk, with three other humans, two males and one female. After landing on the beach below, they did not delay, pulling the boat up above the tide line, shouldering packs, and picking their way up the cliff.

Sounds formed in her brain. "Li," "Anden," "Wicks," and "Shu." Her mind was just sophisticated enough to associate the sound with the humans—each human had a different sound that belonged to them.

She longed for the male, Li, as if he were a mate. The thin one, Aden, was tall and lithe. Wicks was stout and slow. And Shu, the female, she felt towards as she would a sister.

Li led, and when they arrived at the top of the cliff, the Komodo waited. Li's hand went to the sword at his belt, but then he recognized her.

"Kyla," he said, his face showing joy.

The lizard knew that sound was her sound. These humans were hers. They knew where she needed to go. She fell in beside Li as they started their long trek.

Kyla the Komodo dragon could taste the danger in the air before she saw it. They were three days into their journey and seemed to be wandering. They were searching for something, that much was clear to her, but what signs they followed or what they sought was beyond the lizard. She was content to be by Li, his hand often brushing her head as they walked.

As the forest opened up into a meadow covered in tall grass, Kyla-Komodo stopped, her forked tongue licking out. She tasted humans, but not her humans. Li's hand went up and the rest of the humans stopped and quieted.

Three arrows shot forth from those tall grasses, one grazing Kyla-Komodo's shoulder. It was not a wound of consequence and only ignited her rage. She sprinted forth, moving fast as her kind can for short distances, and was on the three bowmen. Using claw, fang, venom, and tail, they died quickly.

After it was done, she heard the clang of steel on steel and turned to find her humans surrounded. She sprinted towards them, but a female human stepped in her way. The sound "Ria" floated in her mind and she felt hate. This human was her enemy and betrayer. She lunged forth, but Ria's hands wove intricate patterns in the air as her tongue formed sounds Kyla-Komodo did not understand.

The great Komodo dragon was frozen in place, an invisible force squeezing her tight.

With a smile on her thin face, Ria pulled a narrow dagger from her belt with her left hand, her right hand continuing to dance in the air.

Air. Kyla-Komodo realized that this Ria was using her air magic to hold her. How could she fight this magic?

Ria smiled as she knelt in front of Kyla-Komodo and pressed the blade to her scaly throat. The Komodo struggled, but could not move, beyond her jaw cracking open and her tongue flicking out. Her innate magic came to her aid and as Ria pushed, the knife skittered off her strengthened scales.

The tall mage rose up, her knife discarded, her chanting growing louder and her hands dancing more intricate designs, and the pressure increased.

Behind Ria, Kyla could see the battle rage with Li, Anden, Wicks, and Shu, surrounded by ten strong men. They did not have a chance.

Memories came to her of humans in stone chairs laughing at her, of the human Li taking her away from her home seeking something important, of the taste of defeat, bitter and rank, of feeling small and weak and insufficient.

But she was Komodo now and all of those memories and feelings burned in the fire of her anger. More than shame came back with those memories, her magic came to life, sounds forming in her mind, a long ago spell resuming.

I am now the dragon.

Lives passed through her mind's eye. As Kyla the human falling from a high cliff desperately trying to turn into a dragon. As a dragonfly, a fearsome hunter and master of the air. As a Draco lizard that loved to fly, so small, so brave. As this powerful Komodo dragon that had found its purpose and its place.

I am now the dragon.

Her body grew many times larger and elongated, becoming more serpentlike. Wings sprouted out of her back, her claws and teeth lengthened, and the chemistry of her venom sacks changed.

Ria backed up, a surprised look on her face, but continued her magic. Kyla was now a dragon, but still could not move, the air pressing her, crushing her. The pain was terrible. She was dying.

Her friends would perish at the hands of Ria's mercenaries. The volcano would erupt and scorch her home of Jango, sending those that survived forth. Ria was winning. Ashna's Heart and the great priestess's sacrifice would be perverted.

She was dragon and still not enough.

But she *was* dragon now and instinct took over, and she forced her mouth open again, this time a gout of flame leaping forth and catching Ria's clothing on fire.

Ria screamed and the spell was broken. Released from the vice of magic, Kyla-dragon leapt forth, biting the mage's head off before going to the rescue of her humans.

There was some green left in the caldera below. Just a few pine trees along the edges of the growing pool of lava, the sulphur smell of it reaching the dragon's nose. After Ria's death and the routing of her mercenaries, it hadn't taken long to find Ashna's Heart. The Komodo lizard turned dragon had found it easily, hidden in a nearby cave. She had invited Li to come along and had flown him back here to the island Jagno, her once-home.

"How can you return the heart?" Li asked, standing beside the dragon on the lip of the volcano. "The chamber must be flooded with lava."

The dragon was Kyla, but many other people too, and insects, and animals, and fish. The dragon had a mind that could see things clearly, could see her past lives all the way back to the time of Ashna.

My sister did it all alone. With her heart. I will find a way. The dragon did not speak, her thoughts entering Li's mind like a whisper carried on the wind.

"Ashna was your sister?" Li pulled Ashna's Heart out of his satchel. It was stone, translucent red, pulsing with power, and looked like a human heart.

The dragon nodded. *I remember it all now.* She remembered being jealous of her older sister and her power. Of being one of Ashna's attendants here on Jagno. And she remembered the jealousy she felt when her sister gave herself for her people. Kyla-dragon knew that the seeds of Ria's betrayal—the stealing of Ashna's Heart—had been sown in her own jealousy and passed down from generation to generation throughout the ages.

It was time to make amends.

The ground rumbled beneath them, a geyser of lava hundreds of feet tall shooting up from the pool below, a blast of heat rushing over them.

The dragon lifted her front leg and held her claw out.

Li swallowed hard and gave her the red stone. "We will find each other…" he said, beginning their ritual.

The dragon studied him. She still felt a longing for him and found comfort in those brown eyes, but the kind of love he professed was now foreign to her.

Her lives made sense now, all leading to this moment, this purpose. The dragon leapt off the volcano, her wings beating the air as she climbed above the island. She could feel the power of the stone in her claw and she could feel her long-ago-sister. No words, just feelings. Pride. Relief. Confidence.

She flew higher and higher until the island was small in the broad ocean with a ragged gash of red-orange lava leaking out the side and nearing the populated coast. Then she dove, folding her wings to her side and using her long tail to guide her, the wind lashing over her scales, down, straight down, towards the pool of lava.

When the island was large again, when she could see Li watching her fall, she finished the ritual and projected to him, *No matter how many lifetimes it takes.*

She didn't know if she believed it, but perhaps a calm life with him would be her reward, or perhaps another life of adventure together.

As the dragon splashed into the lava, she knew it would be all right. One way or another, one lifetime or another.

The cool breeze coming off of the ocean played at Kani's thick, black hair as she held tightly to her mother's hand, her clumsy legs pushing her slowly along the beach's firm, wet sand.

Seagulls flew above, crying and begging for food, while children bigger than her splashed in the waves, laughing. Tall palm trees held court over it all.

Kani was not jealous of the older children, she knew the years would pass quickly, but she was jealous of the seagulls. She knew the feel of the wind under her wings and longed to feel it again.

The mother and daughter walked until they came to a clearing in the trees with a view of the cone-shaped mountain, its black slopes dotted in green. Kani pointed.

"Again?" her mother asked.

The girl nodded and smiled. "Ashna. Kyla." The toddler had learned to speak before she had learned to walk.

The woman squatted down and looked deep in her daughter's eyes. "Kyla had the gift of life-knowing, a great and powerful fire mage she was. It was she who became a dragon and saved us when Ashna's Heart was stolen."

"Sisters," Kani said.

Her mother laughed. "Yes, the legend says that Ashna and Kyla were long-ago-sisters and she made amends for her jealously by saving our beautiful island after Ashna's Heart was stolen."

Kani nodded, for her mother to continue, and because she knew it to not be legend, but the truth.

She remembered it all.

Matt Youngmark is the author of the Arabella Grimsbro series, Chooseomatic Books, and the comic strip Conspiracy Friends. His next novel is *Spellmonkeys*, in which a 22-year-old Frinzil (the girl from his story in this very collection) goes on an epic quest to earn tuition money and remain in magic school as long as she possibly can. To find out more—and to get two free ebooks!—sign up for his author mailing list at www.youngmark.com.

APTITUDE

MATT YOUNGMARK

The great house Frinzil was born in was a stone-by-stone recreation of a much older castle, only cleaner, better ventilated, and plopped down in the inhospitable terrain of the Conquered Lands. It was called Orlehea Manor only because the name Orlehea *Castle* had already been claimed by its architectural ancestor. The Manor itself was utterly immense, employing dozens of servants who got up to any number of shenanigans, indiscretions and intrigues when not properly supervised. Some of these intrigues, as you would imagine, inevitably led to childbirth.

It should be noted that none of the resulting children were the secret offspring of the Master of the house. Lord Orlehea was roughly as gay as it was possible to be, and quite sterile on top of that. He and Lady Orlehea did not at all care for children but permitted the servants to keep their offspring on the property, provided that they caused no trouble and stayed entirely out of sight.

Three such offspring currently enjoying the Orleheas' begrudging hospitality were presently hiding beneath a bush, competing for the best view of the greeting procession about to take place. Two of them are largely inconsequential to our tale, so you needn't concern yourself with their names. The third was Frinzil. She was thirteen years old, and today was the day she would discover what she wanted to do with the rest of her life.

Greeting processions were not rare at Orlehea Manor. In fact, the Lord and Lady entertained an endless stream of guests, since their childlessness meant the castle would eventually be passed down to some as-yet-undesignated relation[1]. According to chatter in the hallways, though, the impending carriage didn't carry yet another favor-currying cousin. The Orleheas would be welcoming *visiting dignitaries*, and visiting dignitaries were a *big deal*.

The children had managed to catch glimpses of many strange visitors from their post beneath the shrubbery—dwarves from valleys

---

1 Assuming, of course, that Westerhelm hadn't lost dominion over the region by then—the Conquered Lands didn't earn their name because they had been conquered *a couple of times.*

between the mountains, elves from the peaks high above them, gnomes from mysterious, hidden cities, and centaurs from their settlements on the plains. Once the Orleheas had hosted a contingent of *werewolves* (they weren't much to look at, but slept in rooms barricaded from the outside, which was particularly terrifying for the manor's younger inhabitants). The territory known as the Conquered Lands was either a gargantuan island or a tiny continent, depending on how one classified such things, and fully twenty-two different civilizations had ruled over it during the past thousand years[2]. Descendants of these various conquerors still populated the countryside, having been raised on legends of past glory and prophecies of the day their people would rise-up and reclaim the lands they had somehow all convinced themselves was their one true ancestral home.

From the bushes, the children saw a single carriage approach the assembled masses lined up outside the castle gates and held their breath in anticipation. The driver reined his horses, stopped the coach, climbed down from his seat and swung open the passenger door.

Out stepped a stout, middle-aged, human man who would have fit in perfectly at any Orlehea family reunion.

"I told you it was just some stupid magistrate or something," the older of the two boys muttered. He was a horrible brat and habitual liar—in fact, he had been speculating wildly about the impending visit all week, and just moments ago had insisted it would surely prove to be hill giants, or possibly a lizard mage.

"Yeah," the younger boy said. He was a fairly sweet child, even if he followed the older one around like a puppy and occasionally soaked up some of his less-appealing characteristics. He was, for his part, entirely failing to hide his own disappointment. "Magistrates are *stupid*," he sniffled.

"Wait," Frinzil said in an exaggerated whisper. "Can you see if he has earlobes? If he doesn't have earlobes, he might not even *be* a magistrate. He might be a changeling."

"Shut up, it's not a *changeling*," the older boy grunted, pushing the younger one's head aside to get a better look. "Do you think it's a *changeling*?"

Frinzil could be fairly certain it wasn't, considering that changelings

2 Twenty-three if you counted the century when it was inhabited exclusively by *ghosts*.

were a story invented to frighten children and didn't actually exist[3]. "Maybe! Look close—you can always tell changelings by their—"

Before she could finish, a second figure emerged from the carriage. He was tall and slender beneath his voluminous robes, and by far the most beautiful creature any of the children had ever set eyes upon, with delicate features and a dark blue complexion the color of twilight on a clear summer's eve. The lobes of his ears, for the record, weren't distinct in any way, but their points rose almost to the top of his head.

The older boy's jaw dropped. "It's a lizard mage!"

The magistrate—or whoever the first man out of the carriage was—spoke. "Lord and Lady Orlehea, it is my great pleasure to introduce Mister Javrael from the Cavern Kingdom of the Deep Elves."

Several distinct populations of sentient creatures thrived far beneath the surface of the Conquered Lands, and technically, the empire didn't have dominion over any of them. In fact, Westerhelm didn't even have *formal relations* with the Deep Elves (Frinzil knew this because she devoured every single book she could get her hands on, and much of the literature she had access to involved the rather dry subject of diplomacy). The guests were traveling with no servants other than their driver, which was unusual. Their tiny contingent was dwarfed by the massive assembly that had turned out to greet them.

Granted, what appeared to be a pair of guests was in fact a trio, since a third visiting dignitary was hiding quietly beneath the elf's robes. More on that particular detail later.

After exchanging complicated bows, Lord Orlehea presented the elf with an ornate, jewel-encrusted book as a gift. It was a copy of the Orlehea family history, and it meant that, as exotic as he may be, Mister Javrael wasn't particularly important. In fact, Lord Orlehea had dozens of copies crated up in his basement and handed them out like boiled sweets.

"It would be my honor to add this volume to my collection," the elf said. His Imperial Common was flawless. "In exchange, I humbly offer a *shrk krael*, the traditional ceremonial dessert of my people."

Lady Orlehea gasped, which led Frinzil to believe the elf must have broken some taboo dessert protocol—and to be fair to her, nobles certainly had very specific rules surrounding what and when they were

---

3 This, it should be noted, made them only slightly more imaginary than *lizard mages*.

supposed to eat. It turned out, though, that the exact opposite was true.

"We couldn't possibly accept so extravagant a gift!" the Lady insisted. "Such a delicacy—"

"—Is not nearly so precious in my own country as it is on the surface," the Elf insisted. "I assure you that I have had the better of this exchange, my Lady. And at any rate, the wyrm larvae can grow upwards of four hundred pounds and must be candied whole, so I daresay I've brought enough that your entire staff might eat their fill."

He looked directly at one of the Lady's handmaidens as he spoke the last part, and the poor girl's knees trembled visibly. Adults were always swooning at the slightest provocation and assuring Frinzil that she would understand why once she became a woman. However, she had become a woman quite unceremoniously more than two months before, just after her thirteenth birthday, and still didn't understand what the big deal was supposed to be.

In fact, despite Mister Javrael's undisputed beauty, it was his *clothing* that had transfixed her. Specifically, an ornate glyph on the breast of his robe. It certainly wasn't Imperial Common, or Gnomish or Elvish or any of the other written languages she was familiar with. Nevertheless, she was certain she had seen that specific mark somewhere before.

Just as she was about to make the connection, a rough hand grasped the back of her blouse, and she was pulled out of the bushes in a single yank.

"Better fetch the poison—looks like we've got hedge rats again."

It was Mister Crosshanks from the gardening staff, and he grasped Frinzil and the older boy by their wrists, quickly hauling them around a corner and out of view of the procession. The younger boy squealed and fled, but he was unlikely to escape whatever punishment lay in store, since Crosshanks was his father.

Frinzil expected to be scolded on the spot, but the groundskeeper kept dragging them all the way around the castle to one of the servant entrances at the rear. The children hadn't simply been caught. They were being *fetched*. Standing just inside the wooden doorway was Missus Parchkuk, a towering, broad-shouldered orcish woman, with her arms crossed and a glare on her face that could have curdled milk.

"These two were right where you said they'd be, along with my little'un," Crosshanks said. "Spying."

"We were keeping out of sight, ma'am," Frinzil said. "I made sure of it."

"I'm certain you did," Missus Parchkuk said, "which is why your heads are still attached to your shoulders." The boy made a little involuntary whimpering sound. Although Lord Orlehea employed a human butler who was technically in charge of the Manor staff, Missus Parchkuk ran the show, and everyone knew it.

"Now, if you want to keep them there, you'll tell me which of you is responsible for *this*."

She strode off down the hall, and Crosshanks shepherded them along behind her. Missus Parchkuk stopped in front of a door that Frinzil had never actually seen open in all of her thirteen years, although she was *acutely* aware of what lay beyond it. It was Lord Orlehea's library, and it housed one of the most extensive collections of books in the Conquered Lands.

The door was ajar, and Frinzil could see a short trail of mud smeared on the floor a few feet past it, and a book laying open, pages down, at the base of one of the massive bookcases.

She was aghast. For children, the library was *the* forbidden room among many, *many* forbidden rooms in Orlehea Manor. It was obvious to her that one of the boys—the younger one, if her hunch was right, after being goaded into it by the elder—had run into the room on a dare, yanked a random book of a shelf and run out just for the thrill of misbehaving.

The boy's expression hardened. He might still be scared, but his survival instinct now overpowered his fear. "I saw Frinzil do it," he said.

Missus Parchkuk's brow fell, her face slipping from her putting-on-a-show-of-being-strict face into what Frinzil recognized as genuine anger. "Is that so?"

"No! I was helping Miss Posey prepare guest suites all morning!" It was the absolute truth—unlike her counterpart, Frinzil was a magnificently poor liar. Even the story she had spun earlier about changelings wouldn't have survived the most casual cross-examination. She was well aware of this shortcoming, so stuck with honesty as a general rule. "Check with her! She'll tell you!"

"Oh, I will," Missus Parchkuk said. "Frinzil, you must know the penalty for this. If *any* of you are caught in that room, you'll be thrown out of this house for good. But the little ones, at least, can drag their parents out the door with them. You do not have that luxury."

Missus Parchkuk was Frinzil's mother. Or adopted mother, at any rate—she and her husband, Mr. Garrkrul the cook, were the only parents Frinzil had ever known. They had taken her in and brought her up as their own when a troubled scullery maid abandoned her baby and her job in the dead of night just days after childbirth, the moment she had recovered enough strength to pack a bag and steal a horse. Parchkuk and Garrkrul were the only two orcs in Orlehea Manor, having come over with the Lord and Lady from the old country. They were treated very nearly the same as the human members of the staff, and it took Frinzil many years to understand the subtle difference: if one of the other servants abandoned their employment, he or she would find it nearly impossible to find other work without a letter to recommend them. If Missus Parchkuk or Mr. Garrkrul did the same thing, they would be hunted down and brought back in chains.

The look in Missus Parchkuk's eyes had shifted again, from anger to concern. She was legendarily fair with the staff, even those who clearly didn't deserve such treatment. Much more than her intimidating appearance, it was the reason she commanded the respect of all but the worst elements of the household. However, Frinzil knew that any infraction she might perpetrate—and there had been plenty, over the years—would result in a harsher punishment than another child might incur, to avoid even the appearance of favoritism. "Look at me, young woman, and tell me you were not in the library today."

Frinzil met her gaze, unflinching. "I have never once set foot in that library."

Frinzil crouched in the darkness, knees pressed against her chest, legs slowly cramping. The things had sprouted like bramblevines over the past year, and if they got much longer, she wouldn't be able to squeeze into her secret waiting space at all.

She had spent the remainder of the day scrubbing floors in the servants' quarters. Once children were judged old enough to work, they were made to earn their keep, and Frinzil had been assisting with various tasks all over the castle for the previous two and a half months[4]. Overall, she didn't mind the work, even if it served as little more than a ten-week tour of all the things she knew for certain she didn't want to spend the rest of her life doing.

After completing her duties, she had been confined to the old storage closet that served as her bedchamber until her father arrived with supper. The whipped custard trifle he had prepared to complete the evening's feast had been supplanted by the visiting dignitary's gift, and he explained with a very serious expression and a twinkle in his eye that as punishment for the day's mischief she would have to make an entire meal of it.

Frinzil's father was the kindest person she had ever known, and her mother was the smartest and wisest. She also benefited greatly from how they envisioned her future, contrasted with their own. As a free, human girl, Frinzil had internalized the idea that she could be anything she wanted to be, even if she was muddledfolk, like the vast majority of the manor staff.

Frinzil belonged to a kind of permanent servant class that blended physical characteristics from every human population the world had to offer. In addition to the Elves, Dwarves, Gnomes Centaurs, and innumerable others[5], human nations from every corner of the globe had ruled over the Conquered Lands at one point or another. The descendants of each of these waves of invaders had commingled with the next (humans would commingle with *anything*, although for the most part the various half-elves, half-dwarves and half-centaurs that resulted couldn't have descendants of their own). The muddledfolk were the closest thing the Conquered Lands had to a native population, even if they generally had the fewest aspirations to rule it.

Frinzil had never thought of her life as any particular hardship. But the day she realized the world could bequeath an entire castle to people like Lord and Lady Orlehea, while designating her brilliant and gentle parents as *their property*, was the day she had truly grown up, regardless of what her internal biology might be up to. Frinzil watched

---

4 She'd been fully prepared for the eventuality for years—orcish children matured much earlier than human ones, and her mother was baffled when she hadn't blossomed into womanhood by the time she turned eight.

---

5 Technically twelve others, including the ghosts, but it still felt like a lot.

as Missus Parkchuk broke her back to keep the household running like clockwork, to satisfy every random whim of her masters while balancing the resulting load as evenly as possible across the backs of the staff. As far as she could tell, her mother cared about *everyone*, and although Frinzil had to assume that Lord and Lady Orlehea cared about something, it certainly didn't appear to be the people who fed them, pampered them, and kept them safe.

Before she could work herself up to full indignation, Frinzil heard a heavy door close at the end of the hallway, and the tiny locking sound which meant this entire wing of the manor would be empty until morning.

That was her cue. She pressed her back against the stone wall, unlatched the iron grate beneath her, and dropped down as smoothly as her cramped legs would allow onto the wooden surface directly underneath, tugging a length of rope with her. Keeping a stone castle ventilated was serious business, and all the fanciest rooms were serviced by a network of shafts that were easily navigated by anyone who could squeeze inside them and didn't weigh much more than eight or nine stone.

Frinzil could swear with absolute sincerity that she had never set foot in Lord Orlehea's library, but if her mother ever asked how much contact her elbows, shins, and knees had made with the tops of the bookcases, she'd be well and truly pounced. And if the distinction between walking on the floor and scampering across the tops of shelving seems an arbitrary line to hang one's residency on, keep in mind that Frinzil was *thirteen*. Senseless, arbitrary rules were all she *had*.

Also, she had finally remembered why the glyph on the elf's robe had looked familiar. She had a hunch to verify, and no power in the Conquered Lands could keep her from doing just that.

Frinzil knew the books in Lord Orlehea's library far better than the Lord himself did—to say that she had devoured every book she had ever come across was to say that she was a *spectacularly* well-read girl. If the master of the house had designated any of his servants as Manor Librarian[6] then she certainly would have seen a future for herself in his

6 And he desperately needed to—by all accounts, he organized his books mostly by *size and color*.

employ.

Most of the cases in the room were easily traversed by climbing from one to the next, but the truly rare books—the ones even Lord Orlehea could tell were of value—were kept in a heavy, ornate display case that sat alone along the front wall. That was why Frinzil had brought the rope. On one end of it was a makeshift grappling hook of her own design, heavy enough to catch the rear lip of the case and support her own weight once the other end was securely tied and padded enough that it would do its job quietly. She had done this so frequently that she could usually get the hook to catch on her first or second try, and in no time, she had bridged the expanse between shelves, hanging from her line and scurrying across it with an efficiency that would impress any common burglar. She waited until she reached the far side before lighting her tiny lamp, so as not to spill a drop of oil along the way.

Of all Lord Orlehea's treasures, the one that fascinated her the most—the one she kept coming back to again and again after all her years of clandestine library raids—didn't even warrant a position on the upper shelves. She climbed down the display case with the utmost care and fetched it from the bottom row. The tome was bound in dark leather and written in a language Frinzil had long struggled to understand. She had mastered Imperial Common and Imperial Proper by the time she was eight and had managed to get reasonably fluent in Elvish and Gnomish—languages she had never heard spoken—just by burying herself in Lord Orlehea's forbidden stacks. The writing in this book, however, was something altogether more arcane, and Frinzil had yet to uncover its secrets.

Once she had reclaimed her perch on top of the case, she flipped to the book's back pages, where the painstakingly-scribed characters and delicate margin decorations ended, and a bolder, less ornate script began. Alone on a page that separated the two sections, scrawled with a heavy brush that had dripped at the edges centuries ago when it marked the parchment, was the very same symbol that adorned the visiting dignitary's robe.

Suddenly, the library door swung open, and the illumination from Frinzil's hand lamp was engulfed by a blinding light.

"It looks as though someone has beaten you to your prize, Horgruth."

It was the elf, his voice empty of all the charm or vigor it had carried earlier at the procession. If anything, he sounded bored. The light was coming from a wand he carried. This was sorcery, which was, as far as Frinzil knew, the exclusive domain of nefarious witches and dangerous thugs. In actuality, more than a dozen schools of magic were practiced throughout the Conquered Lands, some of them considered quite respectable. Lord Orlehea didn't care for sorcery any more than he cared for children, though, so his library didn't contain any books about it, and Frinzil's education on the subject was poor.

As her eyes adjusted to the glare, she saw that the elf's human companion had entered the room as well. He wasn't actually a magistrate, of course, although Frinzil wouldn't have cared much about the difference between a lowly government official and a full-fledged Baron regardless. He reached up and snatched the book out of her hands.

These two had clearly come to Orlehea Manor to rob it.

Her primary concern, of course, was that she was *caught*. She was in the most forbidden room, perched atop the most forbidden shelf, and she knew full well that even speaking to a visiting dignitary was so forbidden that she could be ejected from the house for even joking about it.

"You can take anything you want," Frinzil said. "I won't tell a soul, I swear."

Baron Horgruth ignored her and handed the book to his companion. "Well?"

Mister Javrael flipped immediately to the back pages, his eyes finally betraying just a hint of emotion. "It's real," he said. "The imbecile has the *actual spell*, right here under his nose, and hasn't the *foggiest* notion."

Horgruth was practically drooling. "And you can read it?"

"Of course not. No one can read Archaic Arachnid except the spiders themselves. That's why I had to *bring one*."

His robes shifted, and a massive, eight-legged form emerged from beneath them, crawling up his chest to perch on his shoulders, its eight glowing eyes peeking over the top of his head. If the elf had appeared slender before, he now looked positively emaciated—his total mass must have been at least one-third spider, and the robe now draped over him as if hung from a coat rack.

The spectacle was more than a little disconcerting. "Listen, I—I could be fired just for *being* here," Frinzil stammered. "Trust me when I tell you that, whatever you're doing here, your secret is safe with—"

Horgruth grabbed Frinzil by the arm and dragged her from the display case, knocking everything off the top two shelves in the process. He was much stronger than he looked. And at that moment, at the mercy of two thieves and a giant spider, all Frinzil could think of was the fact that her feet were *touching the floor*. After so many years keeping to the tops of the furniture, the plausible deniability she had worked so hard to maintain was blown.

"What do you think?" Horgruth said to his companion. "Has this one saved us a trip back upstairs for the chambermaid? She looks innocent enough for our purposes."

The elf rolled his eyes. "What is it with surface people and *virgins*? As I said, Ghogg Thamogg requires a living soul and a sufficient quantity of blood. I assure you that he doesn't care the slightest bit how many times his supper has *copulated* before he devours it."

That was the moment Frinzil realized that castle residency and library access were the absolute least of her worries. She took in as much breath as her lungs would hold and screamed. Horgruth winced but did not loosen his grip.

"Go ahead, get it out of your system," he said. "No one in this house is awake to hear it."

"Apparently half-rotten hog livers powdered with sugar and drenched in sleeping potion are the ceremonial dessert of my people," Javrael clarified.

"It worked, didn't it?" the Baron said. "The Orleheas consumed that vile pudding out of obligation, and every single servant sampled it just for the thrill of eating above their station." Frinzil made a desperate swipe at his face with her nails, but he twisted her arm back and clutched her to his torso, facing away from him. The elf had fallen to his knees and was now inscribing a massive circle onto the tiled floor with a lump of charcoal, the massive spider balancing deftly on his back.

"I daresay only a single child escaped our little ruse—sent to bed early with no dessert, I presume?" Struggling was getting her nowhere, so Frinzil went back to screaming—even if everyone in the manor *was* asleep, but she wasn't about to take her captors' word on the matter.

The elf quickly finished his work. "Let's get it done with," he said. "You have the rest of my fee, of course?" He snatched the money sack the Baron tossed him and glanced inside. Then the spider shifted on his shoulders and clamped its mandibles over his face, its eyes glowing in the approximate spot where his own should be. The elf muttered something incomprehensible and sprinkled a bit of powder onto the diagram on the floor.

Frinzil's awareness expanded in a manner that was entirely new to her—she could see the elf and spider through her own eyes, and simultaneously see herself through the eyes of the arachnid (technically she could see through the elf's eyes as well, but since his field of vision was currently limited to the dark interior of the spider's maw, it wasn't nearly as distracting). The elf's spell had linked his own mind with hers and the spider's. A fourth mind, vast and ravenous, nagged at the edge of her consciousness, but at that point Frinzil mistook it for a general sense of dread.

The ritual required free communication between summoner, summoned and sacrifice, and Javrael found the mental link between them unpleasant, but necessary to circumvent various language barriers. This knowledge came to Frinzil along with a wave of emotions, motivations and jumbled thoughts—the elf, she learned, was aiding Baron Horgruth with his power grab because he was *extremely* fond of gold and didn't give a bucket of warm piss about who held dominion over the Conquered Lands. The spider, however, had its own motivations. Its people had retreated deeper and deeper into the caverns over the centuries as fighting on the surface drove entire populations of elves, goblins, and troglodytes[7] underground.

It had no use for gold whatsoever.

Every one of the spider's eyes locked onto the open book, and Frinzil gasped. The words on its pages *made sense to her*. The spider took control of the elf's mouth and tried to use his soft, unfamiliar lips to form them. "Ggglt—Gg-chrl-ch-ch—"

If it had spent as many hours studying the workings of humanoid faces as Frinzil had spent trying to unlock the secrets of Archaic Arachnid, it might have beaten her to the punch, too.

---

7 Also dwarves, who had moved into hollows in the mountains that spiders hadn't been using anyway, but still made a lot of noise, which wasn't great.

"*Grekchikt arkechiktl krkt,*" Frinzil said. "*Chrkriktl rk gikchrect xcht-kt chrt.*" Roughly translated, it was "Undying Ghogg Thamogg, I summon you from the depths beyond depths, tether you to this plane, and bind you to my command."

A circle of flames opened on the spot where the chalk outline had been scrawled, and a huge, malevolent, misshapen thing clawed its way through it. It searched about for its sacrifice, found two beings whose minds were connected to its own but had not spoken the spell of binding, snatched up the elf and spider and devoured them whole. Baron Horgruth screamed.

No one in the house was awake to hear him.

The demon's consciousness was all-encompassing, and Frinzil was far more aware of its hunger, its contempt, and its rage than anything that was happening in the room.

"WHAT IS YOUR WILL?" It demanded. "ALL THE FURY OF GHOGG THAMOGG IS YOURS TO COMMAND." Frinzil had never dreamed she could wield so much power. All the wrongs she had seen in the world could be righted. She now had the means to make sure that everyone, from the noblest and kindest to the most cruel, got *exactly* what they deserved.

"YOU HAVE BUT TO WISH IT," the creature intuited, "AND YOU WILL FIND YOUR EVERY DESIRE AT THE END OF A RIVER OF BLOOD, RESTING ATOP A MOUNTAIN OF DEAD[8]. I HAVE NO POWER TO BREAK THE SHACKLES THAT BIND ME HERE, BUT I WILL UNLEASH MY RAGE UPON THIS CURSED LAND, AND YOU SHALL RULE OVER ANYTHING THAT REMAINS."

Frinzil exhaled. "I command that you go home," she said, "and under no circumstances return to this domain, ever again."

Baron Horgruth was long gone by the time the manor staff awakened the next day, but it didn't take much in the way of sleuthing to realize that he and his companion had been up to no good. He was picked up by the imperial guard at a nearby harbor, still shaking and almost eager

---

8 Ghogg Thamogg was pretty eloquent for a ravenous demon lord, but he was *not* subtle.

to confess his entire plot. As for Frinzil's role in it, she was named in the official account as "one of the servant girls." No one even bothered to question her in an official capacity. Her parents, of course, were aghast when they learned how close the evening had come to tragedy, but she insisted that she had escaped the ordeal unharmed.

And it was true. In fact, her brush with unspeakable temptation and unimaginable evil only drew the line between right and wrong more clearly in her mind. The sort of power Ghogg Thamogg offered came at a price she knew she would never be willing to pay. But the other magic she saw that night—the ability to communicate with someone without speaking or light up a room without oil or flame—seemed to require no blood rivers or corpse mountains at all. The more she thought about them, the more curious she became.

Frinzil knew exactly what she would do with the rest of her life. She intended to study magic, and no power in the Conquered Lands could keep her from doing just that.

Lou J Berger is an Active member of the Science Fiction and Fantasy Writers of America (SFWA) and has published short stories in Galaxy's Edge Magazine, Daily Science Fiction, and a handful of anthologies. Recently, he was a Finalist in the Writers of the Future contest. He can be found on Facebook and on Twitter (@ LouJBerger), and his website is: http://www.LouJBerger.com

Ian R. Berger is fascinated with video games and fighting ogres, and was instrumental in coming up with the overall arc of this story. He is the proud slave to his kitty-cat, Boo, and a jolly dog with a perennial grin, Jack. He shares time between his dad and his mom, and he loves to spend time with his sister and his brother. Although he frequently rolls his eyes at his dad for lame dad jokes, he secretly is very happy to have co-authored a story with him.

WARMASTER

LOU J. BERGER & IAN BERGER

Jillian lay awake until her father's snores reverberated through the bungalow's thin walls, then crept out of bed.

She grabbed a leather knapsack and threw in some dried lamb jerky, a coarse blanket, a goatskin full of water, and some basic camping supplies. Stepping quietly so the floorboards didn't creak, she snuck up to the attic and found the old wooden box with "WarMaster" carved into the top.

Lifting the lid, she pulled a sword from its leather scabbard. The blade gleamed, long and silver, covered in ornate, black runes that she couldn't understand. A ruby the size of a hummingbird's egg lay filigreed in the solid gold pommel.

She buckled the sword around her waist, threw the knapsack over her shoulder and left the house, closing the front door softly behind her.

The sun stained the dark sky with roseate fingers as she walked down the road, through the slumbering village, and into the Dark Woods.

She hiked for most of the day, thinking about her grandpa.

They had spent every summer together, camping under the stars in the Dark Woods. He had taught her how to wield a sword, how to bind wounds, and how to build a fire to keep ogres away.

He told her fantastic stories about assisting fairies and unicorns in their generations-long war with the ogres, healing them with poultices.

When she was eight, he'd let her use WarMaster, practicing on progressively thicker vines, building up her arm strength. By the time she was ten, she was muscled and lean, slicing WarMaster cleanly through thick tree branches as if they were smoke. She had felt like an adult with him, while her parents acted as if she were an incapable child.

So she'd decided to run away from home to find her own adventures in the Dark Woods, and maybe recapture how she'd felt when her grandpa was alive.

When the sun touched the horizon, she stopped beside a small pond. Moving efficiently, she built a fire inside a ring of stones gathered from the pond's edge, boiled some water to replenish her goatskin, and threw a long vine over a high branch on a nearby tree. She fashioned a shelter of cut branches into which she tossed the blanket, ate a meal of jerky washed down with the fresh water, then hauled her knapsack, tied to the vine, up high to prevent bears from getting to it. After completing her preparations, she climbed into the shelter, snuggled under the blanket, and fell asleep, the unsheathed sword on the ground beside her.

Some hours later, white light filled the shelter, waking her. Was it morning already?

The brilliant light that had awakened her wasn't shining through the branches. It came from WarMaster. That had never happened before.

Was it glowing from heat? She licked the end of a finger and touched the glowing blade. There was no hiss.

Something big splashed in the pond.

She thrust the sword back into its scabbard, dousing the light it threw off. Then, she pushed a branch aside and peered out.

The crescent moon's weak light reflected off the wet hide of a massive red unicorn, standing in water up to his fetlocks.

Her mouth fell open.

Unicorns were *real*?

Her grandpa had claimed that unicorns were harmless mythical creatures, not dangerous at all to people. She decided to put that to the test.

She pulled her sword and crawled out of the shelter, holding it high, using it like a lantern. The unicorn, his ivory horn gleaming, stared at her as she approached but made no attempt to flee.

Jillian reached out a hesitant hand and touched his flank. Powerful muscles rippled under his red hide, but he didn't pull away. He danced in place for a moment, rolling his eyes so that the whites showed.

"Careful," she murmured, stroking its mane. "Don't stab me."

Lifting the sword higher for more light, she examined the enormous, red beast.

On its front left leg was a bloody gash. She knelt in the shallow water and brought the sword closer, to better examine the wound. It appeared to be a bite mark from a large creature. Maybe a bear?

Jillian moved back to the tree and lowered her knapsack. She pulled out a healing poultice and a long bandage.

She washed the unicorn's leg wound and applied the poultice, smearing it thickly into and around the torn flesh. She wrapped the leg with the bandage.

"Good as new," she said, proud of her work.

The unicorn nickered and nuzzled her neck with its velvety muzzle. She stood and stretched, then gazed up at thousands of brilliant, pinpoint stars scattered across the sky's black vault.

"I'm going back to sleep."

The unicorn followed her to her shelter, his footsteps soft in the thick grass. She dropped a few logs into the fire, and then crawled into her shelter. Outside, the unicorn kneeled, then lay down near the fire's warmth.

He snorted, and she smiled in the darkness.

"Good night to you, too."

Jillian awoke the next morning, birdsong loud in the nearby trees. Slivers of blue sky peeked through the shelter's branches and she wondered if she'd dreamed about the unicorn. She uncovered the sword, but it wasn't glowing. She sighed and crawled out.

There was no indication that anything big had slept nearby. The grass was untrampled.

She pulled the knapsack down, stirred the coals back to life and dropped another pair of broken sticks into the fire. Maybe just a vivid dream?

The sticks caught and she watched the flames while munching on lamb jerky, the sword beside her.

"Have you seen a carmine monoceros?"

She dropped the jerky and grabbed the sword, pointing it at the voice. The sword glowed with a bright, yellow light and, when she noticed this, her arm trembled.

A small person, maybe two feet high and wearing green slippers made of leaves, stepped back in shock. Behind him stood twelve other people, also very small, all dressed in tunics fashioned from leaves and flowers. Exactly as her grandpa had described them in his stories. Were these really *fairies*?

Her voice trembled. "I don't believe in fairies."

"We don't need you to believe in us," said the fairy standing before her, stamping his feet. "And stop pointing that weapon at me."

One by one, the others knelt to the ground, staring at her sword.

The nearest fairy, clearly annoyed, peered more closely at the sword. The anger melted from his face and his mouth formed a perfect "O."

"Where did you get that?" he asked, his voice reverent. "Is that... WarMaster?"

She shook it at him. "It was my grandfather's," she said in clipped tones. "He died. Now it's mine."

The fairy's face grew sad. "Oh, you must be Jillian. He spoke about you often."

She lowered the sword until its point touched the ground. "You knew him?"

"Of course we did. He was a magnificent man, kept us alive for many years." He flashed a friendly grin. "My name is Auberon. We lost a carmine monoceros nearby and we need to find him. Perhaps you've seen him?"

She shook her head. "A what? I didn't see any mono...whatever. All I know is that a big, red unicorn with a nasty bite on his leg woke me up in the middle of the night."

The other fairies leapt to their feet and talked all at once, their voices tinkling like little bells.

WarMaster pulsed with alternating white and yellow flashes. A twig snapped, and the unicorn stepped out from between two trees.

The fairies cried out in delight and ran to him, climbing him and hugging his legs. One small fairy woman grabbed the unicorn's tail and swung back and forth.

The unicorn didn't seem bothered by this. It tossed its head up and down as if happy.

Jillian's sword continued to pulse.

"Excuse me," she said to Auberon. "Why is this thing glowing?"

He looked impatient.

She pointed to her sword. "It lit up for the first time when the unicorn...er, monoceros came into my camp last night."

Auberon rolled his eyes. "It's WarMaster. See those symbols?" He pointed at the runes on the steel blade. "Those teach the sword how to sense magical creatures."

"Oh." Jillian stared at the runes.

The fairies finished greeting the unicorn and turned to go. Auberon stopped at the edge of the Dark Woods. His little voice was strong, but sad.

"Now that we have found our monoceros friend, will you help us? We are at war with the ogres and may not survive. Your grandpa is gone, and we have nobody else willing to help us."

Fight in a war? Jillian shook her head, and Auberon's face fell.

"I'm sorry to have troubled you. We must go and prepare for battle. Thank you for healing our friend."

"Wait!" she cried, then bit her tongue. Was she really going to help them?

Auberon ran back, searching her face with serious eyes. "Don't promise to help if you are going to back out later. Your grandpa saved us more than once. Nobody here would have made it without him and WarMaster. Most of us owe him our lives."

She stared at him in amazement. Her grandpa had been a hero? Tears filled her eyes.

"I promise," she said.

Her sword burst into bright, red light.

Behind her, a crashing sound came from the clearing's edge. She whirled and lifted her sword.

Auberon screamed. "Ogres!"

Six enormous creatures, each with razor-sharp tusks and giant, muscular arms, headed directly for her.

She took a step back in horror. Time slowed, and she could hear her grandpa's stern voice.

"Put your weight on your back foot, Jillian. Lift the sword. That's it. Watch where you want to strike and the sword will do the work for you."

She blinked, and a metallic taste filled her mouth. It took every bit of courage to not drop the sword and run away.

The first ogre lunged for her, swinging a massive arm tipped with cruel talons. She dropped to one knee, terrified. His arm passed harmlessly by.

In a panic, she lifted the sword and rammed the point into the ogre's chest, just underneath his leather armor. The sword skipped off a rib before burying itself in his heart.

She yanked the sword free and rolled away from the ogre's falling body, scrambling to escape. Her teeth chattered. A high, keening sound filled her ears, and she realized that she was on the verge of screaming.

Snorting, the red unicorn charged into the fight, spearing an ogre through the chest with his ivory horn. He shook his head to the side, hurling the dying ogre into the brush. He arched his crimson neck and screamed, raising the hair on Jillian's neck.

A third ogre stopped, confused, and a fourth ogre, running at full speed behind the third, rammed into him, knocking him off balance.

Flailing his arms to stay upright, he took two giant steps toward Jillian. She swung WarMaster at its thick, trunk-like legs.

Her sword, already green with blood, flashed in the afternoon sunlight, slicing his left leg off. He fell. She swung the sword again and cut off the other leg. The ogre screamed in pain.

Another ogre clasped her hands into a massive double fist, then raised them high, as if to crush Jillian.

She had no time to run, so she feinted to the right and moved into the ogre's shadow.

The ogre's malevolent face loomed and she began to bring down her massive, clenched hands.

Jillian jammed her sword straight through the ogre's chin and out through the top of her skull. The ogre froze, her eyes crossed, and she crumpled lifeless to the ground.

Jillian didn't have time to celebrate. She strode toward the fallen, legless ogre, who screamed in fear as she drew near. She slashed once, and the screaming stopped.

She stared in horror at what she had done.

A rushing sound came from behind. Something heavy struck her. Air whistled by her ears and when she hit the ground her sword flew away. Panicked, she ran out of the clearing, dove under a bush and clutched her knees to her chest, rocking in the dirt while tears wet her cheeks.

The unicorn, which had barreled into her, screamed at the last ogre squatting in the center of the clearing. It leapt high, flipped over and drove its horn down through the ogre's shoulder. The ogre crumpled to the grass, dead.

Jillian crawled out from under the bush and retrieved WarMaster from under a nearby bush, its pommel gleaming in the sunlight.

A crystalline silence descended on the clearing. The fairies gathered around the broken body of a young fairy, his eyes clouded over. One of the ogres had crushed him with a club while Jillian had hid under that bush. Auberon bent and lifted the dead fairy in his arms, then walked to the pond's edge. He stepped into the cool water and waded in waist-deep. Auberon kissed the fairy's forehead, tears shining in his eyes.

"Goodbye, my brother," he said, his voice choking. He released the fairy's broken body and it slowly sank into the pond's murky depths. Auberon, his shoulders slumped, walked out of the water and into the woods.

Jillian started to follow him, but a fairy woman blocked her way.

"You ran away," she said, glaring up at Jillian. "You are a coward."

Jillian stood, rooted to the spot, ashamed.

The unicorn, covered in green ogre blood, stepped up. Jillian ran her hand along his chin.

"You saved my life," she murmured, stroking the massive beast's jaw. "You didn't run away." She stared at the stiff shoulders of the angry fairy. "But I did."

The unicorn nuzzled her neck and whinnied.

They spent the night by the pond's edge, and Jillian lay in her shelter, thinking about the fight. So much had happened since that morning, it was hard for her to believe she could ever fall asleep again. The shame of her cowardice pulsed through her in waves, and she vowed to never run away from danger again.

Eventually, she slept.

She awoke when the sun climbed over the horizon and chirping birdsong filled the air. She stretched, feeling sore, especially in her arms and shoulders.

Around the clearing, the fairies fashioned small clubs from round river rocks wedged into forked sticks and tied with vines.

Auberon stood in front of her and put his hands on his hips. "Ready for the biggest fight of your life?" he demanded.

"No."

He nodded, his face serious. "I saw you run away. You're only a little girl. I can't say that I'm surprised."

"Auberon, I'm so sorry," her words came out in a rush. "I've never been in a fight before. I've never…" She thought about the ogre she'd killed and cut into pieces.

Auberon peered at her, his face serious. "Running away isn't about you, or what you are comfortable with. It's about the people you are abandoning. People who needed you to stand beside them and be strong."

She nodded, searching his eyes for understanding. "I know that now."

Auberon glanced at the pond, where he'd waded with the dead fairy in his arms. "I can't say that your leaving the fight didn't kill our young friend."

Glacial stillness filled her veins.

She kneeled down and took his hands in hers. "Auberon, I swear to you, I will never run from a fight again."

He flashed a tired grin. "Okay. I believe you. But there's something you should know. Those ogres yesterday were just the beginning." He pointed at the pile of dead ogres they'd covered in branches. "We have to destroy them once and for all."

"Maybe they will leave us alone, now that they know we can fight back?"

Auberon shook his head, and his face grew haunted. "You don't know how long we've been running from them. When your grandpa was alive, he did all he could, but we were barely able to keep them at bay. We had to move to a different hiding place every few months, just to survive. And we always seemed to lose at least a dozen or more of us with each move. No, today is when we strike back. Or we'll be killed off completely."

She looked at the unicorn, who had lifted its head and was staring at them as if it could understand them. "And what about your monoceros friend? His leg wound isn't even healed yet."

Auberon walked over to the unicorn. He pointed silently at the leg bandages. She kneeled, removed them and gasped.

What had been a raw, gaping wound yesterday was now healed, with only thin, white lines where the gashes had been. She searched Auberon's face. "How could this be?"

He touched the tip of her nose with a finger. "You're a healer, as well as a fighter. Your grandpa always suspected as much."

She stood and stroked the unicorn's head. "I miss him. He was the best part of my family."

"You're an old soul, child, but you have the heart of a warrior. Your grandpa did all he could to help us, but he was no fighter, really. You're a natural with that sword. If you stay with us, we will be your family. If we destroy the ogres, these Dark Woods will finally be safe for us."

"Then let's do this," she said, her voice loud. "Let's track these ogres to their home and destroy them, once and for all!"

The fairies threw their little hats into the air and let out a mighty cheer.

They finished preparations and marched for an hour through the Dark Woods, following thin paths, barely visible to Jillian but easily spotted by the fairies. Her arms grew tired as she hacked through the thick underbrush. They walked for what seemed like forever.

Finally, Auberon, up front, stopped and raised his fist for silence.

Jillian crept forward, clutching WarMaster, and peered through some bushes. Below them, in a green valley, wood smoke curled up from two dozen small earthen huts' chimneys. The huts encircled a large, stone building. Ogres walked around and between the huts, sharpening weapons and scraping hides mounted on wooden frames. They seemed relaxed, unprepared for an attack.

Jillian whispered. "What's the plan?"

Auberon stared at the ogres, his eyes wide. "I was hoping you might suggest one? That stone building, in the middle, that's where the ogre queen is."

"The queen?"

"She's the one that has been trying to exterminate us for years, encouraging the others to wipe us out."

Jillian scowled, looking first at the large crowd of ogres and then back at their own small, fairy army.

"Well, in a fair fight, we would lose. Badly. What we need is a distraction."

She spotted the red unicorn at the end of the line, munching grass. "Wait here."

She crept to the unicorn. It raised its head and flicked its ears forward.

"Remember when I said I owe you my life?" she whispered.

The unicorn gave a quiet whinny.

"Well, I need your help yet again. I need you to make a distraction, so that we can sneak into that big stone building in the valley. Can you do that?"

The unicorn acted as if it understood what she wanted. It whinnied again and disappeared into the brush. Jillian listened but couldn't hear it move away. Not even a twig snapped.

She returned to Auberon's side. "Okay, now we wait."

The fairies relaxed. Those with spears and knives sharpened them, and those with slingshots crept away to search for more smooth, round stones to stuff in their ammunition sacks.

Twenty minutes later, a shrill scream split the silence. Wide-eyed, Jillian ran to the edge of the Woods and peered across the valley.

A mile away, but yet visible, the red unicorn stood on a grassy hill, proud horn jutting into the sky, its mane billowing in the wind. It threw back its head and screamed, again, then pawed the ground with a black hoof.

Below, in the valley, all the ogres dropped what they were doing and stared open-mouthed at the screaming red animal on the hill. Then they reacted. In groups of two and three, they gathered up weapons and armor. Snarling, they charged out of the small village and up the long hill.

"Now," shouted Auberon, waving them forward. "We attack now!"

The fairies, with Jillian in the lead, burst out of the brush that lined the valley and charged down the hillside.

By the time they reached the village, the ogres who hadn't gone after the unicorn were waiting for them.

Jillian raised WarMaster high. It glowed like a ruddy torch, making the ground and those running beside her look as if they'd been dipped in blood.

She ran directly at the biggest ogre she could see, a giant of a beast, fully seven feet tall and muscled like a fortress. He held a massive club studded with spikes and laughed at her through a mouthful of tusks.

At the last moment, when its club whistled down toward her head, she stepped to the left, spun behind the ogre, and slashed the backs of his knees with WarMaster. He fell to the ground and a swarm of fairies climbed all over him, stabbing and clubbing. His screams grew muffled and then silent.

Jillian was too busy to watch. Weaving a net of glinting steel in front of her with WarMaster's sharpened point, she parried dozens of attacks coming from all sides. Her mind was clear and calm, with no trace of the fear that had made her flee the previous day. Wielding her grandpa's sword in battle had changed her, forever.

She grew confident with every passing moment. WarMaster, like a living thing in her hand, weaved and dodged, shattering ogre swords and turning their clubs into sawdust. When convenient, the sword's tip would dart forward and bury itself in an ogre's chest, drinking the lifeblood deep in its heart, then withdraw to once again block attacks.

First there were only a few ogres on the ground, then eight, then a dozen. When there were twenty dead ogres surrounding her, she glanced up to where the red unicorn stood, high on the hill.

He had charged partway downhill to meet the ogres head-on. Mangled ogre corpses covered the hillside, punched through by his horn and then trampled under his hooves. A shrill scream came to her on the wind, and a small smile tugged at her lips.

She fought, using the sword to carve up her enemies. One by one, the ogres stumbled away, mortally wounded, only to have the fairies swarm them and finish them off.

When there were only ten ogres left to fight, they formed a ring around her. Jillian clenched the sword, slippery with green blood. Her arms trembled. She spun around, wondering whether she had the strength to continue the fight. If she dropped her guard for an instant, she knew the ogres would close in and kill her.

A quick glance up the hill showed that the unicorn was gone. Dark, motionless bodies lay scattered like river pebbles. She killed an ogre, then another, leaving only eight.

Her arms shook, burning with fatigue. She wiped sweat from her eyes with a blood-covered forearm, then feinted forward. The ogres recoiled, either from fear or respect.

It didn't matter. Seeing them back away gave Jillian the spark of energy she needed. Moving WarMaster through the air like a dancer's ribbon, she spun and pirouetted between and amongst the ogres, cutting, slashing, and stabbing. Within the space of a dozen heartbeats, it was over.

Silence descended. The fairies cheered, and Jillian realized that they were surrounded only by dead ogre bodies. No ogre survived.

Except one.

"Don't forget, the queen yet lives," said Auberon, as the red unicorn trotted up to the building and pawed at the entrance.

An enormous ogre, more powerful than any they had yet seen, burst from the open door of the stone building and launched herself onto the red unicorn's back. The unicorn stumbled, then screamed in fear as the queen's weight threatened to crush him.

The ogre queen bunched her powerful muscles and grabbed the unicorn in a powerful headlock, cutting off his fearful scream. The whites of his eyes showed as he tossed his head, seeking escape from the monster on his back.

"Stop!" Jillian shouted.

The unicorn stumbled in one direction, then another, weighted down by the enormous ogre, trying to escape. The queen slashed at the unicorn's hide with a pair of ragged claws, then bit deep into the unicorn's neck.

Blood flowed.

Jillian moved WarMaster to her other hand.

She leapt forward and then dodged their massive, thrashing bodies. The ogre queen's powerful arms crushed around the unicorn's throat. A cold wave of fear flooded through Jillian.

She watched for the right moment, afraid to hurt the unicorn. When they stumbled closer, she saw an opportunity.

With a quick hop and a lightning-fast thrust, she jammed the sword deep into the ogre queen's ribcage, just under her muscled arm.

The ogre queen's eyes flew wide. Her mouth opened. She let out an anguished scream, slid off the unicorn, and crumpled to a heap on the ground.

The unicorn stumbled away, breathing heavily, his sides heaving. Jillian stood, trembling, her sword point touching the ground. Green ogre blood running down the blade made a small puddle.

The fight was over. They had won this battle. But there were more, deep in the Dark Woods.

Two days later, Jillian walked into her parents' home. Her mother burst into tears, then grabbed her in a tight hug. Her father wiped his eyes.

"Where were you?" he said, his voice husky. "We thought you had been taken by kidnappers."

Jillian shrugged. "I'm sorry. I should have told you I was leaving."

Her mother wiped her face. "Young lady, you scared us!"

"I know."

Her father noticed WarMaster hanging from her belt. His eyes widened. "Is that your grandfather's sword? Young lady, you didn't have permission to take that!"

Jillian shrugged. "It's mine now. I only stopped by to pick up the rest of my things."

Her mother stepped back. "What? Where are you going?

Jillian tilted her head. "Back into the Dark Woods."

"I forbid it. I won't have you out there. It's too dangerous. You're only a little girl." Her mother's eyes narrowed in disapproval.

Jillian shook her head. "Not anymore, I'm not. We're at war with the ogres. I can't stay here. If I do, they'll find me…and then they'll come for you, too. I can't let that happen."

Her father frowned. "Jillian, stop this ogre nonsense. It was bad enough that your Grandfather told those ridiculous stories."

She made a dismissive gesture. "They weren't stories. Ogres are real. I've met them. I've killed them. Well, some of them. The rest are waiting for me."

"Don't you back-talk me!" Her father's face twisted in anger and grew red.

Jillian ignored him. "I've brought back some protection. The fairies will watch over you while I'm gone."

Auberon entered the room and Jillian's mother let out a squeal of fright.

"Hello," said Auberon, blushing. "Nice to meet you."

Her father's eyes widened, and his red face grew pale.

She ran to her room and threw the rest of her clothes into the knapsack, then rejoined her parents. "I'm leaving now. I love you. Be careful and do what Auberon says." She walked out the front door.

Her parents followed her outside, not knowing what else to do. Jillian grabbed a handful of red mane and swung up on the unicorn's back. Both her parents glanced at each other, then back to the improbable beast standing before them.

"Are you riding a...unicorn?" her mother asked, voice faint.

Jillian stared into the blood-red sunset before answering. "It isn't safe anymore. It may never be safe again. I love you both, but I have to go."

Jillian tugged on the unicorn's mane and dug her heels into his muscular flanks.

Galloping hard, the unicorn disappeared with his tiny rider into the Dark Woods.

D awn Vogel's academic background is in history, so it's not surprising that much of her fiction is set in earlier times. By day, she edits reports for historians and archaeologists. In her alleged spare time, she runs a craft business, co-edits *Mad Scientist Journal*, and tries to find time for writing. She is a member of Broad Universe, SFWA, and Codex Writers. Her steampunk series, *Brass and Glass*, is being published by Razorgirl Press. She lives in Seattle with her husband, author Jeremy Zimmerman, and their herd of cats. Visit her at http://historythatneverwas.com or on Twitter @historyneverwas.

PRINCESS LAST PICKED

DAWN VOGEL

Princess Alastriona watched as the numbers dwindled. She tried to keep her chin up, but even that became more and more difficult. Finally, there were only two left—herself and Eithne, among the smallest near-grown girls in the settlement.

Darieann was almost always one of the captains for the mock battle the near-grown children organized from time to time, and she had developed a cruel streak in her leadership. She looked over her options and smirked. "Eithne."

Crossing her arms over her chest, Nessa, the other captain, said, "Fine. I guess we get Princess Alastriona." Nessa glared at Alastriona. "You'd better be able to keep up."

Alastriona nodded before she limped over to Nessa's group. Every time the children chose teams for their mock battle, Alastriona was the last one picked. Between her slight build and withered right leg, she was not good at fighting. Most of her peers didn't use her actual name. They called her Princess Last Picked, a nickname that chafed her.

Princess Alastriona was heir to the rulership of the settlement, and her parents assured her that her disability would not matter if she could command the respect of her subjects. But try though she might, she was never chosen to lead either of the teams for the mock battles. And she dared not ask her parents to intervene on her behalf. No one respected a team captain who had been handed the position, rather than earning it through battle prowess.

If she had her way, she wouldn't even be out with the other children. She preferred to spend her days in the library, amongst the books. But her mother insisted that the best way for her to learn to be a leader was to join the other children her age in their mock battles, fought with wooden weapons.

With the teams decided, the captains distributed the scraps of fabric that they used to designate their team members. The bit of blue fabric that Nessa handed Alastriona was barely enough to knot around her walking stick. When Darieann and Nessa had first come up with this game, when they and Alastriona were but seven, there had been enough fabric for everyone to wear a sash. But over the past six years, the supply of scraps had frayed and dwindled, much like Darieann and Nessa's friendliness toward Alastriona.

Alastriona looked over the other members of Nessa's team, hoping to find at least someone she trusted to not leave her behind if the battle became one that ranged across the hills outside the settlement. Bradach could easily carry her on his back, but he'd likely abandon her in pursuit of greater glory.

Her best option was to stick near Seumas, as he wouldn't give chase after the battle. He preferred to watch from the sidelines. Though the other children knew he wouldn't participate in the fighting, they always wanted him on their team, because after the battle, he sang the praises of every member of their team. Even Alastriona, when they were on the same team, received his lauding, typically about how she avoided capture by the enemy. He was kind enough to downplay the fact that she was never in danger, since she rarely made any attacks against the opposing force.

As the two teams sized each other up, a strange quiet fell over them. At first, Princess Alastriona thought of it as the calm before the storm. But this was a deeper sort of silence, muffling even the whispers and giggles of her teammates beside her.

Then a booming voice drifted across the field. "Let those who believe themselves strong be struck weak and bound with the shackles they would cast toward me." There was a strange lilting accent to the words that Alastriona couldn't place. She looked around, trying to find the source, and thinking that she was not strong, unless minds and wills were included.

Dazzling lights flashed before her eyes, causing her to stumble. Her backside landed on something solid, which stung. But then the lights cleared, and she was seated on a stump.

The other children, save Eithne and Seumas, had all fallen to the ground, their bodies rigid and strained. None of them moved an inch, though a faint keening sound came from Darieann's vicinity.

Eithne looked around. "What just happened?"

Alastriona rose from the stump and clumsily sat beside Darieann. She looked over her former friend carefully, placing an ear near Darieann's mouth. The keening quieted, and Darieann's breath came in rasping gasps instead. "I'm not certain," Alastriona said. "Did any of you see anything just now?"

"Shimmering lights," Eithne said. "Like faeries."

Seumas nodded. "Like faeries, or magic."

Princess Alastriona exhaled slowly. That had been her fear as well, and hearing the others say it solidified the idea in her mind.

A heavy scraping sound drew her attention. "The gates," she gasped. "They're opening."

"Someone must have arrived," Eithne said.

"Yes, but who? Normal visitors have a crier to announce who they are."

Seumas looked at the two girls and said, "Wait here." He ran toward the settlement walls. Though he was not particularly fast, he moved more quickly than Alastriona or Eithne.

Alastriona watched until he was out of sight, then slowly began pulling herself up from the ground. Once upright, she straightened her clothing and adjusted her grip on her walking stick.

While Alastriona regained her feet and her dignity, Eithne moved around to the other children, crouching near each one in turn. "They're all alive, but I don't think they can move."

Alastriona recalled the words that had been spoken. "They've been struck weak. They believed themselves strong, so they've been weakened and…oh no, shackled."

"Then they won't have been the only ones," Eithne said, glancing nervously toward the settlement. "If the magic penetrated the walls, there won't be a person left standing. We are the strong."

Alastriona choked back a sob at Eithne's final words. "We are the strong" was the motto of her family and thus the settlement. She had never identified with the words, being as weak as she was. But nearly everyone else who lived there took the words to heart.

Eithne was small for her age, a girl who had not yet grown to her potential strength. Seumas considered himself a teller of tales; his strength lay in that area, much like Alastriona's strength lay in her mind and will. They had not been struck down because they did not possess the type of strength the settlement favored.

"There might be babies, small children, who don't understand the motto. Perhaps a few of the aged and infirm who are past their prime,"

Alastriona said. She looked in the direction where Seumas had run and spotted him returning, moving more slowly than he had when he left.

He was gasping when he reached them, but still managed to speak in between breaths. "Woman in black. In the settlement. Don't know her. Everyone's on the ground."

"Magic, then? Not faeries?" Eithne asked.

Alastriona nodded. "It must be. Are the gates still open?"

"They were closing," Seumas said. His face was still flushed bright pink, but his breathing was less labored now.

Alastriona turned her attention to Eithne. "Eithne, you're small and quiet. Do you think you can sneak back into the settlement and see what's going on?"

"By myself?" Eithne asked, her voice trembling.

Alastriona considered the options, but before she spoke, Seumas said, "I'm the opposite of quiet. I should stay with the Princess."

Eithne nodded at him, then at Alastriona. "Then you and Seumas should wait near the walls. In case anything happens and I need your help."

"What good—" Alastriona began.

"Good idea, Eithne," Seumas said. "We'll come with you to the wall."

Alastriona walked slowly, letting the other children get ahead of her. Seumas kept interrupting her, and now he hadn't let her voice her concerns. Her temper was rising, try as she might to keep herself calm.

Seumas stood a few paces ahead of her, having allowed Eithne to get ahead of him. "Would you like some help?"

"What kind of help can you give me?" she replied, anger seeping into her words.

Seumas frowned. "Have I done something to offend you, Princess?"

"I don't know what help either of us will be if Eithne gets into trouble inside the settlement. I can't keep up, and you don't really know how to fight, do you?"

He shook his head. "I understand the theory, but I'm not practiced. But that's not the point. If we're out in the middle of the field, we're a target. If we're close to the walls, we can hide more easily. And perhaps she'll need us for something other than fighting."

"If there's a witch inside, what else would there be to do other than fight?" Alastriona asked.

Seumas's face grew pale. "You'd fight a witch? You're very brave, Princess."

"There are ways of fighting that don't involve blades and bows, Seumas." Alastriona shook her head, her temper bubbling to the surface. "You know the tales. Do you ever listen, or do you just memorize them so you can recite them to grand applause?"

Seumas began to open his mouth, then closed it. He remained silent the remainder of the way to the settlement walls. Just when Alastriona was certain she'd overstepped the bounds of politeness, Seumas spoke again. "You're right, Princess. There are plenty of ways to fight. I've just never learned anything other than blades and bows and fists." He paused. "The tales say the best way to fight a witch is to trick her."

A smile crept onto Alastriona's face, cooling her anger like a spring rain. "Trickery? That might just be the smartest thing you've ever said, Seumas."

Eithne returned to Alastriona and Seumas after a long while, her face as white as the clouds. "It's Gormflaith."

Princess Alastriona felt like she was falling. Of all the possible witches who might have made an attack on the settlement, Gormflaith was the absolute worst. It was said she was distant kin to the previous king, and she had sworn revenge against Alastriona's family on their ascension to power. In her mind, she was the rightful heir, regardless of her personal skillset. But the other noble families had opted for a shift in leadership, a new family in power, rather than maintaining the previous line of succession.

"She'll be after the crown and the scrolls," Seumas said.

"Scrolls?" Alastriona asked. "What scrolls?"

Seumas's eyes grew wide. "The ones with spells to ensure the loyalty of her servitors, no doubt."

"Servitors?" Alastriona asked, her voice low.

"The people of the settlement," Seamus said.

"It's the only way she can ensure their loyalty," Eithne added.

"The crown will be in your family's chambers, yes?" Seamus asked.

Alastriona nodded. The crown was largely ceremonial, and her

133

father kept it tucked away in a box within a cabinet with many drawers most of the time.

"And the scrolls will be in the library, won't they?" Seumas asked.

Eithne shook her head vigorously. "That's where you'd think to look for them, so they aren't there. There's a cave, outside of the settlement."

Alastriona nodded. "They're safer there." She considered their options. They could retreat to the cave and guard the scrolls there. But if they did so, who knew what sort of destruction the witch would wreak upon her people. Already, Gormflaith had crippled the settlement. Magic worked in ways that defied reality, but people still needed to eat and drink. Gormflaith might leave the inhabitants frozen until they died of thirst if she couldn't find what she wanted.

If Gormflaith believed the scrolls to be in the library, she'd likely go there first. If the three of them could come up with a way to trick the witch, they could put it into action it in the library.

The more Alastriona thought, the more certain she was. "We should go to the library."

Seumas frowned. "But if the scrolls are in a cave—"

"How would Gormflaith learn that information?" Alastriona countered. "If we want to save the settlement, we need to stop her long before she reaches that level of desperation. Already I worry about what her magic will do to the people. We must stop her before she does worse."

"The cave is well hidden," Eithne said, "but the others who know aside from me are aged. If Gormflaith finds them, she may be able to extract the information from them."

"Did you see anyone, anyone at all, moving around when you snuck inside the walls?" Alastriona asked.

Eithne shook her head. "I heard the wails of a few babes, but the only person I saw who still moved was Gormflaith."

"Not even guards?" Seumas asked with a scoff. He stretched his arms out in front of him and tried to crack his knuckles, like the warriors of the settlement often did. Instead of any sound from his knuckles, he let out a soft gasp. "That hurts more than you'd think," he admitted.

"Remember, Gormflaith struck down those who believed themselves strong. We need to use our minds in order to defeat her," Alastriona said. "My family may be the strong, but we are the clever."

"We are the clever," Eithne and Seumas repeated together, laughing as they did.

"Clever will save us," Alastriona assured them.

Eithne slipped through the doors of the library but came back almost immediately. "She's in there, pulling all the books off the shelves."

Princess Alastriona frowned. The library was one of her favorite places, and to hear Gormflaith was treating the books badly was horrid. "We're going to have to stop her. The sooner, the better."

"What can we do to a witch?" Seumas asked.

Princess Alastriona smiled. "What can you do to a witch? Bind her up with iron bars and peony flowers red and orange," she sang. "Like the old rhyme!"

Seumas's jaw dropped. "Yes, I remember that one. Okay, where do we find iron bars and peony flowers?"

"Iron bars are easy," Alastriona said. "We've got plenty of unused swords at the moment."

"And I know where peonies grow," Eithne said.

A shattering sound came from within the library, followed by a fierce sounding wind.

"She's broken a window now," Alastriona said, a note of desperation seeping into her voice as she thought about the damage this witch could do to the precious books. "Who knows what else she might break? I've got to stop her."

"But how?" Seumas asked.

Alastriona took a deep breath. "I'm going to go in there and talk to her."

"What?" the other two children exclaimed in unison.

"I'm going to need to borrow your scarf, Eithne, so she doesn't realize who I am. I'll offer to help, but I'll really just be a nuisance—not enough of one that she'll be cross with me, but just enough to keep her from breaking anything else."

"Then I'll go look for peonies," Eithne said as she unwound her scarf from her hair and shoulders, helping Alastriona to cover up her straight golden-blonde hair that matched that of her parents.

Seumas nodded. "Then I suppose I need to collect swords."

Alastriona nodded. "There's a ring of light colored wood on the floor. I'll keep Gormflaith distracted and within that circle. Lay out all of the swords and flowers in a nine-pointed star. And then she'll be trapped!"

Seumas and Eithne nodded and scurried off, leaving Princess Alastriona to take a deep breath and plunge directly into the belly of the beast.

"Hello?" she called out as she pushed on the heavy library door. "Who's there?" She opened the door all the way, latching it open to make it easier for Seumas and Eithne to sneak in once they'd found the things they needed to trap Gormflaith.

"Who's there?" Gormflaith replied from somewhere in the distance. "I might ask the same of you!" The witch came around a tall bookshelf and peered down at Alastriona. "Oh, I see. I wasn't expecting the strong to keep their weak ones around." She drew out the word "strong" and made it sound mocking.

Princess Alastriona nodded, keeping her eyes down. "I'm just one of the librarian's assistants."

"Excellent. I'm looking for something in particular. Care to help me?"

"What is it you're looking for, my lady?"

"My lady, eh?" Gormflaith laughed. "Well, flattery will get you everywhere, child. I'm looking for an old scroll." The witch held out her hands. "About this long, just a little oath of loyalty."

"Follow me, please," Alastriona said. She kept her gaze on the floor of the library, locating the pale inlaid ring near the center of the library. Within it, several tall cases bearing rolled maps and other tubes stood sentinel, creating a ring of their own within the inlaid ring. If she could keep Gormflaith occupied here until her friends were able to lay out the iron bars and peonies, they'd be able to trap her and find a way to break her spell.

"I don't know which scroll it might be—" Alastriona began.

"Blast," Gormflaith said. "Well, dear, would you be so kind as to help me find the one I'm looking for?"

"I can try," Alastriona said. "Though perhaps you can tell me more about it to help me look for it?"

"You do know how to read, don't you? Being a librarian's assistant and all?"

"Of course, my lady. But can't you tell me anything more at all? As you said, there are so many scrolls here."

Gormflaith muttered something beneath her breath, and the contents of one shelf flew into the air beside one of the bookcases.

Alastriona gasped loudly as the scrolls and maps clattered to the ground. "Oh, my lady, you mustn't just throw these things around. They're all quite old and delicate!"

"What do I care for them? Soon enough, they'll all belong to me anyway, and I can do whatever I like with them then. I think I'll use them for kindling. This settlement needs a good burning to clear the way for my keep."

"But what if you accidentally destroy the very scroll you're looking for?" Alastriona asked.

Gormflaith shrugged, though a look of discomfort flitted across her face. "I'm certain it will be of no consequence."

Alastriona stopped and placed her hands on her hips. "Then why must we find it?"

Gormflaith arched one eyebrow. "Well, you're a spirited one, aren't you?" She frowned, peering more closely at Alastriona. "You look rather familiar."

As Gormflaith reached out a hand toward Alastriona's borrowed scarf, Alastriona stumbled past her, falling to the library floor, but retrieving a scroll from the lowest shelf as she did. It was a much larger scroll than the one Gormflaith had indicated, but Alastriona held it up nonetheless. "Something like this one, perhaps?"

"No, shorter," Gormflaith said. "Though I'll have a look at that one, if you don't mind."

Alastriona clambered up from the floor and brought Gormflaith the scroll.

When the witch unrolled it, she frowned. "Just a map. Keep looking."

Alastriona nodded and glanced past Gormflaith. Seumas tiptoed across the library floor, arms laden with swords. Princess Alastriona wanted to shake her head, to somehow tell him he needn't bring so many swords all at once. As one of the swords began to slip from Seumas's grasp, Alastriona slumped heavily into the bookcase, causing a clatter of scroll and map tubes.

Gormflaith shook her head, scoffing at Alastriona. "And you tell me to be careful with these old things."

Alastriona picked herself up and dusted herself off. "I am ever so clumsy, I fear."

"What's that one there, then?" Gormflaith asked, pointed a slender finger at one of the scrolls that had fallen just out of Alastriona's reach.

Alastriona froze before she recalled that the scroll Gormflaith wanted was not here. She could let the witch look at any scroll she liked, but Gormflaith would never find the scroll to force loyalty from the people of the settlement. Alastriona reached out and handed the scroll to Gormflaith. "This might be it."

Gormflaith took the scroll case from Alastriona and unrolled it carefully, then shook her head. "No, none of these scrolls seem to contain any spells. Where would the ones with the spells be, girl?"

"I can't rightly say, my lady," Alastriona said. The more she considered it, the more certain she was that no scrolls containing magic were kept within the library walls. They likely all resided in the cave. But she needed to keep Gormflaith here and busy for long enough for her friends to complete the warding circle. "I think perhaps the highest shelves might be where the spells would be kept. At least, that's where I think I would keep them if I were the librarian."

"Hmm," Gormflaith said, gesturing toward one of the highest shelves. Several more scrolls flew from the shelf.

"One at a time, my lady!" Alastriona said. "Remember, they are fragile."

"Just like the people here," Gormflaith said, smiling broadly. But she lowered the scrolls she had snatched with her magic slowly into her hands, rather than allowing them to clatter onto the floor.

Alastriona made her way around the circle of bookshelves, pretending to look at the scrolls, but truly checking on the progress of the ward. Seven points of the star were in place, and Eithne was just now hurrying through the door with a basket filled with peony blossoms. Alastriona caught Eithne's gaze and smiled at her friend, and Eithne returned the expression.

As soon as Eithne had finished placing the flowers, she returned to the door to the library and looked out. A frown crossed her features, and then her eyes grew wide.

"Pardon me, my lady," Alastriona said, holding up a finger out of Gormflaith's sight to signal Eithne to wait. "I may have seen another scroll in another part of the library. Please wait here, and I will bring it to you."

"Why can't you just tell me where it is? You move too slowly."

Alastriona took a deep breath. "Well, you'd need to go up the stairs near the stained-glass windows, then turn left at the last ash bookcase, and squeeze through the gap between the bookcases in that aisle to get to the other staircase—" She paused to take another breath and to give herself a chance to make up additional instructions.

"Very well," Gormflaith said, waving her hand at Alastriona. "Hurry back, then."

Alastriona hobbled out of the circle of shelves and met Eithne halfway between there and the door.

"I can't see Seumas," Eithne said. "I don't hear him either."

"Where would he have gone?" Alastriona asked. She glanced back at the swords. "We only need four more to finish the ward."

"Could we make do with a smaller star?" Eithne suggested.

"I can't be certain it would trap her as well as a nine-pointed star," Alastriona said. "I need to go and find a scroll to bring her. You should wait in the hallway. Hopefully Seumas just had to go a bit farther to find more swords. Or perhaps he needed to stop for water."

Eithne nodded and moved out of the library, out of sight of the doors, and Alastriona moved into the portions of the library that were normally the province of the librarian. She found a small scroll easily enough, but beside it were four lengths of iron, of the sort that were used to weight down the edges of a large map. Grinning, Alastriona snatched them up as well, leaving behind her walking stick and bundling the iron rods together to help her make her way back to Gormflaith.

She paused at the edge of the star that Seumas had made, still lacking two of its points, and she let the iron rods clatter to the floor amongst the red and orange peonies. She sat down to arrange the rods just as Gormflaith looked out from the center of the bookcases.

"What are you doing?" Gormflaith shrieked.

Alastriona pushed the tips of two rods together, forming the eighth point of the star.

Gormflaith rushed from within the circle, directly toward Alastriona.

Princess Alastriona's throat tightened with fear. The witch was a terrifying woman. Her anger contorted her face into something even more frightening. Alastriona's withered leg slid across the floor, rigid with fear, and made contact with one of the iron rods.

The rod clattered across the floor and rolled to a stop in just the right position to complete the warding circle.

Gormflaith reached the ring of iron and peonies and fell back as though she had run headlong into a wall. "What? What is this?"

"What can you do to a witch? Bind her up with iron bars and peony flowers red and orange," Alastriona sang, her voice barely escaping her throat.

A moment later, the same words rang out from the hallway, in two voices—Eithne and Seumas. Alastriona's friends appeared in the doorway, each of them carrying a sword in each hand. Eithne's two swords were nearly as tall as she was, but she carried them all the same.

A loud thump drew Alastriona's attention back to Gormflaith. The witch had collapsed onto the floor of the library, atop the scrolls and maps she had pulled out of their shelves. Carefully, Alastriona righted herself as best as she could without her walking stick.

Eithne and Seumas dropped their swords in a clatter and rushed to Alastriona's side.

"What's happened?" Eithne asked, wrapping one of her small arms around Alastriona's waist and draping Alastriona's arm across her shoulders.

"Perhaps the ward put her to sleep?" Seumas asked, supporting Alastriona on the other side in a similar fashion to Eithne.

"I think she got so angry that she tried to defeat the ward and knocked herself out," Alastriona said, as the three children made their way toward Gormflaith.

Footsteps pounded outside of the library, and Alastriona looked up to see Darienne and Nessa rushing past.

The two girls slowed, both of their heads cocked to one side as they spotted the other children standing over Gormflaith. "Alastriona?" Darienne asked.

Alastriona grinned broadly. "The spell is broken, then?"

Darienne nodded slowly, eyes wide.

"Did you stop it?" Nessa asked.

A slower stride outside the library drew the attention of all of the children. Queen Treasa stopped behind Darienne and Nesssa, her head cocked to one side as she spotted her daughter and the other two children standing over Gormflaith. "Alastriona?" the queen asked.

"Hello, Mother! We've warded this part of the library against the witch," Alastriona said.

"You know magic?" Darienne whispered.

Alastriona looked at Seumas and Eithne. "We know stories. And sometimes knowledge is strength."

"Quite right, daughter," Queen Treasa said. She touched Darienne and Nessa on their shoulders, gently parting them so she could step into the library. She paused, looking down at the witch, a gasp escaping her lips. "Gormflaith?"

Alastriona nodded. "She cast a spell to make the settlement trapped by its own strength. Except for us," she said, glancing at her friends.

Queen Treasa smiled at Princess Alastriona, and then at Eithne and Seumas. "Well done, all three of you. It shows wisdom to know when one must rely on one's wits rather than one's physical strength." She glanced back at Darienne and Nessa. "Perhaps there is something to be said for a leader who can make that decision when times are difficult."

Alastriona blushed under her mother's praise, but she also reveled in it, particularly as Darienne and Nessa considered the queen's words.

Nessa glanced at Darienne, then back toward Alastriona. "Will you tell us how you trapped the witch at dinner tonight?"

Princess Alastriona smiled at her old friends, then at Eithne and Seumas. "I'm not a teller of tales, but I think Seumas would gladly share our story with the settlement."

Elmdea Adams lives on a windy ridge near Berkeley Springs, WV, where dragon's-breath fogs often rise from the valleys. Her previous adventures include Fortune 500 management and work as a past-life therapist, which are more related to one another than one might initially think. She and her husband appreciate the skilled supervision of their cat, Miz Alice.

For more information, visit www.ElmdeaAdams.com.

YENDY LOVES RATTLESCALE

ELMDEA ADAMS

I'm *a failure as a dragon. I'm not big enough. I can't flame. I'm not even scary.* Tinvo sobbed. She cried so hard her scales and wings rattled, the sound echoing off the walls and small hollows of her cavern. After one huge, gulping wail, a glistening stalactite snapped and crashed on the floor, which was already littered with bits of bone, hide, and shiny treasures she had found.

And I cry. REAL dragons don't cry. It's not my fault I'm small. So here I am, exiled to a cavern in the hinterlands. Tinvo whimpered. Her head was full of acrid snot. Her exhale was pitiful. Not even a flicker of flame, only dripping slime.

Grandmother tried so hard to teach me how to work up a strong, searing flame. She made me sleep on gold, and nibble on it, enough that it turned my teeth gold. Nothing worked. Grandmother never said she was ashamed of me, but I think she was. She despaired of me. I've never worked up a proper blue and white fire-breath. All I've ever managed are measly trickles of yellow and orange flame. Nowhere near hot enough.

If I were a proper dragon, I'd be raiding the countryside for all the gold, silver, and jewels. They're mine by right, after all, even if humans try to hide them. Only we dragons know that treasure's proper use is fueling fire breath to keep the world warm.

Tinvo did raid, but not the way she was supposed to. Sheep, cows, horses, pigs, deer, dogs, cats—those she could easily kill. They were there to be eaten. Just snap their necks and tuck right in. She preferred the larger ones, though. More food, less effort, and much tastier. Cats were vile, only to be eaten in dire circumstances.

Humans were the ultimate prey. No claws, mostly furless, often quite plump. Their clothes singed off in a flash and there you had it: an ideal dragon meal. And so they were, for other dragons. But Tinvo couldn't bring herself to kill humans.

The sobs rose from her belly again. She had made the mistake of watching humans. They acted like dragons in their love of treasure and their fierceness in protecting it. The oldsters led the youngsters around, teaching them how to walk and talk, just like dragons did. Watching young humans play and tumble reminded her of the days when she and her four nest mates did the same. When the four of them were sent out into the world, she was assigned here, to the least favored, most remote, long-abandoned cavern and lands. Abandoned so long that there was a village at the bottom of the hill. She could not make the world-warming flame and she had a strange fascination with humans.

A soft, sweet voice interrupted her wallowing.

"Pretty bird. Pretty bird."

Tinvo flinched and whirled toward the entrance. She saw a middle sized girl who wasn't as tall as Tinvo's front legs.

Wait! What? A girl? In my cavern? How did I not hear her come in? How dare she! I'll show her. She drew in a deep breath, ready to flame. Except her head and nose were still filled with goo. *Well, I didn't want to flame her anyway.*

"Pretty bird. Pretty bird."

Tinvo studied the girl's face. Her nose was flat, her cheeks were round and rosy, and her wide eyes, with red around them, slanted up. Tinvo knew that red meant the child had been crying, but she didn't look a bit afraid. Not even a little. Her eyes sparkled in spite of their red rims.

The girl came closer, hands reaching out. "Pretty bird. Pretty bird. Pretty bird fly high. I see."

Tinvo was stunned. *What sort of human was this?* She had long suspected the villagers were not properly scared of her, but this? To actually come into her cavern?

The girl reached up and patted her, using her whole forearm. Thump, thump, thump.

"Pretty bird. Pretty bird. Love pretty bird." The girl emitted soft waves of a sweet, warm energy. Tinvo squinted and she could see those waves of love. They were just like the ones she remembered from her mother.

Tears welled in Tinvo's eyes again and her nose started dripping.

"Pretty bird sad. Love pretty bird." The girl patted her, sending out even more comforting waves of love.

"Who are you?" She tried to roar, but it only came out as a weak rumble.

"I Yendy. Love pretty bird."

"What are you doing here?" she growled.

"Yendy need your help. Scare mean ones away who make fun and call Yendy names. Pretty bird never make Yendy scared. Love pretty bird. Yendy imagine what village look like up high. What village look like?"

What an odd question.

"The houses look like bits of blue and yellow and white, peeking out from under red tile and thatched roofs. Each house has a little garden and chickens. Sometimes the cows run away when my shadow passes over them."

Tinvo stopped mid-breath, horrified. She rumbled again, this time louder. "Go away. I don't want you here." She still didn't sound very impressive because of the crying goo.

"Yendy love pretty bird."

"I'm a dragon, not a bird! I'm Tinvo Rattlescale." She gulped. Some dragons might share their last names. They never shared their nest name with humans, ever! *It's those waves coming from that girl, it has to be.* Tinvo rose on her haunches and rattled her gleaming scales, sending iridescent green and yellow flashes across the walls and ceiling. As a hatchling, she'd been the best at scale-rattling and quite proud of it. The rattle shivered and echoed around the cavern, making a few, smaller stalactites fall with faint crashes.

"Oooo. Make sound again?" Yendy paused, cocking her head as she looked at the dragon. "Fly like bird. Pretty."

"You're supposed to be afraid of me."

"Why?"

"Because dragons eat humans."

Yendy's eyes opened wide as she stopped patting. She stepped back and looked at Tinvo from nostril to tail-tip and back. She shook her head.

"No, pretty bird not eat Yendy. We friends." Old wisdom shone from her eyes. "We for each other. Tinvo not like other dragons, Yendy not like other people. We like each other."

Tinvo stifled the "humph" rising up her throat as what Yendy said sank in. *The girl is right. She's too simple, too trusting, unlike most of the humans I've observed. I guess some might call her stupid. But she's not. She's wise in her heart. She's full of love. I can see it rolling out from her in waves. We aren't like our own kind.*

"Tinvo come with me."

"Come with you where?"

"Home. Meet Granfer. Granfer nice, like you."

"No. I'll stay here."

Yendy put her hands on her hips and cocked her head. "Okay. I come back tomorrow. You like cookies?"

Tinvo glared and turned away. *Cookies. Hmpfff.* She curled into herself, lay down, and closed her eyes.

The girl sighed. Tinvo heard her light steps as she left the cavern. In spite of herself, Tinvo had to get up and watch the girl walk down the long hill. She'd overheard villagers say it was a long mile. That was nothing. Tinvo could see a kid goat in the hilltop field on the other side of the village. It was why dragons were such fearsome hunters.

Just as Yendy reached the first house in the village, some boys darted out and started poking and taunting her. Then they began pulling at her clothes. Yendy stood firm, swatting back. They pulled her braid, Yendy lost her balance, and they pushed her down.

The dragon's heart rolled over. Those boys were overwhelming that girl. The same thing had happened to Tinvo and she hadn't liked it. *I might be a small dragon, but I'm dragon enough for this. That girl is pure love. She doesn't deserve this.* Tinvo launched herself into the air and felt unaccustomed warmth on her nose when she blew a bit of real flame, blue and white. That didn't stop her. Four wing strokes brought her close to the gates. Tinvo chortled as she watched the boys trip over each other as they scattered. She landed next to Yendy and folded her wings. "You all right?"

Yendy nodded, mouth clenched, tear tracks plain on her dusty face. "They meaner this time."

Tinvo curled herself around Yendy before she knew what she was doing. "They're all gone. You're safe."

"They run and stumble when see pretty bird," Yendy said as she steadied herself against the dragon's flank and looked up to meet Tinvo's eyes.

Tinvo bent her head down. *I'm now a complete and utter failure as a dragon and I don't care. This little one is special. She's stronger than she looks. Got real fire in her. She's teaching me, a dragon, about courage!*

146

And those boys, those boys will never hurt her again. I'll make sure.

"I'll send them running again, maybe scorch them, if I see them hurting you." Tinvo stood on her hind quarters, crossed her arms on her chest, rattled her scales, and bared her teeth. Her long pointed gold fangs gleamed and her scales glistened in the afternoon sun.

"Come meet Granfer now." Yendy said.

And so it was that Tinvo found herself walking through the village for the first time. She shook her head, knowing she should return to her cavern, even as she padded along beside the girl. *I like how I feel with Yendy. She makes me feel special. She doesn't care I'm a small dragon. She just cares that I'm me. I feel more me than I've felt since, well, since I got sent here all those years ago.*

The world looked new and bright. Tinvo's body felt fit and strong. Her nostrils cleared and she could smell the grasses, earth, and smoke from the village hearth fires.

People scattered as Yendy and Tinvo walked down the street. Parents grabbed children and pulled them into houses. Shutters banged closed and doors slammed, followed by the *thunk* of lowered bars. Tinvo saw two boys pulling a third into an alley.

Yendy pointed at him. "That's the mean one." Her voice shook.

Tinvo felt quite brave. There was something about Yendy, more than the love, that made Tinvo want to protect her. Something that made Tinvo feel like a real dragon and washed her self-doubts away. *Yendy believes in me! That's it. She believes in me.*

Tinvo turned toward the alley and released a short jet of blue and white fire. The mean one bolted with his friends, banging on doors until one gave way and they dove inside. Tinvo grinned when she heard the thump of a lowered door bar.

Twice! I've made blue and white fire breath twice, without even thinking about it. It really doesn't burn me. I thought it would.

Tinvo's mind jumped back to when she was a nestling. *I've never forgotten Zulee, how he tumbled from the sky, blue and white flame around him.* Tinvo shuddered, which made her scales rustle. The sound of Zulee's neck snapping when he hit the ground was as clear now as it was then. Nobody talked about it, at least in her hearing, and Tinvo hadn't asked. Now she wished she had. She was beginning to think Zulee's death had everything to do with his boasting recklessness and nothing to do with blue and white fire breath.

"Tinvo okay?"

"Tinvo okay. I'm better than okay. You're good for me, Yendy."

Yendy clapped her hands and patted Tinvo. She pressed her mouth to the dragon's leg, making a smacking sound. Tinvo had heard and observed humans doing this. From the best she could tell, it was how humans let each other know they cared. She'd overheard it called "kissing." Tinvo felt oddly blessed.

"Tell Yendy more about flying. Please?"

Images flashed through Tinvo's mind as her body felt, again, the freedom of the skies.

"From up in the sky, colors are brighter than they are on the ground. Roads are smooth brown ribbons through green and yellow. The air cools as you rise up. You know how the wind feels? It feels like that."

"Oohhhhhh."

Tinvo looked at her, noting that Yendy barely came to her shoulder. *I wonder if I could pick her up in my front claws. No, I might hurt her. I use them when I take off and land.* Tinvo shook herself, scales rattling. *What am I thinking? Carrying a live human is not like carrying prey to my cavern. And dragons do not carry humans!*

By the time they reached Yendy's house, Tinvo's mood was brighter than it had been for years. It had been quite satisfying to watch humans scatter for shelter. It had been downright exciting to scare those mean boys, especially the meanest one. It had been exhilarating when she produced a hot blue and white fire-breath, twice! She felt quite draconian: eyes sparkling, scales rattling, and fire leaking out her nostrils. Tinvo felt real and good. *It's those waves of love that Yendy sends out. And she believes in me. I've never felt that before. She doesn't need me to be different. I'm enough just the way I am.*

Before the pastures and fields began, they reached the last house on the right. Yendy called out. "Yendy home, Granfer." The house door opened immediately.

A man with whispy white hair stepped out, bending slightly so he would not hit his head on the top of the door frame. "I see you've brought a friend." Granfer's eyes narrowed, lips pursed, as his arms crossed over his chest.

Yendy walked over, eyes wide, and reached up to put her hand on

Granfer's arm.

"Tinvo Rattlescale Yendy's friend, Granfer. Mean ones scared of her. Tinvo and Yendy both different. We help each other."

Granfer's eyes widened as he looked from Yendy to the dragon and back to Yendy. He shook his head and sighed.

Tinvo saw the man clench his hands, then relax them. Granfer stepped up to her.

"She's a fine, brave dragon, is Mistress Rattlescale." Granfer walked around Tinvo, studying her from nose flange to tail tip.

He offered his hand, with a slight tremble, for her to smell, as if she were a dog. Tinvo should have been insulted, except it was quite clear Granfer loved his Yendy very much.

"Yes, a fine dragon, this one. A good friend for my Yendy."

Granfer looked at his hand. It was not scorched or bitten. The dragon had twitched once or twice. Yendy was grinning from ear to ear, clapping her hands.

"Yendy want to fly with Tinvo. Granfer help?"

Tinvo's eyes widened. *What is this?*

"I can help," said Granfer, "but there's another who needs to approve. Have you asked your friend?"

"No. I forgot." Yendy bowed her head a moment, then straightened and turned to Tinvo. "Please, Tinvo, let Yendy fly with you? I want to see village high up."

Fly with her? Tinvo chuckled, which sounded more like a growl. "Humans can't fly, not that I've ever seen." Tinvo paused as the sparkle left Yendy's eyes. Tinvo sighed.

"I've never seen a dragon fly a human. I would fly you if I could, but I can't think how." Tinvo looked from Yendy to Granfer. Tinvo was grateful no other dragons could see her, as she fell even further away from what a proper dragon should be.

Granfer frowned, fingers on his chin, then nodded. "Hmmmm. If you're sure, Mistress Rattlescale, I think I know what we need. I can make you a saddle. It'll take a few days, six or seven at least."

"Saddle? What's a saddle?"

"You've seen humans on horses? Most sit in a saddle, so they don't fall off when the horse runs. It straps around the horse's ribs, with a seat for the human."

149

Straps around her body? Never! Not her, dragon and queen of the air.
Tinvo was about to say no, but then she saw Yendy's serene face. Tinvo
nodded her head once.

"Mistress Rattlescale, you're sure? I've never heard of this being
done." Granfer said.

Tinvo shrugged and tidied her wings. She never had fit in, so why
worry now? "Yes, if there's a way Yendy can be safe."

"If you please, Mistress Rattlescale, I'll be right back." Granfer
ducked into the cottage and came out a few minutes later with a thin
board, a little skinny stick, and a long ribbon.

"If you'll be still a bit, I'll take some measurements, so I know what
I need to do." Tinvo felt the long ribbon when Granfer flipped it over
her back. It was times like this that reminded her how sensitive her
hide was and how much information came to her through her scales
and their movements through wind, rain, and air.

"Mistress, if you would extend this wing out a moment? Now the
other one? Thank you."

Granfer seemed to have forgotten Tinvo was a dragon. He nibbled
the end of the skinny stick, scratched the thin board with it, looked up
at her, head tilted, then scratched the thin board with the skinny stick
again.

"I think I see what to do."

Yendy and Tinvo spent the next few days traipsing between the
cavern and the village. On the third day, they noticed the villagers
nodding at them as they walked through the village square. They
walked a little further and two of the mean boys smiled and waved. The
meanest boy, though, scowled even more. Yendy and Tinvo ignored
him.

Granfer, a leathersmith known far and wide, spent those days
making a simple saddle and harness of soft leather. When it was done,
he placed it on Tinvo's back, tightening here, pulling there, then walking
around her, nodding his head.

"How does it feel?"

"Strange, but not uncomfortable." Tinvo said.

"If you would, please fly to your cavern and back, to see how it feels in the air."

In all of twelve wing beats, Tinvo was back.

"It moved up toward my neck. And it rubs against the front of my wings."

Granfer nodded and pulled sheepskin strips out of the bag by his side. He settled them around the areas Tinvo mentioned. "There. Try that."

Tinvo obliged. She'd given up being surprised.

"It still felt like it moved and it still rubs against my wings, it just isn't as rough?"

"I'll make some adjustments that will help. Thank you, Mistress Rattlescale, for letting me see how it sits on you as you fly." Granfer took off the saddle and harness and went back into the house.

When Tinvo returned the next morning, Yendy was jumping with excitement, pulling Granfer's hand. "Granfer says fly today."

"You might fly today. We don't want to hurt Mistress Rattlescale, now, do we?" He turned to Tinvo. "If you would allow, Mistress, let's see how last night's little adjustments worked."

Tinvo lowered herself to the ground so Granfer could get the saddle over her back, then stood up. Granfer tightened various bits, then patted Tinvo. "Take to the skies, Mistress. Let me know how it is."

Tinvo flew to the cavern and back. "Much better, but still strange."

"That's to be expected."

Granfer turned to Yendy. "Come here, little one. If Mistress Rattlescale is agreeable, step in this stirrup and pull yourself up."

Yendy and Tinvo looked at each other for a long moment.

"Tinvo let me fly with her? Let me get in saddle so I safe?" Yendy said.

"Yes, Tinvo is happy and honored to have Yendy see the world astride her back." She crouched down and Yendy, grinning so wide it split her face and nearly hid her sparkling eyes, climbed onto Tinvo's back and settled herself.

As she felt Yendy's slight weight on her back, something unfurled inside Tinvo. She took a deep breath. She felt herself bigger and stronger and braver, while self-pity and sorrow drained away.

"Here, little one. Buckle these straps just so. These will make sure you don't fall off, in case Rattlescale needs to dodge and dart." Yendy nodded and watched as Granfer buckled one.

"Buckles pretty, shiny. Now me." Yendy said. She pulled up the other strap and fastened it, hands shaking with excitement. She looked at the buckled straps and nodded. "I did right. Watch." She bounced and tried to fall off. "I on safe." Her face fell. "Oh. Tinvo, I not hurt you?"

"No, Yendy. You didn't hurt me."

"You did that buckle just right, Yendy." said Granfer. "And you were wise to make sure. You're ready to go. Only a short trip today, just to Mistress Rattlescale's cavern and back. You must learn to fly together and it will take more than a day or a week." He patted Tinvo's side and stepped back. "Off you go."

Tinvo started walking toward the fields beyond Yendy and Granfer's house.

"We not fly? Why walk?"

"I need to get used to having you and the saddle on my back." Tinvo stretched, paused, turned, stretched again, then shivered. "There. It feels all settled now."

"I not too big?"

"No." Tinvo unfurled her wings and jumped. And landed with a thump. "I need more air under my wings." She jumped again, bringing her wings further forward, and they were flying.

"Oh! Oh, Tinvo! This better than anything."

Tinvo brought her wings down again, remembering to cup them. They rose higher. There was a small flicker of flame streaming from her nose. Startled, she forgot to cup her wings and she felt herself losing altitude and control. She quickly brought her wings back up, cupped, and pushed down. That worked. "This will get easier with practice."

They came back from their first flight all smiles and laughter.

"You are only to fly from here to Tinvo's cave and back, and not every day. This will make Tinvo's muscles stronger and you, Yendy, you will learn to be still." Granfer's eyes twinkled, while his voice kept its seriousness. "And Tinvo, I want to hear about any problems you have with this saddle."

Tinvo nodded.

Over the following week, Tinvo and Yendy made several short flights and Granfer made slight adjustments to the saddle. After two more flights with no adjustments, Granfer nodded. "Now I'll make you a new saddle, one you can use for many years and wear with pride."

In the next weeks, sometimes Yendy walked up to the cavern and Tinvo walked her home. Sometimes Tinvo flew to Yendy's and they flew back and forth. They worked out a communication of touch for the roar of the wind swept their words away. Thus nearly four weeks passed.

"Granfer, me and Tinvo like these." Yendy held out a small bag. "You put on new saddle? Please?"

Granfer opened the bag and poured out a few golden trinkets and a string of glowing pearls. "I believe I can."

The day finally arrived. Granfer brought out a beautiful custom saddle and harness of brown and red leathers. It was trimmed with what they had brought, as well as some trinkets Tinvo had never seen.

"Oh, those." Granfer waved his hand. "Just a few bits and pieces the villagers gave me. The word got out what I was doing. They just came and dropped them in my hand." He shook his head. "I don't know what's got into them, even Old Knarl, who's so tight-fisted he won't share a seed for planting."

Tinvo and Yendy flew a little further each day. Tinvo got ever stronger, and Yendy more confident. Their joy blossomed. They ranged far afield and called themselves Yendy-Rattlescale.

Katie Cross has a passion for writing stories about women finding themselves. Also food. Magic captivated her the moment she held her first book. She has lived many lives scouring story after story, searching for adventure, dragons, and magic. Now, she writes fantasy books so you can seize the light, hold magic in your fingertips, and forget the shadows of real life to live your wildest adventure.

WATER AND LIGHT

KATIE CROSS

Rocking waves woke Avelina before the cawing gulls pecked her skin off. A whisper washed through her mind.

Avelina.

She popped one eye open.

Streams of light barreled through slants in a wooden box that surrounded her. No gulls, then. She must have just heard them.

She lay curled on her back, knees tucked into her chest, strands of thick black hair clinging to the boards. She recalled only a few memories. Running as fast as she could. Blood roaring in her ears. Footsteps following. The Royal Guards tailing her. *"You and your crazy Papa…you'll die, magic holder. Just like the rest!"*

Papa's twisted, horrified expression. Blood spraying behind him in crimson arcs. The screams of those dying in the massacre. Papa sliding the wooden lid shut, encasing her in darkness, before she'd passed out.

It must be, he said, lost to his usual ramblings. *What they don't have is the key.*

She blinked.

He was gone. She knew he was gone. She shoved it away. Papa was gone and the most recent Wielder massacre was behind her—she hoped. Now she had to get away, to the promised lands. She'd be safe there. Safe to work as much magic as she wanted. Maybe even safe to swim in the ocean.

The distant sound of male voices filled her ears. She felt around her prison with her fingertips. Hard wooden boards. Sun streamed from above, which meant nothing blocked her from escaping. Her body ached. A hot pit, like liquid fire, burned in her stomach. Weak. Tepid. With her mind, she reached out, feeling. A few blips of magic spoke back to her.

Swish swish.

Reassured, she pressed her fingertips into the boards above and pushed them up an inch. They gave way soundlessly, allowing a ribbon of light to spill across her face. Avelina peered out. As expected, she rode on a ship. Merchant ship, if the rigging meant anything. Broad canvas unfurled above her, rippling in a steady wind. Beyond it, an endless expanse of sapphire waters stretched out. When she attempted to look to the side, a wooden wall blocked her view. From what she could see, no land lay in sight.

Another good sign.

There was no way of knowing what ship she was on, whether they'd be friendly to a magic holder or a stowaway, or if she was any safer here than fighting the Royal Guards. Had Papa known the captain? Or had he simply stuffed her in a crate to spare her life, then gave his own? With Papa, one could never tell.

Like a heartbeat, the magic reminded her of its presence.

Swish swish.

Growing bolder—and with her throat aching for fresh water—she slid the lid off enough to allow her head through. After ducking down, expecting to be caught any moment, she peeked over the top again. Only two sailors in sight, near the wheel. She was at the back. Ahead, the wheel and poop deck were just barely in sight. Certainly not a navy vessel. Didn't have the appearance of a pirate crew, though one could never tell these days, what with the Wielder imprisoning or killing all the magic holders to take their powers.

Nothing for it. She'd have to make a break when the sun went down.

Legs twitchy, she settled back in the box, leaving it open just enough to admit light, casting the darkness off for a swampy dim. The whisper, *Avelina*, quieted as she did.

Just as she found a tolerable position, the top disappeared. Light poured over her with blinding force. She recoiled. Seconds later, a hand reached down, circling her arm. Someone jerked her out of the box. She bit back a cry of pain to glare instead.

An odious man with a swollen nose and beady eyes stared at her. His white skin, pockmarked and bright red from the sun, seemed to ooze grease.

"Well, well," he muttered. "What have we here?"

She snarled. He sniffed. Then he turned to the side, to another odious man.

"Magic holder. Smells like cinnamon."

Someone guffawed. Avelina attempted to wrench her arm free without success. The foul man shoved her in front of him. He stared hard at her, eyes narrowed.

"So familiar," he murmured. His head tilted back. "What's your name?"

She spat in his face.

He shoved her ahead of him with a growl. "Get walking, little girl. Cap'n will be happy to see you."

Avelina struggled as she walked, but only because the idea of following *his* orders made her want to vomit. She stumbled along, tripping over her sluggish feet, which had fallen asleep in the crate. Firm hands jerked her along.

They carted her across the deck, toward an open doorway near the main mast. A relentless sun beat down, heating the air, making it swampy. Not even the occasional cool mist blowing up off the side could soothe her. Every droplet that touched her sank into her skin. The burn in her belly awakened for a moment with a little sigh.

"Get on your knees," her captor growled. He shoved her down. Her knees slammed into the deck. She gritted her teeth and suppressed a cry.

A man with oily black hair and glittering eyes stared at her with a narrowed gaze. A dingy gray shirt with a black vest covered meaty shoulders. Criss-crossing lines slashed over the vest, as if he'd been hacked by a knife. Resting in the middle of his chest was a massive bauble, glowing a bright sapphire. It was dim. Low on magic. Of course such a filthy man wore a medallion.

Pirates, for sure. No doubt in a stolen merchant vessel.

"What have we here?" he drawled. His fingers twitched, as if they wanted to reach for something. His nose lifted. He sniffed. "Ah, a magic holder. Cinnamon, is it? What is your power, girl?"

"Turning ugly men into more attractive toads."

He barked a laugh. Someone nudged her in between the shoulder blades with a boot—none too softly. She snuck a quick glance outside. An empty horizon on the left. Distant hints of land on the right. A pirate and a coward. Not even he, whoever he was, dared to sail into empty waters and encounter the Wielder Queen.

The captain stared at her with a studious gaze.

"Who are you?"

"I can't remember."

His brow lifted. He swept one hand in front of him, ruffling a tuft of fabric at the wrist.

"Your name?"

"No."

He pressed a hand to his chest. "Drake, if you were wanting to know. Your father is Ansel, magic holder with wind. Madman."

She kept from flinching by sheer willpower. Papa wasn't a *madman*... although he wasn't well.

"Odd," Drake murmured, shaking his head. "Very odd."

He exchanged a look with his servant, one she couldn't read.

"The chances," the man whispered, but it trailed away.

"You're going the wrong way," she said. "The magic supplier is the other direction."

The land was on the right side of the boat. If he was going to the magic supplier to fill his medallion, the land should have been on the left. She could smell the acrid, vinegary stench of his breath from steps away.

"I'm not going to the magic supplier."

Her forehead creased in silent question. She tried to smooth it back out, but it was too late. He grinned.

"I'm taking *you* to the Wielder Queen."

His wicked, wild laugh rang out through the air. All the blood drained from her face. The Wielder Queen. The wicked magic holder that had betrayed her race. She consumed the magic of other holders, sometimes to murderous effect, and had started a war on the mainland that was affecting *everything*.

A mere touch.

They grabbed her by the arms and dragged her back. She kicked and flailed all the way back to the crate. After they'd stunned her with a blow across the cheek, they shoved her back into the box.

All fell into darkness.

Avelina.

They had always underestimated her.

Avelina had lived her life expecting people to believe her capable of less than she really was. A girl. Under fifteen. Black skin. Full lips. Bright blue eyes. No mother. Daughter to a magic holder—but a weak, half-crazed one at that. Papa had too much heart to really use it. Instead he walked around, mumbling under his breath. *It isn't ours. It isn't ours. Surrender. It's the only way.*

Once she recovered from her daze, her thoughts gelled into different paths. Something about their conversation didn't sit right. Several moments of wiggling, cursing, and attempting to recall the snippets passed.

Then it clicked.

He'd been sailing the direction of the Wielder Queen *before* he spoke with her. That meant he'd lied. Or he'd been planning to see the Wielders before he knew about her. He must have someone else.

In the darkness of the crate—which was almost complete now—the whisper returned. *Avelina.*

She mentally reached into her belly. The magic was still weak, but there was a fraction more. She kicked the top of the crate.

"Let me out! If you want to keep your ship, you better let me free."

Someone chortled. She thumped it with her flat palm, but it didn't even budge. Some chubby sailor sat on it, no doubt.

"I have more power than you know!"

Another laugh. Her nostrils flared. She *could* have more power. If they were attuned to magic holders, they would have known that she was running low the moment they saw her. Or smelled her. But what they didn't know would hurt them.

Avelina felt in her belly with her mind again.

Not enough, she thought.

Then she banged again.

"Let me go! This is your warning. If you don't listen, you'll regret it!"

She screamed, warned, and banged for an hour before someone dumped a pail of dirty water on the top of the crate.

"Shaddup!" they yelled. "Or I'll fill yer crate 'till ya drown."

Yes! She wanted to shout. *You fools!*

She sputtered as water streamed into the small space, then sloshed around her back and shoulders. Magic activated, flaring like heat as it lapped up water like a dying man.

Swish swish.

Avelina sank her fingers into the water, drew in a deep breath, and relaxed. Just a little sleep, a little time to let the magic calm. Then she'd act. She fell to sleep on the only reassuring thought she had.

When she woke, they'd regret their decision.

Hours passed.

When she woke up, still in the crate, her head rolling groggily to and fro, she had the impression that evening had settled. Cool night air poured through the holes in the crates, admitting no light whatsoever.

Avelina, whispered the voice.

As always, she ignored it.

The water sloshing around her was gone—the wood bone dry in its place. Almost *too* dry. Cracks and ridges formed along the bottom. Her belly burned hot as a furnace now. Not full. Not empty. By no means satiated.

But better.

Her ankles were numb. Her knees prickling. She flicked her skin to wake it, then swallowed. She should have demanded water. Said she was on the brink of death. She wouldn't be any good if she were dead.

Something she may have to count on.

Avelina closed her eyes and forced out a long breath, then released a portion of the magic. The top of the box shot away like an arrow. Overhead, a thousand stars sparkled. Her confinement disappeared. A rush of wind swept up her back. She rose above the ship, belly flaring with heat, her arms and legs spread wide.

The magic burned deep inside. For all that men coveted magic, would do anything to be able to control it, they knew nothing of what it cost. The scooped, wrung out feeling of her soul. The weariness.

The constant, constant burn.

Sailors moved about their duties, seeing nothing unusual at first. She observed beyond them. Past them. Behind them. Through pursed lips, she let out a single note. A high pitched trill. The water around the boat started to vibrate. Life hummed, squealing in her ears.

The magic burned hot, hot, hot.

Come to me, she sang from her mind. *Release my bonds, set me free. Take me to the places promised, where magic can be.*

The song floated past her, over to the sea. She couldn't go to the water—to submerge herself in the ocean would kill her. Too much magic, too much power.

Never go, Papa had always said. *Never, never. Surrender only. Never, never.*

The magic hovered like a delicate glass over the water. Then it cracked, shattering, and littered the waves with a staccato. Several crewman whipped around. The water had grown agitated. They shouted. Someone spun, pointing to her. Avelina felt a bit of air moving past her feet—they were grabbing for her. But she hovered too far above them. They couldn't get her.

Come to me.

Fins appeared on the surface of the water. Glinting flashes of silver. Then thousands of bodies—small, but nimble. A snarl. White caps. Blown air. The water filled with new life around the boat. Avelina reached deep into the magic, setting it free. It always did what it wanted. Instead of coming to her in the air—replenishing her reserves—it sent creatures.

Come to me, she pleaded.

She didn't have enough to maintain this.

Crewman darted around the deck, stumbling to their knees when the ship pitched side to side. A swarm of fish moved below it, spinning in a circle.

The magic in her belly dimmed.

Come to me, she sang, frantic. *Take me to the lands promised, where magic can be.*

A sailor screamed. Another fell into the jaws of a great white shark. Blood blossomed in the water. Avelina sucked in a sharp breath when a cool wiggle cut through her stomach. A warning.

No, she said. *Not yet.*

Another.

"No!" she cried.

Something dark broke out from the boat, near the main mast. A shadow. No, a cloud of black. It climbed the sky, then covered the moon. Darkness fell with a gust of wind and a breath of disbelief.

Drake's remaining magic in the medallion.

He wielded darkness.

Avelina, came the whisper.

Below her, the sea stirred. Clashing waves slammed against the hull of the boat with wild slaps. Her body dropped. The burn ceased. Blood tinged the white capped waves to a frothy pink, staining the ocean with inky spots.

Her song stopped.

Frantically, she clung to the final tendrils of magic still humming through her body.

Come t—

She gasped and hurtled through the air until she landed on the deck with a heavy *thud*. The rocking stopped. Avelina shoved herself to her feet, but fell again, feeling as if all the blood had been drained from her limbs. She crawled toward the side of the boat.

She'd have to get *in* the water.

Just as she scrambled to her feet near the edge, a hand clamped around her ankle. She whipped around with a cry. Drake's rotting teeth smiled. The white caps disappeared back into the ocean. Only the occasional flash of a shark fin continued.

"Where do you think you're going?" he murmured. The final, dying glow of the medallion faded as darkness swept through her body, ice cold and racing like lightning.

Avelina fainted.

Avelina.

At some point, rain had come.

It slanted through the small port hole in the room where they'd locked her, hands bound in front of her. Drops pattered on her skin. Beneath her, the floorboards were dry. Bone dry. Warmth flowed through her skin. Healing heat. Avelina woke up, looked around, then passed out before the whisper finished.

Avel—

Many times she woke, felt the magic coursing through her as it greedily gobbled the rain, then fell back to sleep. The magic healed her. It banished the darkness.

Without the rain, she would have died.

The room—more like a closet— was empty. No accident. No fool, not even Drake, would leave a magic holder in a room with any sort of supplies if he didn't know their source. The fact that the window was open meant he *didn't* know.

The promised lands, she thought, desperately. *Must get to the promised lands or all is lost.*

Whenever she'd talked about the promised lands to Papa, he'd shake his head. *Surrender. It's not ours. You'll be fine. Surrender.*

The memory sent a ripple of grief through her. She shoved it away.

A thud outside the door made her jerk. She rolled onto her other side and peered at the thin sliver of light peeking in.

"When?" came a low, gravelly tone.

"An hour."

"Think she'll take her?"

"Dunno."

The two voices were low and quiet. *She.* Her blood ran cold. The Wielder Queen, for certain. The thought of feeling part of her body and soul drained from her, ripped out like smoke and gas, sent a shudder through her. She bent her fingertips. The rope was thick. Thick and tied separately. Too thick to work out of now, but she could loosen it for later.

A thud hit the door.

"Get the girl," came a third voice. "We've arrived."

They shoved her onto sand with a sneer and a blindfold.

The sand was gritty against her knees, and hot. A sword pressed against the back of her neck. Behind her, water swelled from the ocean and ticked her toes. The moment the cool liquid touched her skin, it hissed. The heat flowed into her. She burrowed her toes deeper and kept her head bowed. A minuscule amount of water lingered in the grains of sand, then slid through her blood as magic.

The sound of shifting sand came, as if someone had walked closer. Avelina kept her head bowed, even though her eyes were covered. They were on an inlet, far from the mainland, with nothing but ocean and sand around them.

"This is the girl?" came a deep, resonant voice. Female. Cold as ice and twice as sharp.

The Wielder Queen.

"The one," Drake said.

"Cinnamon," she purred. "She wields the power of the ocean."

"What?" he hissed.

"Her father is dead?" the Wielder asked.

"Confirmed dead," he muttered. "My crew killed him."

"Her mother?"

"Still on the ship."

A silence stretched around them. Avelina felt it all the way into her bones, as if her very soul had been rocked.

Mother?

"The other is in your ship as well, I presume?"

"Yes."

"Bring them to me."

The sound of fingers snapping followed, but Avelina sensed that Drake remained. She had no mother. Her mother had died in birth. And how did Drake know about her father? Who was *the other*? No, Drake must be lying. Or he assumed that she was someone she wasn't.

But were there any magic holders her age left?

Drake made his life out of killing, stealing, and trading for magic. He would know what holders were still alive. He'd track the announcements. The list of holder deaths was tacked to most village walls. He'd hunt the remaining powerful down.

She had to escape.

If she died, the last of the magic holders would go. There would be no promised lands, no free practice of magic.

No freedom.

Slowly, a mere inch, she scooted back. The feeling of something cold touched the back of her neck and sliced her skin.

His sword.

"Where do you think you are going?" Drake asked.

Avelina swallowed hard. She pushed her fingers as far into the sand as they'd go. A tepid warmth met her fingertips. She pulled on it, yanking it into her belly.

Grow, she pleaded to the magic. *Grow, please.*

Minutes later, the sound of several pairs of feet and grunts followed. Someone landed in the sand on her left. Then another beyond that person.

"They are the ones," the Wielder Queen said. Surprise colored her tone. "You have done well. We have been searching for them for a long time. How you managed to bring in all three at the same time, I'll never know."

"And shall be paid well, I assume?"

"As you deserve."

The sound of a slicing sword followed. Gurgling, then shouts of outrage, came next. More swords. Cries of pain. Something hot fell on Avelina's skin. She could immediately taste copper in her mouth.

Blood.

Chaos ensued in a heated battle. But who fought for the Wielder Queen? Likely no one. Someone that had taken so much magic from everyone else could fight a crowd of sailors. Avelina ducked her head closer to her arms and inched her blindfold off. Two people lay prostrate on their knees next to her.

A pair of eyes met hers

She almost gasped—would have—if the power of breath remained in her. She stared into a near perfect imitation of herself, only this was a boy. The same sloping forehead, bright eyes, full lips. Dark, ebony skin. Something about him was difficult to look at. Difficult to see. His eyes tapered into slashes. She had to look away.

Her mouth went dry.

A woman cried out. The boy spun to face a middle aged woman, thin, frail, with delicate, familiar features in her face. It could have been Avelina in so many years.

Mother, Avelina thought.

The woman stared at her, stricken, tears in her eyes. The battle continued around them. Sand flew in the air. Blood. Men streamed from the boat to fight the Queen. Knives flew with sharp whistles and the staccato of them hitting bodies.

"You," Mother whispered.

A flash of white caught Avelina's attention. She looked up. The Wielder Queen stood above her, looming with terrible presence. Strands of white hair, like strings of sand, trailed out on the breeze. Her skin, as alabaster as clouds, was almost translucent. Even her eyes were white, colored over as if by fog. No blood stained her robes, which were black as pitch and flowed to the ground.

"Avelina," she murmured. Her gaze slipped to the boy. "Avel. I have been searching for you for…so long."

Clouds built in the restless air, towering with dark promise behind them. The screams of the sailors had faded. All of them lay dead in the sand, their hot blood pouring into the grit. Avelina didn't take her eyes off the Wielder Queen. One simple touch is all it would take to erase Avelina's magic. To steal her soul.

But the Wielder didn't reach for her.

She didn't even move. Nothing but the restless shift of her garment in the growing breeze gave any movement. The sun faded behind the clouds. A murky darkness fell.

Avelina, whispered a distant voice.

The Wielder Queen's voice.

"You may call me Mari," she murmured. "You are the twins, are you not? Oh, but you wouldn't even know, would you? Your parents split you up to keep you safe."

Avel stared straight ahead, lips pressed, expression rigid. Just like Papa. Mari shifted forward a step. The sand didn't move underneath her feet.

"I've been searching for you for a while now. Without you, I have no hope of completing my goal."

"Of ultimate power?" Avel said. His voice was deep, even for someone so young. Avelina rubbed her hands together. Still bound, but there was some give in the tension.

Mari gestured to Avelina. "The power of water." Then she gestured to Avel. "And the power of light. Without your gifts, I have no hope of controlling the magic of the four seas and five lands. Here you come.

Together. Isn't it…odd?"

Stalling, Avelina thought. *She's stalling.*

Thunder raged overhead. Wind whipped sand into her eyes. The clouds thickened, filling the whole sky as if they encircled them in a tomb. The darkness deepened. Avelina sucked in a sharp breath. *What they don't have is the key!* Papa had shouted once. *What they don't have is the key!*

There was no reason for the Wielder Queen to delay. Why didn't she grab them and take her magic right away?

Because she *couldn't,* perhaps.

The Wielder Queen *didn't* have the magic of the ocean.

"What do you plan to do with your power?" Avelina asked, spitting it out as if she were enraged. Her fingers burrowed deeper. The ropes rubbed against her wrists, raw, but movable. Her toes dug into the cool sand. She unleashed some of the magic in her belly.

Come to me, she sang. *Set me free.*

"Rule, of course." Mari flicked an annoyed glance at them. "Create equality where there is none. When one person holds all the magic, no other can die for it."

Water pooled at Avelina's fingertips. Her skin greedily absorbed it. The heat in her belly soared. More water came. She pulled it all in. Next to her, Avel hummed. His lips didn't move. His stony expression never faded.

The darkness became palpable now. Avelina couldn't see the ship, the bodies, or even her…*mother.* Just the Wielder Queen. Her stark white skin stood in heavy contrast to the puddled sky.

"That's why your sacrifice will be so appreciated," the Wielder Queen continued. Her eyes flickered to the sky, where the sun had been. A blanket of clouds covered it now. Only a few remnants of gray slipped through.

When Avelina tried to look to Avel, her eyes recoiled. He was too bright. He teemed with light. It crawled through him like roots, illuminating his ebony skin from the inside. His eyes were closed, his body tense. The humming had increased into something like a painful moan. His eyes opened.

They locked gazes.

Avelina loosed her magic. It burned from her belly to her heart, then tore free.

The ocean surged.

Light split the air.

Water rushed around her. She dropped into it. Her skin soaked up each molecule. The power in her belly doubled. The bonds dropped from her hands. The Wielder Queen screamed, recoiling. Avel found his feet. His humming had increased into a song without words that came from deep in his throat. Avelina rolled away, blinded by his light.

The Queen fell back, collapsing on a dead sailor.

"Cease!" she screamed.

"Run!" Avel yelled. Avelina looked up, barely seeing the woman—her mother—scramble away. He turned to Avelina next, fear in his eyes. Something inside him dimmed. The song lessened.

Light. He had the power of light—which the Wielder Queen had blocked with darkness.

Avelina sprinted to the water and released the torrent in her belly.

Come to me, she sang. The waters collected, snaked onto the shore, and grabbed the Queen. She flailed, screaming. Coats of darkness pummeled the water that enveloped her, driving it back. One of them gripped Avel, who had fallen. The light ebbed from his body. His mother threw herself on top of him, beating back the strange wraiths.

Avelina threw her body into the water. Magic swept through her with breathless intensity. The Wielder Queen leapt to her feet, snarling.

"I will have *all* the power."

So do I, Avelina thought. The pulse of the ocean banged behind her. Despite the breathless, out-of-control feeling, she tapped into the heavy current. The Wielder Queen lunged. Her bony fingers clamped around Avelina's wrist.

Avelina gave herself to the waves.

The heat of what felt like a thousand suns poured through her body when the water closed over her head. The magic no longer resided in her belly, but in her very soul. It radiated out. She heard the call of the water. The crash of the waves synced with her heart. Avelina *became* the water.

The magic is not mine, she thought as the water swept her away from the beach. *I am but a holder. The magic belongs to the sea.*

It isn't ours, Papa had always said. *It isn't ours. Surrender. It's the only way.*

The ocean bore them away, down, down to the depths by a swift current. Down where the sand didn't interfere. Where the surge of ocean could take the Queen, and all her horrible, stolen magic, into the depths.

It isn't ours, Avelina. Surrender that and you'll find your way.

The magic.

Papa always meant the magic.

She had no choice. The ocean closed over her head now. The magic infused every particle of her body, threatening to tear her apart. Even the Wielder Queen held onto her, as if terrified herself.

Avelina shut her mind to the magic. The burn stalled, as if confused. When it tried to surge again, she forced it back.

Go to your home, she said. *You are not mine.*

For a moment, everything seemed to calm. Then, one vein at a time, all the heat left her body. It dissipated into the ocean, leeching away one morsel after another. Her body weakened. Drained. Darkness overcame her.

She surrendered to it.

The hiss of the ocean woke her.

Avelina felt the water curl around her body, then disappeared. The warm, lapping feeling surrounded her. Gritty sand irritated her back. Warmth, sunshine, light beckoned overhead.

"Dead?"

"Naw. Barely breathing."

"She moved."

Avelina sucked in a sharp breath and opened one eye. Two men hovered over her with long, salty beards.

She screamed.

They leaped back, wielding broken oars. Avelina jumped to her feet and crouched.

"Not a magic holder," one of them said, nose halfway in the air. "Can't smell anything."

In a panic, Avelina turned to her mind, but nothing was there. No extra life teemed inside her. Nothing else moved and flowed. One of the men dropped an oar and held up both hands in a gesture of peace.

"Calm down. We won't hurt you. Came to see if you were part of the massacre."

One muscle at a time, she calmed. Her breathing came faster; the memories faster. The Wielder Queen. The ocean. The sheer power of the magic...then nothing.

It isn't ours...

"Massacre?" she said carefully.

They gestured to the beach. "All those filthy pirates left dead."

Avelina straightened. Empty. She felt...empty. But strangely...free. As if she owned herself for the first time. She touched her arms, her face, then her belly. It growled.

Empty.

The magic had forsaken her.

"There were two people," she said. "A boy, a woman—"

"Gone."

"Everyone is gone! They've all gone to the mainland to celebrate."

"Thought I saw a boy, though," said the other. "Looked like you."

"Sure. With an older lady. They left this morning but hovered around for a while. How long have you been here?"

"I-I don't know. Why is everyone celebrating?"

They nudged each other in the ribs, scoffing. Avelina felt like she'd been turning cartwheels over and over again, her mind whirled. There were so many pieces...so many things that didn't *quite* come together.

One of the fishermen scoffed. "Where've ya been? The war is over. All the magic holders are getting their gifts back."

"If they're still alive," muttered the other one.

"Rumors saying the Wielder Queen is dead."

Her thoughts spun. The magic had gone back to the ocean—but the ocean must have claimed the Queen.

The magic holders were free.

Her family would still be alive.

She pressed her fingertips together, missing the buzz of energy that had hummed in her body. When she looked up, both men had lifted their oars again, as if shielding her off.

"Where is the mainland?" she asked. "I need to find my family."

Fulvio Gatti is an Italian journalist, writer and global geek, author of graphic novels, nonfiction books and short stories published in Italy and France. As you read, he is taking his first steps as a writer into the English-speaking market. In the northwestern part of Italy where he lives he works as an event organizer, translator, radio speaker, and even deputy mayor of his town. *Low is the Land* is set in a fantasy version the real history struggle for freedom that happened in the wine hills of Piemonte during the late World War Two.

LOW IS THE LAND

FULVIO GATTI

The day Luigi left the family to join the freedom fighters, Ida felt there was something wrong in the air. As the oldest son of Giovanni and Jolanda Cassola hugged everyone goodbye, in the windy spring morning, big dark clouds slid over the sun. As a result, the bright colors of the countryside, from the bare lawn that surrounded the humble Cassola family shack, up to the blooming vineyard, seemed to vanish in the blink of an eye.

It was a feeling that went beyond the obvious worry that Ida felt for her older brother. Before disappearing three years ago, taken away at night by the Elves, their father, Giovanni, had been able to teach Luigi how to use a sword. Now, sixteen years old, the oldest child in the family was tall and strong enough to overwhelm any human servant of the Elves. Chances were high that he could even survive a fight with an Elf warrior.

No, Ida didn't fear that Luigi could be killed in a terrorist attack. At thirteen, she was old enough to know that many leaders of the Rebellion were former Elf servants who had switched sides, bringing to the freedom force both their military skills and a deep knowledge of the enemy. Hopes that soon the humans would be able to kick the pointed eared demons out of their land were growing day after day.

When Luigi finally hugged his mom Jolanda, after kissing or talking to each one of his siblings, from Giulia to the barely talking Quartiglio, Ida couldn't help shivering. She got one puzzled look by her sister Teresa and ignored her as usual. Luigi might never come back, Ida thought, like their father hadn't. Outside their poor home, beyond the hill that held their vineyard, dwelt sinister presences compared to which the Elf occupation army was just a bunch of noisy kids. Ida could feel them. She had inherited from her grandmother, and her dad, the ancient power of nature. That power, when she was old and strong enough, would free them all.

"Are you still awake, little Ida?" The voice of Grandma Maria, rough and familiar, was emphasizing her feelings as usual. Ida couldn't help but smile at the old lady, even if there was no need to worry. She had decided to stay up late once more, sewing in front of the faint light of a candle. Moving her hands between needle and fabric relaxed her after a long day in the fields, but also the concentration made her feel closer to the Path.

It was just a matter of listening. Keep quiet, free the mind and let it flow. A soft pulse, coming straight from nature, a wave she had been perceiving clearer every day. The other season, by concentrating, she had been able to strengthen some tomato and carrot plants. To her, it was just like giving the love and care she usually reserved to her siblings. The harvest, as a result, had been great. With a simple caress, she had also rid the vineyard of an illness among the leaves. Without anyone knowing, Ida was training herself to control magic.

"I'm all right, Nona, I simply couldn't sleep," Ida said in a sweet voice.

"I know that!" Grandma exclaimed. "Both your dad and his mother were night owls. I even feared her, when I was young. Did I ever told you?"

"Many times, Nona," Ida commented with a grin.

Grandma Maria got closer. She caressed her granddaughter's cheek. "You have the same eyes, so...out of this world."

Hearing that, Ida lowered her gaze.

"But you've been ill as a child, Ida!" Maria continued. "You should not expect to be stronger than you are. Here..." The old woman took the candle, strolled to the other end of the room and lit another candle. She put a pot on the stove and with the same flame she lit a small fire. Maria gave the candle back to Ida, then took an egg from the cupboard. She broke the shell, let its content slip into the pot, mixed it with a spoon as it crackled over the fire.

Ida, oblivious of needle and thread, had been watching the operations. It was nothing new. Still, it was made with love. Ida wondered which, between the throb of the earth she could feel deep inside and that simple gesture of care, was the real magic. Grandma Maria got back to her with the cooked egg in a cup and gave it to Ida.

"Please eat, my little Ida. Get some fresh energy," the old woman suggested.

The delightful scent of the cooked egg grabbed Ida by her nose and she took the cup and the spoon under her grandmother's pleased eyes. But a cracking sound from the door prevented her from beginning her night meal. The two women froze and waited in the dark. Was it possible that some stray animal, or something worse, had chosen to visit them in the middle of the night?

Ida heard a loud breath and a cough, then her brother Paolo limped into the room. The relief left room for worry as she saw the hunched and balding young man barely standing. Ida and Grandma Maria ran to him and grabbed him by his shoulders before he fell on the ground with all of his sickly body. Paolo was stinking so strongly that Ida felt pain in her guts as she approached. His clothes were torn and stained, and he had grass and dirt all over himself.

"Paolo! What happened? They beat you?" Ida asked in distress.

"Oh yeah", the older brother replied in a drunken slur. "That Barbera was stronger than a bunch of horses!"

Ida sighed. "Paolo, why do you do that? This is such a bad example for the kids…"

The older brother seemed to regain enough control to look at her in scorn. "The opposite, sister. By seeing me, they learn the man they don't want to become." He limped away in the dark, leaving an astonished Ida behind.

"Don't bother, little Ida," Grandma Maria said. "Paolo has always been naughty ever since he was a baby."

"I only hope he doesn't get himself killed some day," Ida complained.

A friend had told Jolanda at the market that the Elves were going door to door, looking for every single adult male in the region. They needed new recruits for their war, which seemed to be intensifying on the Western border. Some said that men who had been found in their homes had been taken away and forcibly recruited. Hearing the news, Ida was relieved that Luigi had already left to join the freedom fighters.

Paolo wasn't happy, though. He went mad and, during a frantic Sunday morning, he urged the whole family to reopen the hole in the wall. It was a narrow niche that had come out after a building mistake between the shack and the barn. Since the Elves were expected to recruit every adult male, able or not for fighting, Paolo would need a place to hide whenever they came. Teresa spent all day crying since the home works had prevented her from going to church.

"Lord will get angry and will send me to hell!" she screamed.

Ida grinned and ignored her like every other member of the family. She was the only one, probably, that knew Teresa only wanted to go to the church to meet Tonino, the baker's son she had fancied since last summer. The silliness of her siblings was not an issue to Ida. She didn't care much about the church, either. She knew there was a stronger power that could really protect them all, and she was growing stronger day by day.

The hideout for Paolo hadn't been built in vain. Just a couple of days later, in a gray afternoon where a soft rain was pouring invisible cold drips of water all over the country, the rumble of trotting horses reverberated among the hills. Piero, Aldo and the other kids were playing in the courtyard. They froze in awe as three huge horses headed in, mounted by tall men in black clothes. Four more were following on foot, the same dark clothes reflecting their grim determination. Ida saw them from the window and noticed there were no Elves among them. Still the troop looked very frightening. Teresa burst into loud sobs and Paolo limped as quickly as possible to his hideout.

Ida followed her mom Jolanda and her grandmother Maria as they went to the courtyard, staring at the newcomers. The three riders stopped the horses and climbed off the saddle. The other men stood around on guard. The tallest rider had a hat, a black scruffy beard and a scar just over his left brow. He took a step ahead towards Jolanda and Maria.

"Greetings, ladies. I'm Captain Ivaldi of the Republican Forces. I'm here to recruit your men for the war, in name of the Duke," said the bearded man.

As the stranger spoke, Ida caught Piero, eleven years old, staring at the newcomers in a defiant look. She grabbed him and pushed him behind the elders with the other children. He hissed in anger but then kept silent after Ida gave him a death stare.

"We have no men, here, your excellency," Jolanda said in a calm voice.

Captain Ivaldi frowned. He looked around. "How is it possible that such a big and happy family have no men?"

"Thank you, your excellency. But we are no longer a happy family since my husband Giovanni died of a disease three years ago," Jolanda explained without losing eye contact.

The Captain casually stepped around the two women, reaching the children. His thugs didn't move but followed him with their eyes. Little Piero had detached from the group again and was facing the stranger. Ida tried to pull him back but Captain Ivaldi noticed the kid. He approached, knelt and grabbed Pietro's chin with his hand, looking into the boy's eyes.

"Hey, we have a young lion here!" Captain Ivaldi said in appreciation. "Too bad you are still a bit young for war. But I'll keep a place for you in my army." The bearded man looked up at Jolanda. "This is the eldest boy here?"

"Yes, your excellency," Jolanda replied way too quickly.

The Captain stood up and exchanged a look with one of his men, a short, auburn boy that Ida remembered having seen at the church. Most of the servants of the Elves came from the capital city, many miles away. But the pointed eared demons had found sympathizers among the locals.

"There were...others," the boy said, hesitant.

Captain Ivaldi stepped in front of Jolanda. "You're not lying to me, sweet lady, are you?"

"No, your excellency."

The Captain grinned. "Let's say I believe you. Still, there may be things about your family you might be oblivious of. Let's say some fake deaths."

Ida was hushing the children when she was grabbed by her arm by Captain Ivaldi. Jolanda couldn't keep from sighing loud. "No!" she said.

The Captain kept talking like he hadn't heard. "This girl looks smart and very committed to her family," he said, still speaking to Jolanda. He drew his sword under the terrified eyes of Jolanda and Maria. "I wonder if she would be so kind to be my guide inside this comfortable house of yours."

Ivaldi's grasp was very strong and Ida felt waves of pain spreading from her arm all over her slim body. Pain was energy and she could use it. She simply had to collect it, the throb of nature growing in intensity inside her. She kept staring at the ground, pretending not to be there, her back on him. Was this the time to react?

In an angry move, Captain Ivaldi pulled Ida closer, forcing her to face him. "I think you are old enough to answer, young lady." Their eyes met for a moment, before Ida looked away. The Captain paused, contemplating her face. "Too bad you are not as pretty as your sister over there. But there is some strength in you as well, like your little brother. What a great family! What great soldiers you'd be!"

Ida bit her tongue. If she unleashed her powers now, her siblings could get hurt. It was too early.

"But your fierce attitude shouldn't keep you from behaving," Captain Ivaldi hissed. "Would you be my guide in your house, now?"

"Yes," Ida replied, still looking away. "I mean, your excellency," she added.

The Captain gloated for his little victory. He stared at her for a few seconds in a predatory way. Then he seemed to get back in control. He let Ida's arm free.

"Let's go," he said, pointing at the door.

Ida took a careful step ahead. Seeing the bearded man waiting, she forced herself to go on. She was about to cross the doorway when she felt the tip of the sword biting her back.

"Fornaro, Severino, stay here and keep an eye on the children," Captain Ivaldi ordered. "The others, with me. Mom and gran, you as well. Pray God I do not find any adult male in here, or the not-so-pretty girl dies."

Ida realized, feeling the beat strong through her body, she could unleash her power at any moment. She had been carefully collecting all the emotions. Now the fear and the horror of her mom and grandma, sisters and brothers buzzed in the air in a crimson cloud. But she had to wait. Everybody was still too close. Unleashing the magic didn't guarantee her being able to control the consequences.

She stepped into her house, turned right, slowly walked into the bare dining room. The big table had a green and yellow cloth covering it, held in place by a big bottle of red wine. There wasn't much more on it besides two dirty dishes, one mouthful of stale bread. Below it, a roach crawled over an apple core. In the corner, two empty pots rested on the stove.

"Nothing interesting here, let's move on," Captain Ivaldi ordered.

They stepped around the table and headed back to the hallway. Ida's eyes went to the old wardrobe that was closing Paolo's secret hideout. Ida could perceive her brother's fear behind the wall. Luckily, nobody else could feel it. Still, she needed to keep the Captain away from Paolo, or they would capture him.

Passing in front of the stairs, Ida quickly turned and stepped on. The tip of the sword dug deeper into her flesh. She ground her teeth, recalling the throb of the earth. But she stopped. What if she could get out of the situation without using her power? If she could bring the Captain upstairs first, long enough for Paolo to sneak out of his hideout, they wouldn't find him. And by not using her magic, she wouldn't even risk jeopardizing her beloved ones.

"Upstairs, already?" Captain Ivaldi commented, unaware of the power about to unleash below his feet. But the bearded man's voice suddenly seemed to relax. "It's all right, girl, you are my guide. You choose. We will come back here later."

They climbed the stairs in a few, quick steps and they were in the kids' bedroom. There, the Captain stopped and mumbled. The room was a mess. Between the beds, the dirty blankets and the box of silkworms there were many places to hide. Also, because of the closed blinds, very little light filtered in the room.

Captain Ivaldi ordered Ida to open the blinds, then pushed her around with his sword moving each and every blanket or mattress.

"Your siblings are very messy," he eventually commented in an annoyed voice. "You should beat them harder."

They did the same careful search in the other bedroom. Aside from a harsh comment on the dark skin of Giovanni Cassola, in his picture over Jolanda's beside table, the Captain didn't find anything interesting in that room either.

"So, time to go back downstairs," the bearded man said. As they walked, Ida hoped her brother had had the time to flee. She did her best to give him a chance. But sneaking out would mean being caught by the Captain's thugs. A silent escape was something very far from Paolo's typical behavior.

Jolanda stood in the doorway, with Grandma Maria and Giulia behind her. Her mother tried to meet Ida's eyes but she was lost in her thoughts. Her back was aching, hit by the frantic tip of the Captain's sword. The rage was mounting inside her soul. She would make use of the power of nature only as a very last resort. But she felt they were getting close.

This other ground floor room was a collection of farming tools. One side of the floor was filled with goods like eggs, floor and wood. In the middle stood another box of silkworms. Behind it, a few steps away, there was the big heavy wardrobe. Ida was trying not to think about the hidden Paolo when a crack broke the awkward silence.

"What was that?" the Captain asked.

"The silkworms," Ida replied. "They are always very noisy."

Captain Ivaldi grunted. "What's in that wardrobe?" He had her open it and rummaged inside. Old and ripped clothes, a small anvil, a rusty scoop. The Captain pushed Ida away to look better. He grabbed a broken knife, weighed it, then reached to a decorated porcelain box occupying almost one full shelf of the wardrobe. He took it and saw it was covering a hole in the back of the wardrobe.

Ida was struck by the sudden feeling of terror of Paolo. If only he had stood still, he might have still had a chance. Instead, out of fear, he had moved. Behind the wardrobe a loud crack rumbled in the room once again.

"What?" the Captain muttered. "Morando, Ferrero, here!" he called his thugs. Quickly two of the men reached him. Captain Ivaldi grasped one side of the wardrobe and started pulling. The thugs pushed from the other side. The huge piece of furniture screeched as being dragged through the floor. Dust blurred Ida's eyes as the inevitable was happening.

The three black clothed men let go of the wardrobe and simultaneously looked at the hole in the door. A pale and horrified Paolo looked back. He sat, frozen, over an old rusty chair. The same thing that had been cracking all over.

"Not exactly a man, here, but still…" the Captain started speaking. He couldn't finish his sentence because the anvil had come out flying from the wardrobe shelf, hitting him hard on his head. He screamed in pain. The box of silkworms trembled in front of the two other men.

Under their astonished eyes it fell on them, lifting a cloud of dust.

They would not get out of there alive. That was Ida's only thought as she finally let herself ask nature for help. What followed was a hell of screams, dust and pain. Seeing her concentration, Captain Ivaldi pointed his sword at Ida. He yelled in anger. But the metal the weapon was made of felt the call of its furnace and started trembling in his hand. The sword fell on the ground. He couldn't see the heavy wood and iron wardrobe collapsing on him from behind. The Captain disappeared under the big piece of furniture as the floor started shaking like during an earthquake.

Ida ran outside, shocked by the extreme power she had unleashed. The scene she faced was even worse than expected. None of the other thugs had had the time to react. Long ropes of vine crawled through the ground and grabbed the black clothed men at their ankles. They were drawn to the ground and stumbled against it. As they screamed in pain, the land seemed to swallow their bodies inch after inch. In the blink of an eye they were gone.

The horses, left without their riders, started running wildly through the courtyard, neighing frantically. The kids were heading to the house for protection but little Quartiglio was last in line. Jolanda yelled to her children to reach him, but they couldn't hear. Ida started running towards him, but she was too far. Grandma Maria, who was still outside, was the one acting faster. She stumbled in the middle of the courtyard, grabbed Quartiglio and pushed him ahead to his family. She didn't see the horses coming and was run over by one of them. Jolanda covered the eyes of the little girls. Teresa saw the scene and started sobbing again. Ida got close to comfort her, but then remembered about Paolo and got back inside the house.

The older brother was still inside his hideout, paralyzed by fear. The Captain and his men had disappeared, swallowed by holes in the floor. The house shook and rubble fell from the ceiling. Ida jumped over the broken pieces of furniture and stretched her hand, shouting her brother's name. Their eyes met. Paolo regained control, took his sister's hand. Ida pulled him out of the hideout and he fell on the broken floor.

"Come on!" Ida yelled.

Paolo, taking a long breath, stood up and limped toward his sister. Together they were able to stumble outside. They found the rest of the family crying in despair. Grandma Maria was gone. It was the most painful way for Ida to learn that every victory comes at a cost.

That very night, while everybody was sleeping upstairs, Ida snuck into the living room. It had been a long day. The hardest part had been calming down the kids, explaining to them that the danger was over. But even the grown-ups were shocked. One of the ground floor rooms was in complete havoc but it was nothing the family couldn't fix. The overall structure of the house was strong. After a careful inspection they couldn't find any sign of Captain Ivaldi or his men's corpses.

When finally the dusk had come, the younger kids fell asleep and were brought upstairs by Ida, Giulia and Teresa. Paolo had vanished as always. He was probably at the tavern, totally drunk. When only Ida and Giulia were still awake, Jolanda eventually burst into tears. She couldn't believe her mother was gone in such a crazy way. The two daughters made a chamomile tea for their mother and, together, they went to sleep.

Only Ida knew that nothing, from then on, would be the same. The Elves used to kill ten humans for each one of their soldiers who were murdered. Retaliation, they called it. Even if nobody knew Ida was the one who could use the power of nature, her very presence would endanger her loved ones. So, alone in the kitchen, she cooked herself an egg like her grandmother used to do. She ate it voraciously, thinking about how much Maria would forever be with her, like her dad and her other grandmother.

Ida put a headscarf on her head, some food in the basket and headed outside. In a quiet night, brightened a full moon, she gave a silent farewell to her childhood and her family. The freedom fighters would soon have a new member.

Edward J. Knight's wife has been bugging him to write more about *Calamity*'s Beth since she appeared in his novel *Sidekick*, the first novel in his Mythic West Universe. He loves writing adventure stories that don't rely on idiot plots and also playing with historical figures in fantastic settings. The actual reported romance between Calamity Jane and Wild Bill Hickok was the basis for this story. When he's not writing, Edward J. Knight designs satellites by day and co-parents two young children by night. More of his work can be found at www.edwardjknight.com.

CALAMITY

EDWARD J. KNIGHT

B eth nearly dropped the water pitcher. The long-haired man at the parlor's back table—*it had to be him!*

Fortunately, the pewter pitcher just slipped in her hand and she only sloshed water over her faded gingham dress. It'd dry fine, and if she held the pitcher just so, she could block anyone from seeing the wet splotch.

But no one else in the Astor's crowded parlor, the finest boarding house in Golden City, Colorado Territory, had even noticed. The teamsters and traders and miners all ignored her and the other serving staff as if they were part of the decor. Which they were, she thought with a grimace.

So, since no one was watching, she took a longer look.

Yes! It was Wild Bill Hickok himself!

He had to be fresh from the front, fighting the giants, but it couldn't be anyone else. His long brown hair curled about his shoulders, just like in the pictures. His eyes twinkled as he spoke with his companion, a plain-looking man in brown—

—no, a *woman* in brown.

Beth sucked in her breath and trembled. The woman wore a man's white shirt with silver buttons under a brown buckskin coat. She'd tied her chestnut brown hair up into a small bun and she smiled at whatever Hickok had said. A Colt .45 rested on the wooden table near her elbow.

A woman! In man's clothes!

The flush of imagined impropriety began to fill her cheeks, but Beth forced it down by looking away. Not that a woman in man's clothes was really improper here in Golden City. There were too many war widows just struggling to make it on their own for there to be a good sense of what was improper.

But none wore men's clothes. Well, Widow Genovese did when she was planting, but never when she came to town.

Beth steadied her nerves and looked back at Wild Bill and his companion.

And found them looking at her. The woman smiled, held up a glass, and gave Beth a meaningful look.

She took a deep breath and wound her way past the other tables of drinkers to them.

"More water, Ma'am?" she asked once she'd arrive.

"Beer," the woman said. "I understand Mr. Lake received a shipment from Mr. Coors earlier this evening…?"

"Yes, Ma'am," Beth said, eagerly nodding her head. "I'll fetch it for you immediately."

"And ask Mr. Lake if he still has some of those raspberry muffins from this morning," Hickok added.

"Yes, Sir." Beth nodded once again and quickly headed for the kitchen.

Once through the door, she relayed the order to the cook and forced herself to take a deep breath. *She had to talk to the woman. Had to!*

She continued to calm herself until the cook gave her the muffins and traded her pitcher of water for beer. When she returned to the parlor she moved slowly so as not to spill a drop.

They smiled when they saw her approach. She carefully set the muffins down.

"Ah, good!" Hickok said as he eyed the muffins. He rubbed his hands together and slid his glass over towards Beth.

She poured slowly and glanced at the woman again. Her warm smile led Beth to steel herself.

"Uh, excuse me Ma'am," she said. "Is that your gun?"

"Why yes," the woman said. "Why do you ask?"

"They let you— I mean, you can…" Beth stopped herself and took a deep breath. "How'd you learn to shoot?"

"Practice," the woman said with a chuckle. "Like anything."

"But now you're good, right?"

Hickok leaned over. "You're what, young lady? Twelve?"

"Thirteen," Beth said. "But that's old enough!"

"That it is," said the woman. She looked at Hickok. "I was fourteen." She reached out and fingered the ivory handle of her pistol. Then she extended a hand to Beth.

"Calamity Jane," the woman said as they shook. "And you are…?"

Beth started in surprise. *Her too!*

"Beth Armstrong," she said. "My ma's the laundress for Mr. Lake."

"Ah," Hickok said. "No pa?"

Beth shook her head and the familiar pang of grief grabbed her heart for a moment.

"But you want to shoot," Hickok continued. "Let me guess, you want to be a gunfighter."

Beth couldn't hide her blush. She focused on filling their glasses and not spilling a drop.

"Why don't you stop by my room upstairs later," Jane said. "We'll talk then."

Beth nodded as the giddy smile drove her blush to an even deeper shade of pink.

Beth tried not to bound up the narrow stairs to the Astor's second floor. Given the hour, it just wouldn't do to wake any of the other guests, though she suspected few were yet asleep. The faint sound of Mr. Lake playing Chopin on the parlor piano followed her up the stairs and mixed with the coughing and snorting of the guest in Room 2. Foul tobacco smoke wafted out of the cracks around the door to Room 3, which she thought was Hickok's. Beth trod carefully, avoiding the squeaky planks in the floor, as she made her way to Room 4.

Calamity Jane's.

Beth's heart raced as she lifted her fist to knock. She hesitated for just a long breath, and then rapped the door.

Instead of calling out, Calamity Jane opened the door.

"Why Miss Armstrong," she said. "How do you do?"

"Well. And you, Miss… Jane?"

"Miss Jane will do fine. And I am fine, considering the circumstances. Do come in." She stepped back to allow Beth to enter.

The room was well lit from an oil lamp on the short dresser. Like all the Astor rooms, the small space contained only a straw mattress bed, a dresser, and a simple chair. Most guests used hooks on the wall for their clothes and on one, hung a frilly pale blue dress.

A gorgeous dress. With white lace and silver stitches all down the sleeves.

"You like it?" Jane asked. "I don't normally carry on with such impractical attire, but Bill says it will be good when we meet with the President."

"You're going to meet the President?" Beth asked, her eyes wide. "Oh, my."

"We are," Jane said with an exasperated sigh. "Can't be helped, I'm afraid. We have to show him something."

"You don't like him?"

"I don't like most politicians. But as I said, it can't be helped." Jane sat on the bed and gestured toward the chair. "Now Miss Armstrong, what do you wish to know about gunfighting?"

"So much," Beth gushed. "So much I don't know where to begin."

"Then one beginning's as good as the next." Jane smiled indulgently and tilted her head, waiting.

"What's it like?" Beth asked eagerly. "Holding a gun? Shooting? Or fighting? How do you do it? It's not like I don't have *some* idea, but—"

"Now hold on," Jane said with a chuckle. "One question at a time." She rubbed her chin. "Have you ever even held a gun?"

"Only once," Beth said, "when I was ten. But I didn't have a chance to fire it. I was just keeping it safe for a minute."

Jane chuckled again. "Well, then that's the first step." She pulled her Colt out, checked it, and passed it handle first over to Beth.

"Now unless you're planning to use it soon," Jane said, "you should leave one chamber empty and lower the hammer on that empty chamber. That way you can't accidentally shoot your foot off."

Beth carefully wrapped her hands around the revolver. She ran one finger down the cool barrel and hefted it slowly, feeling its unexpected weight.

"Flip the barrel out," Jane said. "Here." She took the gun briefly, demonstrated the flip, and passed it back to Beth. "See how that chamber is empty?"

Beth nodded and ran her thumb over the empty hole, and then over the backs of the other bullets. A small shiver ran up her spine. The room felt cool, despite the warm flickers from the lamp. She pushed the cylinder back into place and then wrapped her hand around the grip, with her index finger just to the side of the trigger.

"Now you want to sight down the barrel," Jane said. "Don't aim at me! Point it at the wall."

Beth nodded and raised the gun. Her wrist trembled under the weight, but it was a good weight—a weight that felt right.

"Now—"

The door burst open.

A burly cowboy rushed in. He pointed a fat revolver at Jane.

"Don't move!" he growled, surprisingly soft.

Jane and Beth both froze.

The cowboy stepped in and closed the door behind him. He glared at them. A jagged scar ran along his cheek and disappeared into his scruffy beard. He looked fierce and serious.

Beth's pulse raced. She fought to keep her breathing calm, to not start panting or crying.

"Hand it over," he said. With the barrel of his gun, he gestured toward the Colt in Beth's hand.

Beth glanced at Jane, who calmly nodded. Reluctantly, she passed the gun to the cowboy, who jammed it in his belt.

Jane cleared her throat. "And what might we do for you, Mr...?"

"Smith," he said reflexively, and then scowled when he'd realized what he'd done. "Just give me the Governor's ledger."

"Hickok has it," Jane said calmly.

He grunted, and his eyes darted from Jane to Beth and back again. His gun wavered and sweat beaded on his forehead.

A quick knock sounded on the door before it opened an inch. Smith moved away and another cowboy with curly black hair poked his head in.

"Hickok's gone!" Curly said, as Beth immediately thought of him. "Jumped out the window and took off!"

"Probably took the ledger with him," Jane said. Her hands stayed firmly in her lap.

"Might've," Curly said.

"Let's go!" Smith said. He waved his gun at Jane. "You too. Move slow and keep your hands where I can see 'em."

"Leave the girl," Jane said as she stood. "She has nothing to do with this."

"She knows my name," Smith growled. "She comes too."

Jane carefully stood and gestured for Beth to do the same. Smith stepped to the side and indicated for them to lead the way.

They walked down the stairs without encountering anyone, to Beth's surprise. It was almost a shuffle, with Curly looking around wild-eyed in front and Smith bringing up the rear with his gun pressed into the small of Jane's back.

Beth couldn't hear the piano, which unnerved her as much as the men did. Had something happened to her boss? They didn't go into the parlor though—just hustled right by it and out the door. Wherever Mr. Lake was, she hoped he was safe.

Outside, the cold night air stung Beth's cheeks and bare arms. Only a few lights spilled from the Astor, and the nearby buildings were dark. It took a moment for her eyes to adjust to the bright moonlight as the cowboys pushed them along, up the road, into the mountains.

Beth stumbled on a half-buried stone, but Smith pushed them on. He cursed and slapped the back of Jane's head. She started to swing back with her elbow but cut it short when he pressed the gun firmly into her back.

Ahead of them Curly hustled up the street, his head darting side to side. He looked back.

"Keep up, will ya?"

Smith shoved Jane and growled at Beth. "You heard 'em."

They left the last building behind and the road meandered around a curve in the hill. The night wind picked up, and Beth shivered.

Don't give into fear, she thought. *Don't give in.*

She'd survived worse, when the giants collapsed the cabin on her and killed her Pa. She could survive this. She just needed to keep her head.

But her heart still threatened to pound so hard as to leap out of her chest.

Curly froze. His head popped up like a prairie dog and then he yelled. "I see him!" He took off running up the road.

"Go on ahead," Jane said to Beth. She nodded up the road.

Beth took a deep breath. There was something in Jane's eyes, something she wanted to say. She couldn't, though, not with Smith pushing the gun in her back.

Beth ran.

Her legs wobbled like rubber. They held, though.

She kept her eyes on the road, making sure each step was sound so she wouldn't fall. The dirt crunched under her steps.

Behind her, Smith shouted and cursed. Jane yelled. Beth lowered her head and forced her legs to move faster.

And then the gunshot.

She skidded to a stop and turned.

Jane and Smith seemed to be in a clench, almost an obscene dance in the moonlight, distant town lights silhouetting them against the sky.

But then Jane slid to her knees and toppled to her face.

Smith jumped back, a gun still in each hand, a look of shock on his face. His own was held high. Jane's—pulled from his belt—still pointed at the fallen woman.

He recovered quickly. With a jerk, he leveled both guns at Beth. "Come back here, girlie."

Eyes wide, Beth just stood, until he growled and cocked the guns. Slowly, she trudged back toward the killer.

He glared at her, but then looked down at Jane's body. "Killed with her own gun," he said with a smirk. He shoved the Colt back into his waistband but kept his own revolver pointed at Beth. He gave her an evil, wolfish grin.

Beth froze. Her knees locked. She struggled to breathe.

"C'mon," he said. He waved his gun. "I won't hurt ya if you do as you're told."

He's lying, Beth thought. She glanced around—the few scraggly pine trees near the road stood too far back. He'd shoot her down if she ran.

She took a deep breath and took a step toward him. Then another. Then another. Slowly, as her legs failed to collapse, she made her way forward.

Near Jane's body, a small fog formed. Grey, and almost transparent, it slowly stretched up and solidified.

Beth's eyes went wide.

The fog took the form of a person, with arms and legs and a head. Slowly the features filled in, becoming a face.

Beth gasped.

Calamity Jane.

Her ghost, actually.

The ghost stared down at her body. She put her hands on her hips and frowned.

"C'mon!" Smith called. He didn't seem to notice the ghost standing right next to him.

He can't see it, Beth realized. *He doesn't know.*

To her surprise, she felt calmer. She picked up her pace but paused about three feet from the body and the ghost.

Smith sneered at Beth. "Search the body," he said. "Make sure she doesn't have any pages of the ledger on her." He stepped back, out of reach, to give her room.

Beth knelt. Her heart still pounded. Her eyes darted from Smith to the ghost to the body. She gently put on hand on the corpse's back and checked on Smith. He was watching the road ahead more than her.

She looked questioningly at the ghost. It pointed urgently toward the body's right boot.

Beth nodded. Smith's eyes were on her again, so she made a show of patting down the corpse's back and sides. She tried not to vomit—the body was still warm, but the smell of the released bowels stank up the air.

She inched her hand down, slowly, over the hip, down the thigh. She took deep breaths to suppress the trembles in her arms. When she glanced at the ghost, it still pointed at the boot.

They heard yells from up the road and Smith's head jerked that direction. Shots followed.

Beth jammed her hand into the boot. Her fingers wrapped around the handle of a small derringer.

She yanked it out and pointed it at Smith. She squeezed the trigger. It clicked on an empty chamber.

Smith had been looking down the road, his revolver pointed in that direction, but he instantly snapped his eyes down and pointed his own gun at her.

"Well," he drawled. "It looks like the girl's got some spirit. Too bad."

Beth pulled the trigger again.

The bang surprised her. The kick of the gun, too. Her arm flew back and, startled, she fell.

Smith's eyes went wide. His gun slipped from his fingers and clattered to the dirt. Crimson red blood soaked his shirt.

He collapsed into a lifeless pile.

Beth sat up, panting. Her arm ached, and she'd bruised her hand somehow.

I'm alive! I'm alive!

As she watched, a dark cloud formed above Smith's body. Instead of solidifying, it shifted and wavered like smoke, before fading into nothingness.

Jane's ghost smiled at her. It put its hands on its hips and nodded happily.

Behind her, she heard pounding footsteps on the road. She tensed, and then scrambled around, bringing the gun to bear.

She let out a relieved breath. Hickok raced down the road toward her.

He skidded to a stop a few feet from her. "Are you hurt?" he asked before dropping to one knee by Jane's side. Shock and grief raged across his face.

"I'm fine," Beth said.

Hickok rolled Jane's body onto its back and felt for a pulse on her neck. He cursed softly. Then he sat back on his haunches. His voice cracked when he spoke.

"She's gone," he said. He bit his lip, as if fighting back tears.

"Mostly," Jane said. "Her ghost's here." She gestured to where the ghost stood, smiling sadly at Hickok.

"Where?" Hickok turned wildly, looking all around. His gaze went right through the ghost not more than five feet from him.

"She's right there," Beth said, pointing.

He sighed. "Sorry," he said. "You must be one of the special ones that can see them."

Beth blinked as that sunk in. She stared at the ghost, wondering.

Calamity Jane's ghost cupped her hands over her heart and pressed them in. Then she pointed at Hickok. She repeated the hands on her heart gesture.

Beth nodded. She turned to Hickok. "She says she loves you."

He snorted softly, but the edges of his mouth still softened at the news.

"Tell her I love her, too," he said at last.

The ghost nodded, and her face beamed with an almost heavenly glow.

"She knows," Beth said.

Then the ghost drifted over to Smith's body. She pointed at something. Insistently.

Beth scrambled to her knees and crawled over to it.

"What it is?" Hickok called.

"She wants me to get something," Beth said. "Maybe the ledger?"

"I have the ledger," he said. "Or at least the pages that prove the Governor's been stealing the Army's money."

The ghost knelt and pointed at Jane's Colt. Beth looked at the ghost to make sure, and it nodded. She gingerly picked up the gun.

The ghost pointed at the revolver, and then at Beth. She repeated the gestures several times.

"You...want me to have this?"

The ghost nodded.

With a deep breath, she squeezed the revolver tight. "Thank you."

The ghost smiled.

And then slowly faded away.

"She still here?" Hickok asked. He scrambled to his feet and extended a hand to pull Beth up.

Beth shook her head. She didn't relax her grip on the gun as she got up.

"She want you to have that?" he asked.

"I think so."

He nodded. "Then I suppose you oughtta keep it."

"Can I?" she asked. A gift from a ghost was gonna be trouble, but she didn't feel she could refuse.

"C'mon," he said and gestured back toward town. "We need to make sure everyone else is all right and get some help with these bodies."

"Then what?"

"Then," he said, "I teach you how to shoot. It's what she would've wanted."

Beth nodded solemnly. She gave the spot where Jane's ghost had stood one last look before they started back to town. Hickok would need some time to grieve...but then, after he taught her to shoot...?

She'd have to find some trousers that fit.

At Castell Henllys in Wales, a little girl sneaking a bottle of Dr. Pepper in her Iron Age costume told Sarah she sounded like Buffy (the Vampire Slayer). She's not, however, from California. Then, after spending years training in Shotokan karate with no serious injuries, Sarah fractured her finger taking soil samples in Northern Ireland, so that's one vote for martial arts being safer than archaeology.

It's still debatable where writing and cats fit on the danger spectrum, but she tries to test both every day.

NOT A WHISPER

SARAH BARTSCH

Kate stopped mentioning the ghosts when people realized she *meant* it, she really heard their voices. The word spread how she'd gone mad, even her parents said it, so Kate stopped talking about the ghosts.

Then she stopped talking altogether.

Her words drowned, caught in her throat whenever she opened her mouth, forced the breath…even with her family. Especially with family. It hadn't always been like this. She used to say everything that came to mind, and her voice itself functioned. She still spoke out loud in the deep forest where only the animals and trees listened, and she chatted up a storm with the strangers who passed through, each and every one. Traders, thieves, farmers, vagrant soldiers—she *sought out* conversations with strangers.

Today, Trader Efram headed out of town with his creaking cart, heavy with all sorts of sweets and spices, sparkling—but cheap—jewelry on display and fancy fabrics from foreign lands as well as the medicines Kate tried so hard to learn about. Once past the last couple farmholds, she knew he'd board up the sides and hide his goods before taking the road to Arlinn, the village where the green-eyed people lived.

Efram always put up with her incessant questioning with smiles, so she searched him out every time he came to the village. But this time she'd wandered, exploring the forest for days, and if the deer hadn't wandered near the road, she would have missed her chance. He had kind blue eyes and sun-wrinkled skin making him seem much older than he really was, and he looked concerned as she approached.

"Katie, lass. What's this I hear about you being a simpleton?" He stopped the horse and leaned to peer at her from the cart's single seat, sun-bleached blue cushion fraying at the edges, his pudgy forearm resting on his knee. "I asked after you yesterday. I stopped some of the girls in town, who I thought were your friends, but they sounded… cruel. Said you were a crazy mute and the forest was stealing your soul. I told 'em they got it wrong, that you talk to me all the time, but—"

"You got the truth, Efram. They aren't my friends, just silly gossips."

Though she had been away from home for days with only plants and creatures for company. Her hair was snarled, her pointy elbows skinned, and dried mud splattered her clothes where it wasn't completely caked-on. She bit her lip, and her throat tightened up.

"Is there trouble?" he asked. "Maybe I could help."

A silent shake of her head answered no because the word refused to shake free. But a ghost nudged her, let her know Efram was a good guy. She tried again and said, "I'll be fine." His offer to help was sincere, and so she went further and decided to share her secret plan, eager to hear someone agree it was a great idea. "I'm fifteen in a few years, and then I'll run off to join Archer's Company."

His reaction wasn't right at all. He *frowned.* "Not sure that's going to work out, kiddo."

"No, no, you don't understand! I know I'm skinny and short now, but I'm gonna grow tall like my parents soon—they're both so huge—and I'm already great with my bow and I can throw knives—"

"You could be the best of the best, but it wouldn't matter if your pop won't let you go."

"He doesn't want…doesn't need me when he's got Ally."

"Ah, yes. See, that's the problem. The whole village is abuzz since your sister ran off."

"She'd *never*…" But Kate hadn't been home herself for nearly three days. What could have happened in the space of three days? "Sorry, Trader Efram. Thank you for… Safe travels to you, but I've got to go."

She ran all the way back and ended up so winded she couldn't force words through her scratchy throat even if she'd wanted to. In town it was harder. Not only did people stare, but the ghosts were louder, there were more of them, and it got confusing. She wished she understood what they meant. They didn't actually have voices most of the time, more like feelings and sometimes the words manifested like thoughts in her head—but they weren't hers, and she knew it. She knew the difference. Her own thoughts came from a different place.

Her lungs burned and sweat stuck her filthy clothes to her body as she headed through the inn's taproom. Her mother wasn't there. A few pro drinkers had already taken their pre-lunch spots and glared at her as she passed, probably worried that without Ally to take over from their father, the inn would fail, and they'd have nowhere to go. One of those regulars grabbed her arm as she passed.

"Is it true? Your sister's gone?"

Kate shrugged and squirmed loose.

"She was sweet on that minstrel a few weeks back, I remember." He laughed. "Hell, everyone remembers! That girl is gettin' all…uh… grown up." For Kate he only gave a dismissive once-over and went back to contemplating his beer.

That couldn't be it, though. She barely remembered the minstrel, and Ally wasn't some bubbleheaded twit willing to give up her good life for a guy like him. She was the smart one. She knew minstrels had a girl in every town, the villages in between, and even a wife and babies back home in the city. They weren't for serious. Catching up with him would just be beggin' for a brutal rejection, *everyone* knew, especially the smart one herself, Ally.

"What do you have to say to explain yourself?"

Her mother had found her, and Kate just sighed.

"Right, right." Her mother sighed in return. "Say nothing because you hate me." As though Kate's silence was a weapon to hurt her mother, which it wasn't, but no amount of explanation would be enough. Even the ghosts who haunted the inn vehemently agreed with that, so she didn't bother, and her mother went on. "Your sister's been gone for almost two whole days, and I know she got the idea from you."

Ally had run away, but it was Kate's fault? She hadn't seen her sister in a week, hadn't spoken to her since the middle of winter, and it was nearly harvest. There was a time she and Ally were allies, whispering secrets to each other, a united front against their parents, but ever since Ally started helping Dad around the inn, learning the books and numbers and filling in to serve the drinks, she'd changed. The way things were now with all the praise she got and the future she was promised, she was less likely to leave than ever…

On her own.

The only explanation that made sense was not the minstrel, not some streak of moon-induced, bloody insanity. No. She'd been *taken*. Kate forced her throat to work. "Mama—"

"I'll tell you what you're going to do until Ally comes back—which she will, any day now—but until that happens, we've got to keep up appearances, which means you'll start pulling your own weight and fill in for her." Her mother grabbed at her waist, groped her hips and sighed. "Not only a dimwit but built like a boy, and that isn't what keeps the men drinking. Eat more and try harder."

Doubtful she'd be able to grow a woman's body overnight on willpower and buttered bread alone, but her mother had a point. The men liked the way Ally looked, always watching her walk, dropping things so she'd bend over to pick them up while they ogled. They teased her and stayed late when she was there and spent more money since she started serving the drinks. Rees, the drifter, most of all, and Kate realized what had happened. Rees took Ally. He wasn't from around here, showed up with a limp after serving in the Wind Wars, he'd *said*. Had the look of a soldier about him but didn't try to settle down proper even after a couple years. No woman to keep him warm at night. No man, for that matter, and he'd watched Ally fierce enough to burn holes in her flesh.

So…was Kate right?

The ghosts didn't answer one way or the other.

After cleaning up and changing clothes, Kate quietly served drinks and food and wiped down tables while Dad repeated the lie her mother had concocted: Ally went up the mountain to help their sick aunt and would be back in a few days or so. Nothing wrong here. No, the girl wasn't disobeying her parents over a boy. How *dare* anyone suggest otherwise?

Rees appeared for dinner, sweaty and tired after helping out at the mill—or whatever odd job he had this week. Kate watched him and listened for the ghosts' feelings about him, but they were too many, distracted and conflicted like they often were inside buildings. He ordered the same as most other customers, pig roast and greens and a beer to wash it down, and nothing suggested he'd stolen a girl in the past few days. He didn't want extra food to take home. He stayed after eating to swap stories with his friends, who liked him—even admired him—and from the outside she could see why no one would suspect him when he was so charismatic and friendly and *relaxed*.

But when he left, she followed. Patrons still filled the tables, were lined up along the bar, and her father would be furious with her, but Kate was the only one who realized Rees took Ally. She had to go. The ghosts agreed once she was out in the dark street and she could sense them clearer. She would track the unsuspecting kidnapper to his lair, and the spirits urged her on, the faint hint of a whisper drawing her closer to Ally. Over the years she learned that while sometimes the ghosts didn't have all the answers or weren't sure… They never lied.

Ally was nearby and needed help.

But Rees just went home. He lived in a room at Widow Carigie's big stone house right in the center of town where the street lamps lit the way through the dark and certainly not where Kate expected him to keep her sister captive. Of course, if no one suspected him and even Kate doubted this was the place, then maybe it was the perfect hiding spot. A light came on in a second story window, and she climbed the wall beside the house to get a peek inside. There Rees chewed on a piece of jerky as he set about patching a hole in his trousers in the faint lamplight. Alone. The damp night air seeped into her stiff muscles as she waited and watched while Rees finished sewing the one patch and started on another.

Ally was close, the ghosts chanted in the back of her head. But not in Rees' room. Where else could she be? Was there a basement under the big house? The walled garden might have a tool shed or…

"What are you doing?"

Startled, Kate fell off the wall. She landed at Dad's feet, her wrist bent too far, too hard a slam against the paving stones, but she didn't shout. Dad looked around, ashamed of his crazy daughter. "I left the inn to follow you, and we've got to get back before your mother notices, you hear me? Get up and let's go." She struggled to her feet, cradling her aching arm, but Dad carried on. "Why do you keep trying to hurt me and your mother? Both you girls, so irresponsible, going out of your way to be difficult. I left people waiting to come after you, important customers who deserve respect, and you don't even care enough to say you're sorry."

Kate *was* sorry. It was embarrassing how guilty she felt, and now she'd hurt herself, too. How was she going to help out in the inn one-handed? But she'd come this far, and Ally needed her, so she sucked in a deep breath, pushed Dad down, and ran for Widow Carigie's door where she knocked with her good hand, *pounded*, and held her breath until Widow Carigie finally appeared.

The woman hesitated to open the door wide until she saw it was

Kate waiting. Widow was still fairly young but rich and well respected throughout the town. Word was she turned away suitor after suitor, stating they weren't good enough to replace her husband, and Kate imagined growing up to be like her someday, strong enough to say what she meant and hold out for what she really wanted no matter what other people thought.

Widow hunkered down to look Kate in the eye and put a comforting hand on her shoulder. "What is it, honey?"

But standing there now, Widow's expectant eyes focused on her, Kate's throat squeezed tight. If she said the wrong thing or admitted to hearing the ghosts, Widow Carigie would look at her the way everyone else did, and she wasn't sure she could bear that.

Dad came up behind her and apologized. "She's a handful of a child. I'm sorry for bothering you at this hour for no reason. Come on, Kate."

"Looks to me like *she* thinks there's a reason. Come on, sweetie, tell me what's happened."

Her throat eased up as she relaxed a little, but Dad beat her to it. "She's always upset about something, the sensitive little thing, but she doesn't talk anymore. I know you've heard. Everyone knows this girl's gone quiet." Then he grabbed her shoulders and turned her away.

"It looks like she's hurt," Widow mentioned.

"I'll take care of it."

Then Widow stood and backed away, unable—or unwilling—to stop Dad from dragging Kate all the way home without a good reason. Kate had to explain what was happening, why she needed to stay, but Dad was guiding her away, hampered by reluctant steps, and Widow Carigie closed her door, shutting them out before Kate finally shouted. "The ghosts say Ally's here!"

Dad jerked her arm and started walking faster. "I knew it. I knew you could talk this whole time."

And Widow Carigie didn't come out. Maybe she hadn't heard? Or more likely she didn't believe Crazy Kate was worth listening to, just like everyone else. Kate bowed her head, watching her feet tackle the cobblestones faster and faster as Dad raced to get back to the inn before they were both in worse trouble.

But then footsteps clattered up behind them.

"What ghosts?" Widow caught up. She'd run after them because she *had* listened. "Isn't Ally the girl who ran off?"

"My sister."

Dad snorted. "Don't waste your—"

Widow glared at her father and spoke directly to Kate. "What ghosts?"

"I hear them—always have, I guess—speaking to me. They don't use words or voices, exactly, but they tell me the truth, and they say Ally didn't run off, she was taken. To your house."

Dad shook her arm. "She's sick in the head, this girl, pretending to be mute half the time and saying she hears things that aren't there."

"Well… She's not hearing ghosts, that's for sure," Widow said, and Kate's heart fell sick into her stomach. "Sweetie, they're not ghosts."

Kate swallowed around a growing lump. "You don't know—"

"Not ghosts, you hear me? Ghosts are the trapped spirits of the dead, and maybe they're real, I couldn't say. But I've heard of folks talented like you. It's rare, but… They're not ghosts. I think what you're hearing are the loose, drifting thoughts of *living people*."

Dad said what Kate was thinking. "That's impossible."

But it made so much sense. Thoughts. That's why the forest was so quiet, why the barroom at dinnertime was so confusing—too many people thinking all the different things. Not ghosts after all. "Does that mean…outside your house, I was hearing Ally?"

"I believe so." Widow's gaze darted back home and then critically at Dad before settling back on Kate. "Why don't we go save your sister and prove the impossible?"

Ignoring the pain in her probably-broken wrist, jostled with every step, Kate ran full tilt back the way they'd come, Widow and Dad trailing behind. The closer she got to the house, the stronger the sense of Ally became, but at the house she was stumped, unable to pinpoint the feeling…Ally's thoughts…any further. When Widow caught up, Kate told her. "She's here *somewhere*, but I can't tell exactly. It's dark, scary."

"But she's okay?" Dad asked like he finally maybe believed her.

"For now, but we have to hurry. That's all I know." To get more, since she could sense thoughts, she wanted to ask Rees what he knew and listen to behind his words. That's how she'd find Ally. "Widow Carigie, can you take me to Rees's room? I want to ask him a question."

203

Widow let out a slow angry breath and nodded, jaw clenched. "This way."

It only took one look at them as Rees answered his door. Kate didn't even get a chance to ask about Ally before the worry and guilt flooded the area, then the confidence that they couldn't actually know. The girl was hidden too well. She wasn't in his room where she'd make noise to give him away, and she wasn't even in Widow's house. They'd never find her...

In the abandoned storeroom of the building next door.

Kate grinned. "I'll get her!"

And as she rushed away, she heard Rees—confused, guilty Rees—commenting. "Isn't that the dimwit? What bad luck you have, innkeeper! One girl's crazy and the other runs off with a minstrel—"

She was pretty sure the next sound was Dad's fist slamming into Rees's face, but she just focused on finding Ally. Now that she knew where to go, it was easy to find Rees's trail through the fence at the back of the garden onto the neighboring property, overgrown with weeds. Kate pushed on the door, which didn't budge, but the boards blocking the window were loose and only rested leaning against the empty space. Climbing in, she sensed Ally's anxiety, her exhaustion and fear, and Kate was able to go straight to the right storeroom, unlatch the lock on the outside, and free her big sister.

She silently led Ally out to the street where Dad and the Widow were waiting. A guardsman held onto Rees and cursed when he saw Ally, saw the proof of what Rees had done. He tied Rees's hands and led him away, and Ally started crying harder—but in relief, now—and Dad just hugged her and patted her hair and promised to protect her forever. They started towards the inn, Ally limping a little. Dad helped her walk but didn't look back to see if Kate was following. Much less thank her for not giving up, for saving Ally's life, for being the good daughter for once.

"Some people are too fragile to admit when they're wrong," Widow said, watching alongside her.

"Do you think things will change, now that he knows I've been telling the truth all along?"

Widow just shrugged, and Kate sighed. At least she was used to it, and while they didn't need her there, it was probably time to go home.

She made to leave, but Widow Carigie stopped her. "Wait, listen." Widow put an arm around her shoulders and squeezed. "Tomorrow I'll send letters to some friends who know things, and we'll work together to get you placed immediately in a good school where you'll be trained to use this power you have. There you can learn all about that and about everything else you'll need. If you want."

It didn't sound right. Well, it sounded amazing to leave town to attend a school where she could study and belong and talk and maybe people would even listen to her sometimes like Widow Carigie did. Could she learn to control the ghosts? Hear them clearly or shut them out whenever she wanted? And she'd be able to join the Company when she was old enough or go and do *anything* without Dad or her mother telling her she wasn't good enough.

Too good to be true, it sounded.

But was it?

The ghosts said... No, *Widow's thoughts* confirmed the offer was real. Kate smiled and answered, loud and clear, "Yes, please."

J eremy Zimmerman is a teller of tales who dislikes cute euphemisms for writing like "teller of tales." He is the author of the young adult superhero book, *Kensei* and its sequel, *The Love of Danger*. In his copious spare time he is the co-editor of *Mad Scientist Journal*. He lives in Seattle with a herd of cats and his lovely wife (and fellow author) Dawn Vogel. Visit him online at bolthy.com

HOPE BEYOND DEATH

JEREMY ZIMMERMAN

Morna had died waiting for someone to rescue her, wasting away in a tower cell seemingly without doors. The wizard who had kidnapped her stopped showing up with food and water, and she died far from home in an unfamiliar land.

In death, she wandered the abandoned castle, wailing in her dismay. The sun would set, she would rise and begin her mournful cry afresh. She couldn't say how long she had been dead. Countless nights of moaning blurred into each other. She no longer noticed seasons, and she didn't keep a journal.

One night, a boy appeared on the blasted heath that surrounded the castle and watched her.

Normally she didn't see people. There was no settlement visible and people rarely passed near the castle. When she did see people, they didn't want to see her. Some averted their eyes, made a sign of warding against evil. Some were children, daring each other to touch the wall of the fortress and then run giggling from their fear.

But this boy seemed fearless, and he returned most nights. When he wasn't looking at the castle walls, he was looking at her. She walked along the battlements, sounding her mournful cry, and he watched.

Even in death, she learned, she still felt self-conscious.

On one trip to the castle, the boy arrived carrying a heavy sack. Morna paused in her wailing, curious about the change in his routine. The boy pulled out a strange looking crossbow that was nearly as long as he was tall. After wrestling with it, he cocked the bowstring and placed a multi-pronged hook on top of it.

He staggered to lift it, then fired it toward the battlement near where she stood. The hook, which trailed a rope behind it, hit the wall and clattered back down to the ground. He cursed and reset the whole process. After several more tries, the hook caught on the wall, and he began climbing.

In all the time Morna had haunted this castle, no one had ever tried to break in. Since she had died, no one had tried to leave, either. She didn't know if she should assure him that he didn't need to go through all this effort for her. It was too late to rescue her, and the wizard was missing.

It was hard to monitor his progress along the wall. She could walk through everything in the castle except the exterior walls and the space above them. She couldn't lean out over the crenellations to see how the boy was doing.

With a grunt of effort, the boy reached the top of the wall and pulled himself onto the battlements. He sat there panting, then looked up as she drew close, smiling a lopsided smile. She was so baffled by his arrival that she didn't know how to respond. It didn't occur to her to smile back.

"I can't believe it," he said. "I can't believe I swiped you right from under Gill's nose. You're going to make me rich beyond my wildest dreams."

Morna frowned, not certain what he meant.

"You probably don't understand me at all," he said as he rummaged through his bag. He pulled out a box with a brass screen on one side and a crank handle on another. "I just need you to hold still while I put you in this box, and then I'll get you off to market."

Though she didn't know what the box was, she suspected it was bad. Even in death, she felt fear. And she ran.

She shot through the nearest wall, gliding down the stairs and through the next wall at the bottom. Since she no longer drew breath, she wasn't winded from the effort or tight-chested from the fear. And yet she couldn't remember the last time she had been this afraid. Certainly not since she died. And even then, she had been more delirious from hunger than actually afraid.

She paused in the garden and lurked between the trees and the overgrown flowerbeds, listening for her pursuer. No sound reached her ears. She would have sighed with relief if she breathed, but she felt certain she had escaped whatever bizarre fate the boy had in mind for her.

And then his footsteps rang in the corridor. He glanced into the garden from the hall he ran down before running past. Then he doubled back and paused in the doorway with his smile. He lifted the box with the mesh aimed toward her and began walking her way.

He made shushing noises. "It's alright, Princess. It's alright. Just get in the box, and I'll get you out of here to a new home."

"What kind of new home?" she asked. She hadn't spoken since her death, and the sound of her moaning words alarmed her.

The boy's expression fell. "I guess you can understand me after all. I don't know what you heard me say earlier. But it's a nice place, definitely not weird or uncomfortable. Probably."

Morna shrieked and ran through the nearest wall and down the corridors again. She didn't have a plan, she just ran through rooms, desperate to get away from the boy. In each room, she looked around for something useful. The castle was not large, and she had been through almost every room multiple times in the past. She had seen everything in those rooms, but she kept darting through them in hopes of finding something new.

She spotted the boy sneaking around the corridors of the castle, peeking into each room before creeping on to the next door. Each time she saw him, her fear went up another notch.

Eventually she willed herself to enter one of the two rooms she hadn't returned to since she had died: the library.

It had been her first memory when she was kidnapped by the wizard. He had brought her there, tied up, while he gloated about the ransom he was extorting from her father the king. She'd wept and begged, but to no avail. He had dragged her up into the tower and sealed her in her doorless prison.

But in her fear, she grew desperate, and ventured into the library.

It was the largest room of the castle. Most of the walls were lined with books. Tucked into one corner was a small writing desk. The center held a large work table with stacks of books and a large glass bottle resting on its side in a wooden cradle. As she moved about the room, she noticed someone had painted dozens of symbols in a circle. Next to it stood a lectern with an open book turned toward the circle. A shadowy smudge of some sort hovered inside the circle near the book.

As she drew near it, the smudge shifted and a cold and alien awareness focused on her.

Morna retreated from the circle and bumped into something in the process. From one of the shelves, a tiny voice yelled, "Mek!"

She had moved through the table and collided with the bottle. It teetered in its perch until a winged imp the size of her fist landed on it

209

to stablize it. The imp glared at her and again said, "Mek!"

"Aha!" the boy shouted from the doorway. He smiled, trying to catch his breath, and stepped into the room. "Look, I get it. Change is hard. But you're a sad princess, and this is your chance to get away from here. Just hold still, I'll crank this handle, and then we can leave together."

A derisive snort came from the circle of symbols. "Spookmonger," a grating voice said from within the shadows.

"Who said that?" the boy asked, looking about frantically.

"What…what is a spookmonger?" Morna asked.

The boy's attention whipped back to her. "Not me. No. I'm definitely not one."

"They capture ghosts and sell them," the shadow said. When it spoke, Morna thought she caught a glimpse of white specks flashing. Like teeth.

"People buy ghosts?" she asked. "Who? And why?"

"No one," the boy tried to answer as the shadow said, "People with a lot of money and desperate for a cure of dubious quality."

The boy glanced around the room, still not recognizing where the grating voice came from. He began working the crank again on the box. "Quiet, you. It's nothing like that. What you'll be doing is helping me. I have a wife and three kids to feed."

Morna no longer had a stomach, and yet she felt increasingly nauseated as the boy cranked the handle on the box. She doubled over and tried to back away, but he pressed closer to her. In frustration, she shoved at the glass bottle, forcing it out of its cradle and over the edge of the table.

"Mek!" the imp cried in dismay.

If the glass made any noise when it was shattered, it was immediately overwhelmed and forgotten by the shrieking that erupted. A yellow miasma swam up around the boy and soon he screamed as well. Eyes wide, he dropped his box and swatted at the smoke that shrieked all around him. He staggered farther into the room and into the circle of symbols.

And into the shadow.

More teeth than seemed plausible flashed in the darkness. At the first sign of blood, Morna fled the room.

It was many nights before Morna returned to the library. Instead, she skulked around the battlements and stared at the horizon. The sorrow that had prompted her years of wailing had abated. It was replaced by a cold dread.

She'd never heard of spookmongers before, or that ghosts could be bought and sold. She'd thought starving to death was as bad as it could get, but clearly there were more cruelties than she imagined. And the only one who seemed to know anything about these spookmongers was in her second least favorite room in the castle.

But finally, her fears motivated her enough to seek out the shadow. She worried that there would be blood and gore all over the study. But instead, the room was returned to its previous state. The bottle that she had broken had been replaced with a different bottle, the swirling yellow mist once more inside.

"Hello?" she called out.

The tiny imp reappeared and positioned itself between her and the bottle, arms spread wide as though it would block her from accessing it.

The darkness said, "You returned faster than I expected."

"I need help," Morna said. "The boy—the spookmonger—he said something about beating someone else here. There are more people, more spookmongers coming."

"That will not end well for you," the darkness said.

"You aren't worried?" she asked.

"I'm not a ghost. And they wouldn't be able to do anything with me. The old wizard had trouble binding me, and he was an actual practitioner of the arts, unlike ruffians like the spookmongers. If someone damages the circle, I'll return to my own plane. Which is a shame, but not lethal. I'll miss having books to read, but I will survive."

"Can you help me, umm—I beg your pardon, I do not know your name."

"You would not be able to speak my actual name. But I have many sobriquets. My favorite has always been 'The Empress of Teeth.'" White danced in the darkness, which Morna wanted to believe was a smile.

"My name is Morna," the girl said. "Princess of—"

"Yes, I know who you are. And no, I cannot help. It is nothing personal. I simply cannot leave the circle. The best I could do is be available for you to lure people in here again."

Morna wrung her hands and paced in front of the Empress. "What can I do then?"

The Empress was quiet for a while before asking, "What abilities have you cultivated?"

"Abilities?"

"Can you move physical objects? Possess living things? Sway emotions?"

"No. I can walk through walls?"

"Any ghost can do that, and I'm sure those cretins will be prepared for such."

"What about castle defenses? He was a powerful wizard. He must have had something."

"Yes, he did."

Hope blossomed in Morna's absent heart. "Wonderful. How can we use them?"

"You need to wield his staff. I don't know why the wizard disappeared, but he probably took his staff with him. Even if you were able to find it, you have no ability to wield it because you are insubstantial."

"He could be dead," Morna said. "And left the staff behind."

"Have you seen a body? I thought not. Plus, even if he had died, he has contingency plans. His soul is bound to some hidden location far from here. He would just return as soon as he regrew his body."

"He can do that?"

"Anyone can, if they know how. But that's a more complicated prospect."

"What about that bottle?" she asked. "I was able to touch that."

"Of course you were. It's warded. Much like my circle and, I gather, the outer walls. It keeps the screaming madness inside, and you out. Which makes it a physical thing for you."

"Is the staff warded then?" she asked.

"Potentially, but this assumes the staff is still here. The wizard never left without it."

"Where could I look?"

After a long pause, the Empress said, "Mek, can you bring us the master's staff?"

The imp said, "Mek!" and flapped out of the library. After a few moments, the imp returned, wings laboring to keep it aloft while it carried the staff.

Morna reached out and took the staff. It was light in her hands, though she didn't really feel it. Like the outer walls and glass bottle, it resisted her passing through it. She didn't feel wood grain, just a force pushing back against her hands.

But if the staff was still in the castle, Morna wondered what had become of the wizard who had left her to starve. "Mek, where did you find this?"

Mek flapped off, and she followed in its wake. She found she couldn't walk through the walls while holding the staff, so she had to navigate the castle through the actual doors. When she caught up with Mek, the imp sat next to the bottom of a flight of stairs.

She looked around for some obvious sign of why the staff was at this location but found nothing. "Mek, where's your master?"

The imp flew off again and led her to a small courtyard with a midden heap. Mek sat next to it and looked up at her expectantly. At one point, the midden was probably used for whatever food scraps the wizard had left behind. Now it was the place where the boy lay. There wasn't much left after the Empress had gotten hold of him, but what remained was left to compost.

It only took a moment of poking with the staff before an old skull tumbled into sight, part of it crushed inward.

Her own body was in her doorless tower cell, where Mek couldn't get to it. But if the wizard had fallen down the stairs and smashed his brains against the landing, it was another mess for Mek to tidy up.

Morna stared at the skull long into the night. As the eastern sky began to lighten, she turned and headed back inside. She needed to understand the staff.

For several months, the staff brought her peace. But such security was fleeting.

When the spookmongers arrived, Morna was prepared. With some experimentation, she had learned to open and close the hidden doors that could only be accessed with the staff, including the entry into her "doorless" tower cell. She was still unwilling to enter the room where her remains lay, though it pained Mek to have a room the imp couldn't clean. She woke the stone sentinels that used brute force to repel invaders and the enchantments that harmed or repelled mortals.

Under the advice of the Empress, Morna made certain that none of the spookmongers remained in the castle walls. Those who ran in terror from the defenses were allowed to flee. Those who died were dumped outside of the walls in case they themselves came back as ghosts. Morna didn't want to spend her unlife trapped in the castle with someone who had tried to capture and sell her.

She remained vigilant, but she felt safer than she had since before she died. She watched the horizon for new intruders and read the old wizard's books. She wanted to understand what it meant to be a ghost, and how she might move beyond that state, and she studied diligently on the castle walls. In time, she worked her way up to turning the pages of the books with her spectral hands instead of fumbling with the tip of the staff to do so.

And then the wizard returned.

He stood across the blasted heath, flanked by men she recognized as spookmongers she had chased off. His hair was different from when she last saw him, but she knew his face. Even in death, it haunted her.

Morna didn't want to abandon the wall, afraid the wizard would sneak up on her, but she needed advice more. So she fled to the library.

"I believe I suggested he had such a thing." The Empress of Teeth did not look up from her book.

"Can he get in without the staff?" she asked.

The Empress shifted back in the circle and regarded Morna. "Most likely. He created all the enchantments in here. I doubt his plans for immortality would leave him locked out of his own home."

"Do you think the guardians would still attack him?" she asked.

"He's had a few apprentices try to kill him by taking control of the staff, but it seems the more physical threats will not harm their master."

"And I guess Mek is in the same category?"

"Essentially."

214

Morna's shoulders drooped. "Then what can I do?"

The Empress drifted around the circle, a habit Morna recognized as one the Empress used when deep in contemplation.

Morna paced as well, hoping for some sort of insight but hoping even more that the Empress had a better suggestion. The princess poked at the bottle on the work table until Mek flew over and glared at her. "What about the screaming madness?"

The Empress paused. "What? No. It is dangerous to normal humans but easily corralled by the wizard."

The pacing resumed. After a long time, the Empress simply said, "The best I can think of is that the apprentices were inexperienced in using the staff. You have used it for some time now and may be able to outthink the wizard."

This left Morna with little hope, but it was all she had.

In the end, it was hopeless.

When the night rose and she manifested, Morna heard men's voices in the castle. She drifted through the walls and found the wizard speaking with the spookmongers in the library. He held the staff in his hand, and the other men were preparing their ghost-catching boxes.

In the circle, the Empress roiled in anger. Morna was not certain if it was because of the wizard's return or that the Empress's book had been taken away.

One of the spookmongers spotted her and called out, "There she is, lads!"

Morna fled, slipping through the walls as quickly as she could. She tried to think of some place to hide, but in her fear, she couldn't think of anything.

She fled through one of the spookmongers before realizing what she had done. Soon, all she saw were spookmongers. Every wall she passed through put her on a path with another spookmonger with another crank box. She zigged and zagged through the walls, trying to evade them, until finally she was penned in a corner of the castle, which she couldn't pass through.

Pain and nausea overwhelmed her, and soon there was only

darkness. She no longer had a sense of her limbs or her body, her spectral form instead reduced to a small but intense cramped muscle. Straining against her prison, she tried to reach out with what were once her hands and legs. She moved, but not enough to provide any relief from her pain.

The spookmongers laughed and chatted unintelligibly and seemed happy with themselves while she suffered.

For a moment, her prison contracted, and the pain of her existence intensified. Then it relaxed. It contracted again, more forcefully, and then relaxed. She could shift slightly, the boundaries of her existence not as rigid as they once were.

The spookmongers argued in the distance. Voices became more heated.

Morna pushed out again, and something snapped. Wood splintered, and metal banged against metal. One person screamed in pain, while others screamed in terror.

As she reformed her spectral body, she found herself, on the threshold of the main gate the shattered remains of one of the boxes scattered around her. One man, the one who had captured her in the end, lay on the ground and writhed in pain. Pieces of the box pierced his torso, while his hands and face carried huge lacerations.

The others backed away from her, making warding signs against evil.

"She broke the trap," one said. "I ain't never seen a ghost break the trap."

"The wizard tricked us," another said. "This ain't a ghost. You saw those demons he had. She must be another demon. He's having a laugh at us. He said he wanted help with the ghost here, but it was all to torture us."

Morna said, "Yes. I am a demon."

The spookmongers jolted with surprise at the sound of her voice, taking steps away from her.

"And if you linger here," she said, "I am allowed to feed on you."

The spookmongers fled, pausing only to pick up their injured friend. Out across the blasted heath they ran, not looking back.

Morna pushed her hand up against the open air, and felt the wards that kept her in. She assumed they had prevented her from being removed from the castle. It left her wondering what kept her in the box.

The trap lay in broken pieces around her. Most of it was lacquered wood and brass gears. But there were also pieces of crystal and a metal she couldn't identify. She reached down and picked up a piece of it.

It was a jagged shard, with an oily sheen and symbols painted on it. Touching it, she knew this was what she had been inside of. Warded, like the walls and the bottle and the Empress's circle. And under enough strain, it had shattered with great force.

She looked at the metal and then up at the castle. Then she headed in.

The wizard was in the library at the work table, looking at a book and frowning. His staff rested against the shelves behind him. The Empress regarded Morna as she drifted in but said nothing. The wizard did not notice the princess's arrival.

Morna delicately set her metal shard near the door, then slipped out of the room to come back in through the wall behind the wizard. She didn't enter all the way but passed through enough to watch him. When she felt certain he wouldn't look back, she came into the room, picked up the staff, and shot through the door with it.

The wizard grunted in alarm, but by the time he got to his feet, Morna had used the staff to seal the door. Up the stairs she fled, to her old tower cell. She used the staff to open an entrance to the sealed room, slipped inside, and closed it behind her.

She avoided looking at her remains, left the staff against the wall, and flitted back down to the library. When she arrived, the wizard was cursing loudly and feeling along the door with his hands. She slipped over to where she had left her metal shard and picked it up. He turned at the sound of metal scraping on the wooden shelf.

"Hello child," the wizard said. "You've been busy, haven't you?"

Morna's fear pushed back against her anger, and her sorrow got tangled in between. She tightened her grip on the metal, hesitating to strike out at him.

"I might owe you an apology for letting you die. That wasn't part of the plan."

Morna spat back, "You owe me an apology for abducting me in the first place."

The wizard frowned. "That was just a mercantile matter, not

negligence. The supplies needed for my work cost, well, a king's ransom. But braining myself on the stairs and neglecting to manage my possessions—"

Morna's anger pushed past her fear, and she slashed out at the wizard's face with her jagged shard.

He staggered back in disbelief, clutching at his bloodied face. Only then did his expression show that he understood the trouble he faced. The wizard shot a look at the door, widened his eyes, then cast his glance about the room. He scampered away from Morna, snatching up a bag of something from his work table and backing into the corner next to his writing desk. As she drifted closer, he scattered a powder in front of himself.

From the circle, the Empress chuckled.

When Morna reached the wizard, she couldn't cross the line of powder.

The wizard laughed hysterically. "It seems we've reached a dead end, princess. Perhaps we can negotiate a different option than your bloody vengeance? I could create a new body for you. Or steal one. We could give you a fresh new body, a fresh new life."

Morna ignored the wizard. She didn't need his help, she needed her revenge. Kneeling near the powder that formed the wall in front of her, she found she couldn't get her hand near it, but the shard of metal was a different. It proved very simple to scrape the powder away with her crude tool.

The wizard began a droning chant, causing Morna to slide backward as though an invisible wall pushed her away. Desperate, she flung the shard of metal at the wizard and struck his forehead. Blood flowed from the gash, but he maintained his incantation.

She grabbed the bottle of screaming madness on the work table. She felt bad destroying another bottle, but Mek wasn't there to tell her "mek." The barrier halted even the motion of her throw, much like how the trap had been stopped by the castle wards.

But that had also caused the trap to explode.

"I'm sorry for what I'm about to do, screaming madness." She pushed the bottle up against the barrier and continued pushing as hard as she could. Inside the bottle, the invisible wall pressed the yellow smoke into a thick mass at the end of the bottle.

Morna gave up hope that her mad scheme would work, but then there was a crack, and she lost her perception. As she coalesced back into awareness, the wizard stumbled, bloody and wounded, while trying to fend off the yellow miasma that shrieked around him.

She snatched up her metal shard again and charged the wizard, slashing at him and trying to herd him back toward the circle. The madness drifted off to scream elsewhere.

"Do you think me a fool?" he asked, raising his injured hands to protect his face from Morna's attacks. "Do you think I'd be so dumb as to cross over into the summoning circle?"

"I think you're out of options," Morna said. "I am tireless, and you're bleeding a lot. How do you think this is going to end?"

"I won't have my soul devoured by that demon. You may as well strike me down. Just know that this is not the en—"

Morna struck him down.

"Mek!" the tiny imp said as it came into the room. It dithered for a moment, surveying the mess, before it descended upon the broken glass to begin tidying.

"That was exciting," the Empress said. "I can get back to reading now."

Morna had never felt so tired in all her death. "Is that really your biggest concern?"

"I care about you in my own way, Princess," the Empress replied. "Though I will need to wait for Mek to finish tidying up before it will get me another book. I imagine the wizard's soul was snatched back to his hidden artifact, and he'll be back again in a few years."

"Hopefully I won't be here by then," Morna said.

"Have you puzzled out a route past the wards?" the Empress asked.

"They stop spiritual entities. Not people. If I can create a body for myself, I could leave here. And there are presumably all the ingredients I would need in this castle."

"An interesting idea," the Empress said.

"I could make two bodies, if you wanted to come with me. See far off libraries."

The Empress smiled with a million teeth visible.

Frog and Esther Jones are a husband-and-wife writing/editing/publishing team living deep in the rain forests of the Olympic Peninsula. They are primarily known for their running urban fantasy series, The Gift of Grace, and they appear in many anthologies including this one. They can be found online at www.jonestales.com or www.impulsivewalrusbooks.com.

BALANCING THE SCALES

FROG AND ESTHER JONES

Tertia's throat felt dry and scratchy as the cart evacuating her father, mother, two sisters, and all of the Scipiones family's wealth, rattled out of the courtyard. The Gallic barbarians had already overtaken and slaughtered the militia, and they would soon fall upon the city, plundering Rome. According to her father, as the third and least of his children, Tertia must stay and face the barbarians. Tertia thought it unlikely they'd spare one apparently worthless eleven-year-old.

Her eyes burned like coals, full of pain and resentment. Father's clear repudiation of her as he evacuated everything—everyone—else to the Capitoline stung at her like wasps. But her pride wouldn't let her cry. She crouched down where she stood and hid her eyes against her thighs as the wagon creaked away, unwilling to watch her family abandon her.

When she could no longer hear the cart, Tertia opened her eyes. She and the remaining servants stared at each other blankly. Father left no instructions for any of them. One of the servants started looting food and easily carried household items, and the rest followed in a mad rush to flee. There was no way Tertia could halt the thievery and she snatched bread, cheese, and a small jug of water for herself. She fastened her small bundle of spoils around her neck with twine. Then the servants escaped from the house, leaving nothing but a quiet shell that had, minutes ago, been home.

Despite her father's words of impending catastrophe, in the short time that passed, not one invader had yet shown up to tear down walls. Tertia looked around the deserted courtyard she'd known her whole life and felt tears well up. Whether she willed it or no, her breath came in fits and sobs, and Tertia could not stop shaking. Father said she would die today. She took a deep breath, trying to find space in her head to think.

Far in the distance she heard crashing. Then strange chanting mixed with screams fell faintly on her ears. She began to poke about the courtyard, looking for something to do the job properly with; better

221

to die fighting than to meekly accept whatever the barbarians had in store for her.

Tertia found her mother's weaving rod, sturdy and sharply pointed, next to a pile of discarded work, and hefted it experimentally. It only extended her reach a little, but it would have to do. As the crashing and yelling became louder and more distinct, Tertia crept behind one of the tall pantry bins, squeezing herself into the crevice between it and the wall. Acrid smoke began to tinge the air and fill Tertia with dread. She waited, her knuckles white from gripping the weaving rod, as the ruckus grew slowly louder.

A shadow fell across the threshold of the house, snatching her attention away from the gated courtyard entrance. A tall, willowy woman, her short-cropped hair wreathed with laurel leaves, sauntered out from inside the hearth's doorway.

The woman raised her arms above her head, stretching. "Whew, it feels *so* good to be free of all those kill-joys! I thought they would never release their grip on me." Her voice was low-pitched and totally relaxed, at great odds with the dissonant chaos threatening to envelope the courtyard.

Tertia hiccupped in shock, gawking. The embroidered tunic the stranger wore ended at her knees, its edges embellished with grapes and fig leaves. The woman's feet were bare and scarred. She had come out of Tertia's home as if she owned it, but Tertia had never seen her before. The clamor in the distance moved inexorably louder; now Tertia could hear stomping from many feet and the clanking of metal, along with chanting and terrified human or animal screams.

The woman leaned down, eyeing Tertia's hiding spot and weaving rod with a conspiratorial grin. "You may as well come out of there; that hiding place is as weak as a new-born calf," the woman said, still grinning. "It won't fool anyone, least of all those who come after me."

"If you attempt to harm me, I will defend myself," Tertia said, her voice low, thrusting the weaving rod up at the stranger like a sword.

The stranger laughed, a great, booming guffaw. "I do applaud your determination."

The woman's lack of concern would bring the invaders down upon them in minutes if not seconds if she wasn't more careful. "Shhh!" Tertia said, springing forward from her hiding place, attempting to shush the woman's laugh.

Tertia found herself scooped up into a warm embrace instead, the weaving rod deftly twisted out her grip. The woman hefted Tertia up onto one of her shoulders as if Tertia was a much smaller child.

From that vantage, Tertia found herself staring down at laurel leaves nestled in curling dark-brown hair. The woman glanced up at her with a mischievous smile. How could this person be so calm? Tertia wondered.

The air reverberated with the crack of something sundering much too close, and the smoke in the air thickened. Tertia squeezed her eyes shut against the sting of the smoke, and a tear tracked down her cheek.

"Wipe those eyes, Tullia Tertia Scipiones," the woman chided, setting Tertia back on her feet, and straightening Tertia's tunic with an easy twitch of fingers. "Aren't you *so* glad all those obnoxious, unimaginative prudes are gone? 'Be pious!' they said. 'You are a Lar. Stop shaming the family,' they said. Who do they think *established* this family!" The woman snorted a laugh.

Tertia gaped, unable to look away. No one had used her *full* name before. She was always just Tertia. The third, the last. The least.

The woman chucked Tertia under the chin and smiled, appearing to ignore the ever-escalating sounds of destruction, now coming from just outside the courtyard.

"Who are you?" Tertia asked. "Are you one of my ancestors? A Lar?"

"Who am I? Why I'm Scipiones, of course. The first. The original. In fact, this family only exists because of me!" Scipiones chuckled, swinging an arm out to encompass the large Roman villa around them. "Which includes you, of course. Tell me, young Tertia: The world is in front of you. What would you like to do?"

"I want to live." Tertia blurted out immediately. "I want to be reunited with my sisters at the Capitoline and not have any of us be killed."

"Oh, delightful!" Scipiones exclaimed, leaning in with a conspiratorial grin. "You'll need to be *sneaky*. It so happens that particular trait, ah, runs in your blood," Scipiones winked at Tertia, who could only blink in surprise.

"Shall we start with getting to the Capitoline then?" Scipiones continued blithely, appearing unfazed. "Lesson one: People rarely look *up."* She pointed at the villa's ridge line.

Something that sounded similar to distressed metal squealing reached their ears, followed by the thunderous clap of wood breaking.

Scipiones quickly led Tertia to the sheltered wall of the courtyard just behind the cistern, then jumped and grabbed onto the yellow brick, swinging her feet up so her toes were leveraged into the small gaps, and scrabbled up the vertical wall with apparent ease. The goddess then jumped down, showing Tertia how to cling to the small cracks and crevices in the brick. The goddess then guided Tertia up the wall's seemingly sheer surface for the first few feet, until Tertia started to get the hang of it.

Scipiones clung to the brick easily as Tertia labored, then flawlessly transitioned to the upper story of the villa from the top of the courtyard, leading Tertia by example on this trickier ascent. The villa's decorative arches, ledges, and embellishments formed fewer and even more precarious holds, but even so, Tertia persevered.

"Keep your body low, so it's stable, and stay close to the tiles of the roof itself." Scipones instructed as they approached the top of the villa. "It will make you much harder to see from below, as well." With that advice, Scipiones vanished then reappeared, reclining on the roofing tiles—where Tertia would hopefully, eventually, land. Outside the courtyard, the sounds of Rome being breached and looted were becoming deafening, but Tertia could not allow herself to look.

Tertia took a deep breath and slowly, carefully crabbed her way up the rest of the villa's second story, then finally to the roof, refusing to acknowledge whatever happened below.

Once Tertia lay on the roof next to her, Scipiones pointed across the roofs of the patrician district, toward the hill where the Capitoline sat above the rest. "You can use the canopies or archways between structures to transition from one building to the next."

"I don't know if I can do this." Tertia quavered, her muscles burning and exhausted, as she looked across the narrow alley between the next house over. The distance down to the ground made her stomach jump.

"Then you will die," Scipiones pointed out, her tone matter-of-fact.

Tertia's familial villa stood only two stories high, as did the one next to it, but many of the patrician homes were taller than that. Some soared three or even four stories high with pillars under-pinning lower floors, leaving even fewer hand-holds for scaling.

Tertia gritted her teeth, rolling over onto her stomach as she judged the distance to the next house. If she died today, it would not be because she failed to try.

Scipiones nodded in approval. "Now, the trick, young Tertia, is to only allow yourself to be seen when you want to be," she said, "and if you are seen, only let them perceive what you want them to see. A glint of metal, a bird's shadow, the rustle of the wind against the sun. Now, show me you're worthy of my name." With that, Scipiones vanished like smoke buffeted by sudden wind.

Tertia took a moment to center herself and feel the rough brick and tile under her, then launched herself onto the next rooftop, refusing to look at the distant ground. She felt the mud tile slip under her feet, then pitched her body forward to lower her weight once more.

Then she paused and looked back over her shoulder. Mistake.

Her gaze unwillingly riveted on the alien army flooding up the streets of her neighborhood. She knew she absolutely must keep moving, but fear rooted her body. The Gauls looked nothing like any person Tertia had ever seen. Even the shortest of them stood half again her father's height, like a giant of legend. Those behemoths came, breaking down the barred doors on the smaller dwellings, then throwing their contents in the street, simply trampling what they did not want, taking what they did.

One Gaul, who stood taller than the rest, shouted directions, loosely appearing to direct the chaos. His pale shoulders were striped with blood and blue paint, his torso covered in a leather breastplate. Checked and striped fabric peeked out from underneath. His long hair, pulled up into a mane behind his head, was blinding, brilliantly white, like linen that had been bleached by the sun—at least where blood had not dyed it scarlet. Around his neck a golden torque glinted in the early evening light and a massive two-handed, iron sword emanated menace in his hands.

Tertia glanced toward the Capitoline. Gathering her strength, she continued scrabbling and launching herself from rooftop to rooftop, trying to stay ahead of the chaos when she could, waiting until the looters were busy when she could not.

Tertia could not help looking down into the courtyards of the last several very affluent villas that lined the road closest to the Capitoline. Elderly patriarchs from Rome's great houses waited for the barbarians outside their respective domiciles. Just below her and to the left, she could see her father's friend Marius Papirius, and there were more silent statesmen in the courtyards both ahead and behind her. The statesmen she saw had dressed in their ritual best, their long-silvered beards oiled and curled, their cosmetics flawless, ivory staffs held firmly in their weathered and ancient hands. They sat in the carved ivory chairs that overlooked their courtyards and signified their station, but the courtyard gates remained unbarred.

In a whisper Tertia wondered, "Have they been judged too old, too infirm to defend the Capitoline?"

Scipiones suddenly materialized in the courtyard nearest to Tertia, sitting in the lap of elderly Marius Papirius. His gaze stayed fixed straight ahead, not paying the goddess any mind.

Scipiones looked up at Tertia and answered her question, "They look to find favor for their families with the gods by offering their lives as sacrifice. They are old, and wise, and perhaps, some of them may become Lares themselves if their will is strong. Their sacrifice is certainly great enough."

Scipiones kissed the weathered cheek of Papirius above his long, oiled beard and turned back into mist. He did not react; had he not seen the Lar?

Tertia had reached the last mansion before the ascent to the Capitoline. Crouching on that rooftop Tertia considered her options. The thick iron gate into the citadel was only thirty feet away, but the rest of the way was totally out in the open, and it had already been locked and barred. An archway two and a half stories tall spanned the road connecting to the mansions on either side, but nothing connected the archway to the gate.

Behind her, the bulk of the strange warriors had reached the houses of the statesmen. Their footsteps slowed as they stared with awed at the soaring marble mansions. For several minutes, the invading army just milled up and down the street, glancing through the open gates of the mansions, before returning to their fellows as if suspecting trap, instead of continuing their wave of destruction. They stared in seeming confusion at the carved ivory thrones in the elaborate courtyards, at the dignified elderly men who sat unmoving atop them, but they did not attack.

Tertia wondered if the barbarians thought the old men of the city-state looked just as strange, or stranger, than the Gauls did to her, with their blue paint and brilliant-white hair.

One of the Gauls approached Marius Papirius cautiously, walking around his chair of office, inspecting it from all sides. The whole swarming army had come to a hushed stand-still, appearing unsure of what to do with the open courtyards and their silent inhabitants. The barbarians stopped all looting and a strange, tense hush fell. From Tertia's limited vantage point, none of the Roman statesmen appeared to move, sitting in solemn, formal splendor.

Tertia wondered if the alien army had mistaken the elderly men for Lares in their own right.

Just as she was beginning to hope that the whole invading force might turn around and leave the city of their own volition, the invader nearest Papirius reached out, grabbed a handful of the patriarch's long beard and yanked. Hard.

Papirius lashed out with his staff, dealing the Gaul's head an equally hard blow.

The giant roared in anger, unsheathing his sword and drawing it across Papirius' throat in one fluid motion. Blood splattered on the ground of the courtyard like gruesome rain. Tertia squeezed her eyes shut, queasy. The soft sound of blood spattering across brick seemed to wake the whole army from whatever calming influence they had been under. Descending into a fury of carnage, the barbarians butchered the rest of the statesmen in a matter of minutes, bathing the gutters in blood.

Tertia clamped her eyes and mouth shut, fighting against the nausea in her stomach. If she was ill, the smell would eventually lead them to her, even if the sound did not.

The barbarians dispersed amongst the vast mansions, looting them with abandon. Wonton acts of destruction scattered marble and yellow brick in the street alike. Piles of furniture and household goods were put to the match, sending new gouts of flame and plumes of smoke skyward, blocking out much of the late sun's rays. It helped obscure Tertia's hiding place, and she crept out to the large stone arch that spanned the roadway, hopeful she'd find a way to make it the rest of the way to the Capitoline. But her eyes stung with the smoke, making it hard for her to squint down into the ruined streets.

Eventually the commander sauntered under the archway where Tertia hid, surrounded by his cohort of fighters. She breathed slowly through her nose, unwilling to let air pass her lips, lest it somehow alert them to her presence.

Behind the barbarians, the looted wagons carrying all their spoils trundled slowly.

A rain of arrows whistled out of the arrow slits of the citadel, sleeting down over the road and sticking of out of the ground and the Gaul's shields like a particularly lethal hail. A few arrows whistled terrifyingly close to Tertia, but thankfully none struck her. Someone laughed, seeming to find the defense of the citadel comical. Tertia's heart hammered in her throat; the efforts of those in the citadel appeared futile to her.

The wagon creaked to a halt in front of the arch, and Tertia crept forward to get a better vantage point. She found the fighters had gathered at the barred gate to the citadel. The commander stood in front, his army arrayed around him. Glancing about, she noticed the arrows had had no lasting effect on the invaders.

"Open the gate and your deaths shall be quick," the commander called in a heavily-accented voice to those locked inside. Tertia wondered when and where he'd learned their language. "If you do not, we will dismantle your fortress around you, water its stones with your blood, and piss in the dead eyes of your loved ones."

"We will not allow the City of Rome to be conquered by some nameless invader," came the return call.

"I am Brennus, and we shall see who outlasts the other, then. I am willing to bet, be it today, tomorrow, or a month from now, I will still have the advantage. After all, I have the whole city at my disposal, and you do not." The Gaul army spread out, ringing the Capitoline and settling in for a siege.

Scipiones suddenly appeared on the arch next to Tertia, watching the Gauls' preparations with bright eyes.

"You could walk away now, you know," Scipiones said to Tertia. "Your family has abandoned you once. You have no obligation to save

228

them or any of the other Roman patricians."

Tertia looked at Scipiones solemnly. "I know. I could leave; no one would miss me. Perhaps they don't *deserve* to be saved." Her father's cold words and her mother's silence still stabbed at her heart. She closed her eyes and took another deep breath. "Perhaps. But my sisters are there too, and they never did anything to me. The Roman patriarchs did nothing, and yet they died horribly. I cannot leave everyone to die here alone. Not even Father."

"Spoken like a true Scipiones," the Lar said, smiling. "We're going to have to train you as we go. To be successful, you will have to be as imperceptible as the wind. Your father will not know you've changed his fate. None of them will."

"I can live with that," Tertia said.

"So be it. I do *so* love a challenge," Scipiones said. "We can start tonight."

Tertia turned to reply, but the goddess had already vanished.

Tertia woke abruptly, certain she was about to tumble off her precarious perch. Instead she found herself clinging to a very amused-looking Scipiones.

"Are you ready for lesson two?" the goddess asked her, before standing on the archway and stretching. It was as if Scipiones had no concerns. For all Tertia knew, she might the only one able to see the Lar.

Tertia nodded, her stomach twisting with nerves.

"If you control the pieces, you control the game," Scipiones said, looking at Tertia expectantly. Scipiones produced a coin out of thin air and handed it to Tertia.

"Close your fist around the coin," the goddess said. Tertia did so, gripping it tightly.

"That coin is yours now, is it not?" Scipiones asked holding Tertia's hand lightly in hers. "You have it trapped in the palm of your hand, yes?"

"Yes, it's in my hand." Tertia squeezed the coin, feeling it press into her palm.

"Are you certain?" Scipiones asked, nodding significantly toward Tertia's fist.

Tertia opened her hand to find she gripped a smooth stone. Scipiones snapped and the golden coin appeared between the goddess' fingers.

For the next few hours, Scipiones demonstrated it again slower, patiently showing Tertia how to pick up and move the coin while not alerting the person who held it.

"Now," Scipiones said, "We're going to send you down there to play similar tricks. Tiny things at first, larger ones as you improve. The rules are the same as before: go where you will not be seen, move silently like the wind, and always cause as much mischief as possible in your wake."

During the next week, under Scipiones tutelage, Tertia became a haunt of the Roman night, creeping silently through the sleeping Gaul army. One of her first acts dyed the city well an ominous, stinking red using pulverized madder root. None of the Gauls had tried to use it in the days since. They had to trek out to the river for water instead.

Then she'd torched the fields outside the city and started stealing the Gaul's rations. Some she'd kept for her own use. Others she'd trampled into the ground as if a wild animal had roamed the army while they slept. The game the Gauls managed to scrounge was meager, and Tertia took every opportunity to spoil any attempts to preserve it.

As she grew bolder, she started stealing the warriors' personal items. She stole this person's sword, that person's axe, a handy belt-knife, wool blankets, drinking horns, and the list went on. Nothing ever went missing while anyone was looking, but she targeted anything that would be keenly missed soon after the theft. Her stash of stolen items grew and had to be spread out on the forum's roof to avoid detection.

Under Scipones' watchful eye, she grew proficient at climbing and spiriting away large, sometimes sharp, objects that the Gauls needed for the siege. She released horses, emptied purses, and then fouled the Gaul's water, over and over again, with dirt and animal dung, but never when someone might see. Tensions in the camp grew and fights started breaking out at the slightest provocation. Her midnight missions complete, she fell asleep in her eyrie just as the dawn's golden light brought the first squabbling disagreements from the camp below. She felt a brushed kiss on her cheek, and Scipiones whispered, "Well done, young Tertia."

Tertia woke to the Gaul commander yelling through the gate to the citadel. She crawled to the edge of her favorite arch nearest the Capitoline, looking down at the display below.

"I don't know how you keep sneaking men past my guards or if you employ spirits to do your bidding, but your petty tricks will not work. My men grow hungry, but yours starve outright. We walk for our water, but you have none. Only your deaths or a proper ransom will satisfy," Brennus said.

Father's voice, "Ransom? What kind of ransom?"

"One thousand pounds of gold, and we will leave this place and its cursed, pranking, foreign spirits. Take it or die. Either way, we leave today. You decide whether we leave over your corpses or not."

"You will have your ransom," Father said, quickly. The iron door to the citadel slowly groaned open.

"It is done." Brennus confirmed.

Brennus' men produced a giant scale, complete with weights from the depths of his wagon train. They set up the scales in the plaza in front of the forum, between two of the large pillars. The bottom of the scale stood about a foot off the ground until the weights were placed.

A long line of Romans began depositing all their valuables on the scales. But when they had finished, the balance still leaned heavily in the Gaul's favor.

In front of the scales, her father and Brennus argued about the weight of the ransom.

"We have fulfilled the ransom already," father was protesting. "We have provided far more gold than the required amount. The scales are false."

Brennus stared at her father, his face impassive, his eyes lethal. Then the giant Gaul reached for the sword strapped across his back. Father flinched as Brennus drew the sword, clearly convinced the Gaul meant to use it on him.

Instead, Brennus threw his massive sword onto the Gallic side of the scale with a flourish and a hard, mocking smile. The giant, two-handed sword clanged onto his side of the scale, adding a good seventy pounds to the Gaul's counter-weight, growing Rome's debt in a matter of seconds as their side of the scale inched upward. Brennus continued staring at her father in a silent contempt, his gaze unfazed.

"Woe to the vanquished," Brennus said.

Father stared at the Gaul's sword for a moment longer, and then turned, walking off abruptly.

Scipiones appeared next to Tertia, her gaze fixed on the scene below.

"Father is short on gold for the ransom, isn't he?" Tertia asked the goddess. "He's arguing the weights are off because he's already gathered all the gold that Rome has to offer, or so close to it, as makes no difference. Now he must make up the weight somehow or all my efforts will be for naught."

"You have managed much. It's not your fault your father cannot negotiate a workable bargain. You've reduced the Gaul army to a hungry, contentious, rabble that is nearly as big of a danger to itself as it is to Rome," Scipiones said.

"Brennus hungers for gold to make this siege worthwhile, but he's loathe to waste the energy his army has left or test his control of his men in battle," Tertia said slowly. "But he cannot lose face by accepting a lesser amount or appearing weak in front of a vanquished foe."

"I would agree," Scipiones said.

"Then the scales must balance." Tertia said.

Starting from her stash on the roof of the forum, Tertia tied a sack of bronze statues and other odds and ends to her back. She estimated the sack weighed fifty or sixty pounds. It was not enough, but it was a start. She slid a small knife into her belt and wrapped extra rope around her waist.

From her vantage point, Tertia could see the invaders had set a young Gallic guard in the plaza to keep watch on the gold. Using the pillar farthest from him, she crept carefully down, making sure she stayed out of any eye-line.

Once on the ground, as long as she came in from the back, the bulk of the scale should hide her from his sight and from any of the Gauls gathered in front.

Cautiously circling to the front of the pillar, Tertia dove for the senator's podium directly behind the scale, breathing a prayer to Scipiones. She opened her eyes, confirming no one had spotted her.

The plaza guard was sticking to his post like glue. If she tried to tamper with the weights while he stood there, he'd notice. Tertia glanced around and saw her sisters, standing at the edge of the plaza, waiting out of the way of a cart bringing a few more pieces of gold to the scales.

It was risky, but if she could enlist their help… Tertia picked up a pebble, then balanced it in her palm, waiting to throw it until she was *mostly* sure she'd only attract Prima's attention. The pebble hit Prima's shoulder and fell to the ground with a small clack. Tertia winced.

Her sister turned toward her hiding place. Tertia put one of her fingers to her lips and pointed toward the guard in front of the scales. Prima's eyes grew wide and she gripped Secunda's arm, nodding toward Tertia's hiding place. Secunda's mouth opened in a silent "O" before she clapped a hand over it, looking down. Tertia gave a soft sigh of relief and pointed toward the guard once more. *Please understand*, she begged them internally. She used two of her fingers to mimic walking and pointed toward the guard again.

Prima walked toward the young fighter, wringing her hands, "Sir," she said, "My sister's not feeling well. Can you help please?" She batted her eyes at the young guard.

The young man shook his head doubtfully and shrugged. Prima pointed to where Secunda stood with her hand clapped over her mouth. He stepped toward Secunda, peering at her admittedly pale face.

Tertia crept up next to the pile of the gold on the scales, finding her mother's golden trunk, opening it just far enough to retrieve four of her mother's gold body chains and shove her bag of bronze inside. She then wrapped the chains around several of the yellow bricks scattered about, burying the bricks under the gold at the back of the scale, then hurriedly slitting a burlap bag of coins and laying it on top.

She'd just tied another of the smaller bags of gold coins to her belt when Prima signaled her, panicked. Tertia dodged, hiding inside the nearest senator's podium with her contraband seconds before Brennus and her father rounded the corner. A cart loaded with the last of Rome's gold followed in their wake.

She looked back, realizing she'd left the body chains draped on the ground out of her reach. Brennus meant to weigh the ransom, not count it out gold-piece by gold-piece, but she'd still need to remove the bricks from the scale when Brennus unloaded them.

As father turned away from dumping the last of the gold on the scale, Tertia crept out of the senator's podium. She hugged the floor, heart hammering, then silently grabbed the gold chains where they lay.

The scales slowly settled into an unwilling balance. The Gauls looked around at each other, muttering in surprise, and then turned to Brennus for direction.

Brennus signaled for the unloading of the scales to begin, picking up his sword. He stepped away, shouting orders, readying their departure. As the Gallic warriors began rapidly unloading the scales—more than ready to be quit of Rome—Tertia yanked hard on the gold body chains, putting her whole weight into it. The hidden bricks slid off the scale, hitting the ground at the same time the slit burlap sack burst in a raucous shower of coins. Gold cascaded all over the forum floor. Tertia quickly unclasped her gold chains, rolling them up and placing them in her tunic. She waited until the warriors finished picking up the last of the coins, and then slid away to the edge of the plaza, scampering back up a pillar to the safety of the forum's roof.

Scipiones welcomed her there with a beaming smile. "Well done, Tertia. I'm very proud."

Tertia allowed herself a small smile. *Woe to the vanquished*, indeed.

Jeffrey Cook and Katherine Perkins are an Indie Author tag-team that turn weird inspirations into books, especially YA books. Between them, they have 13 novels currently in print, 1 non-fiction book, and numerous short stories in anthologies, with more always on the way. Their latest book together is the YA urban fantasy *You're Not a Real Goth Until You Sack Rome*.

Jeffrey frequently feels like he lives wherever the current sci-fi/fantasy convention is being held. His most frequent stop is Maple Valley, WA, to visit his wife, housemate, and three large dogs. He is a founding member and head organizer of Writerpunk Press. When not working, he has a lifelong interest in role-playing games and watching football.

Katherine, who was born in Lafayette, Louisiana, and will defend its cuisine on any field of honor, currently lives in Ontario, Ohio, with her husband and cat.

Their work can be found at: https://clockworkdragon.net/

REMEMBER TO THANK YOUR HEALER

JEFFREY COOK & KATHERINE PERKINS

In the rough days when life was carved out of chaos, the Golden Maiden, with her sister, came to the vast walls of her divine cousins and knocked with the gilded pommel of her broadsword.

No gate opened, but a voice called, 'What need have we of you?'

'I wish to join my cousins, in luxury and in expertise,' declaimed the Golden Maiden. 'I am mistress of the blade.'

'This we can say that we have.'

'And of saga-telling.'

'This we can say that we have.'

'And of metalcraft.'

'This we can say that we have.'

On and on she listed, from archery to tactics to music, and the voice replied the same.

'But can you say,' asked the Golden Maiden, 'That you have any who so strives in all these things?'

And at last the voice said 'No.'

'Then you shall let me in, and my sister for good measure.'

And they did, for she was a mistress of argument as well.

From the Litany of Gold.

Rota's golden paladin armor shown in the spell-light, and the demons swarmed her. Scaly fingers pried between the panels and pierced skin, but she continued driving the creatures backwards with her shield, keeping the focus on her. One scaly neck was pierced in turn by Hedren's dagger, as the operative from the Guild of Entrymen made every second count. Further back, Tannemyr, the representative from the Collegium Arcanum, was felling more of the creatures with bolts of sorcery. Behind even the sorcerer, Arin, her drab dress the opposite of her temple partner's regalia, knelt quietly off to one side, prepared bandages, and prayed.

When the battle was done, Hedren and Tannemyr were finished collecting demon-heads before Arin was finished dressing all the wounds that had been made under Rota's armor.

"How in the name of every hell known or theorized," Hedren asked, "are we going to get anywhere if you take this long with every nick and cut? And that stuff smells awful." Hedren gestured to Arin's vials of salve as she applied it to Rota's shoulder.

The conversation, such as it was, had become extremely common during the joint operation between the Guild, the Collegium, and the Temple. As usual, Arin stayed focused on her work. She interpreted Hedren's question, at this point, to be as rhetorical as his previous ones, such as 'How much money did the temple waste on gilded armor?' and 'Comfortable hiding back there?' and 'Do the Brass Maiden's priestesses even take vows of chastity, or do they rely on those outfits?' Arin was too busy for rhetorical questions.

The half-armored woman, however, glared at the guild operative. "If she says it's necessary, it's necessary," Rota said.

"We're not getting anywhere," Tannemyr said. "We've barely killed a dozen of the demons. And not because they're all *that* scary. They've gone down to my spells just fine."

"The traps and wards aren't that complex, either," Hedren said.

Arin shook her head, not looking up from Rota's wounds. "Demons. You don't ever know what kind of enchantments they have. The salve is blessed by the Lady of Evercleansing Brass. It will prevent any festering. Even infernal."

"What kind of second-rate priestess of a third-rate goddess needs salves *and* prayer?" Hedren said.

"And if the stuff is so great, why is she getting almost all of it?" Tannemyr said. "Is this a temple thing, or a girl thing, that you always focus on her?"

"She has all the demon-wounds."

"But she's killed what, one…maybe two?"

"Not my job," Rota said.

"Not even our job," Arin said. "We're supposed to deal with the source."

"Which is much easier if all the individuals are dead," Tannemyr said. "You know, as long as they don't have all day to prepare for us.

This entire operation feels like it's dragging a giant heavy anchor."

"With a short, scrawny anchor attached to it," Hedren added. "So much for the vaunted demonsbaney paladins of the Temple of Gold."

"And Brass," Rota said.

"Right. Temple of Gold and Brass. Trust me, some adherents of your religion downplay the runt of the litter," Hedren said.

Rota tensed before Arin put a hand on her less-wounded shoulder. "My Lady's been called worse, and she's proud of her golden sister. Let me help you back into your armor." Rota settled back as Arin set to putting the shoulder piece and arm guards back in place.

"You do that. Then maybe you can catch up," Tannemyr said, starting down the passage. "More of them this way. Let's go, Hedren. No more time for deadweight."

Arin did look at them this time. "That's suicide."

Hedren shook his head. "We haven't had any real trouble so far. As you said yourself, only the golden girl has taken any real demon-wounds, wading into them while you duck. Talk to her about personal safety consciousness. We'll manage."

"You're just going to leave?" Arin looked back to the sorcerer.

"This joint operation needs to be a little less joint and a lot more operating. If you decide you can keep up, maybe we'll cut you in on part of the payday still."

"It's not about the payday. It's about making sure the demonic infestation doesn't settle in," Arin said

"Keep telling yourself that. Or go back and tell your order that some real adventurers handled the demonic infestation for you and collected the bounty on demon skulls too. See how happy they are that the job is done, but the gratitude of towns doesn't flow into the coffers. I know the guild wouldn't like that, so I can't imagine your people would." Hedren followed the sorcerer down the passage, leaving Arin scrambling to re-secure Rota's armor.

Mid-scramble, she paused, glancing down at the golden plate.

Rota looked at her in confusion. "What are you doing? We've got to hurry if we're going to make them see reason."

"They want to face the storm without knowing where the lightning rod is. They won't see reason."

"We've got to try. This mission is important."

"Exactly. I can't ask you to keep protecting them. You're going to get yourself killed like that."

"If need be. That's part of the job," Rota said.

"Yes. And the job might still be deadly, and it's bigger than any two people. We can't grow old banging at a wall that won't open. If we don't have allies, we have to change the plan."

"You know I'll stand with you. What's the idea?"

"The two of them might still be useful."

"So we *do* need to catch up with them?"

Arin shook her head. "We need to take a different approach. And... much as I hate to say it, we're going to need to do it without your armor."

Rota didn't hesitate as she began to remove the next pieces while listening. "No more lightning rod?" she asked.

Arin moved to assist with the removal down to the padded underlayer. "Exactly. We need to move quietly."

Rota raised a brow. "Move more quietly than a guild operative?"

"They'll draw attention off of us. Guildsman or not, you heard him. Bounty on demon skulls."

Rota nodded. "And confident in their ability to kill. While forgetting the first through third laws of demon slaying." As they talked, she dirtied up her shield with mud and blood to hide the shine.

Arin smiled as she finished tucking the armor away, hidden under some of the bodies. She didn't look forward to the cleaning when they came back—if they came back—but it would hopefully keep the eye-catching armor hidden. "Not everyone gets a proper temple education. Just because you learned early that demons always put the cannon fodder near the doors..."

"Then what *do* they teach them at those schools?"

"Backstabbing, of course," Arin said. She started leading the way deeper into the cave. "Shoving a blade into something with its claws in gilded armor is probably in the introductory course, but abandoning colleagues you believe helpless—that's prodigiously advanced study."

Rota snorted. "You'd think sorcerers would learn better."

"You'd think," Arin said. "So...this passage over here looks like it's had more demons come out than go in. Let's go."

After a while they found a nook in the rock, and Arin paused. "Does this seem safe?" she asked.

"I can make it as safe as anywhere's going to be," Rota replied, and she stood guard as Arin sat, took out a small brass mirror and began the divine augury.

Finally, Arin meticulously put the mirror away and rose. "Well," she said. "We haven't headed in the wrong direction yet."

Rota frowned. "That's good. It took you longer than usual, though."

Arin nodded. "That's part of the problem with going the right direction. It takes us closer to the source of the demonic infestation, and further away from my Lady's influence."

Rota nodded, offering Arin a hand up. "But we haven't gone in the wrong direction yet. She's still guiding us."

Arin smiled and rose, clasping the paladin's hand an additional moment. "That's what she does."

It was all too brief a time before the sounds of crackling lightning echoed through the halls. Inhuman screams followed. Rota pulled Arin into another nook to hide as a number of demons, legs longer, scales stonier, rushed past. "Hedren and Tannemyr would have killed quietly where they could. With just the two of them, their attacks are getting bigger and louder as the demons do. I'm hoping the increased numbers of patrols out here heading that way means we're getting close."

"We can hope," Arin said. "And hope also that those two can keep all those patrols occupied a while longer."

Arin hesitated at another scream, mixed with echoes of spellcasting, as she glanced down another hallway.

Rota nudged her. "They made their decision. So did we. We need to stop the incursion while they have the bulk of the attention. Which way?"

Arin led her a little further, with another pause as they ducked out of sight of a patrol.

The next augury took longer still. Rota's guarding proved necessary this time. Thankfully, she was able to silence the two sentries before their alarms rose above the general noises of chaos.

"Tannemyr's pulling out the big spells now. How are we doing?"

"Her voice is faint, but we're close." Arin paused, frowning. "The direction also came with a final warning. We still have a fight ahead of us."

"I would expect no less," Rota said. "I know you don't like fighting, but I'm here."

"You're without your armor. I'm sorry I couldn't think of something better."

Rota smiled. "I have your blessings, and my shield. Stay behind me, and if a fight breaks out, find us a doorway. I'll be fine as long as I can keep them in front of me and keep it down to one or two who can reach me."

Arin smiled. "And you can kill at least one or two of them?"

Rota laughed. "When I've only got one person to look out for, and she knows how to duck, cover, and keep me upright, yes. I can handle a little demon-slaying."

"Good, because there's more demons this way, if I understood my Lady right," Arin said.

"Absolutely perfect. We'll have to collect a few skull-bounties to make up for all those tithes the temple isn't going to get." Rota grinned.

They quieted again, moving through the caverns with regular pauses to duck out of sight. Each time they did so, Arin prayed while Rota checked for signs of patrols.

In the rough days, even divine children could succumb. But the Brass Maiden carried water to keep her younger sister scrubbed free of festering. The Brass Maiden stoked cleansing fires, and her younger sister listened to stories and studied the heat. The Brass Maiden labored, so that her younger sister could train.

"Everyone should have their role. Everyone should do their job," she would tell the little one as they saw the walls from a distance. "But we are out here. And so, you cannot be only mighty, or only radiant, or only keen. You must be everything, for them to admit they need you, for them to let you in."

And when the Golden Maiden was everything, when no wall and no test could keep her out, she brought her sister with her.

"What does she do?" the voices tried to protest.

"She got me here."

From the Copybook of Gold and Brass

Rota peered around a corner, quickly ducking her head back again. "I think we're there, sort of. Down that hallway I can see four sentries around a narrow opening in the wall. They all have some kind of insignias branded into them."

Arin winced. "Have I mentioned that I find it disturbing that some demons indicate promotions with branding?"

"I find a lot of things disturbing about demons. That's one of them."

"Think you can take them?"

"Those four, yes. As long as there's no more inside the chamber. I'll handle the fight. Just make sure it's clear, and get through the door as quick as you can."

"And if there are more?"

"We improvise." Rota said.

"And if they call for help?"

"They will, but the idiots are making plenty of noise. Here's hoping they keep it up for a while longer, and help stays occupied." She took a couple of deep breaths. "That's a lot to hope for."

Arin rested a hand on the big woman's shoulder. "That's why we have faith. We do our jobs, and the Divine Ladies will handle the rest."

Rota nodded and held her sword and shield out. Arin began quietly casting a blessing over both items while Rota talked through the plan. "Time to invoke all you can for me. No use saving anything now. Finishing the mission comes before making it out."

Arin nodded, starting by handing her the second-to-last bottle of water she'd brought from the sacred spring.

"We're going to have to rush them and see if I can drop one, maybe two while we have surprise," Rota said between sips. "Heal what you can, but unless you see more demons inside, get through the passage, and I'll follow and hold the way. Eventually, the other fight will end, and more will show up. I'll buy you time, but you need to figure out the source of the incursion and undo it."

"Which will be trickier without the sorcerer's help, and take a while," Arin said.

"You'll have the time you need. I promise you. Take note of

243

what kind of symbols they've inscribed, and if we hit the worst-case scenario—"

Arin shook her head. "Before the worst-case scenario. We need to prepare for if we're not going to make it. I'm going to Commune with the Mirror as soon as I've looked at everything. I'll focus on the symbols—and on location and vague impressions of numbers—so that the next person who Communes might come in with better information."

"Bring better help, anyway," Rota said. "But yes. It would be a lot harder on anyone else, though. The infestation will have set in." One more deep breath as she readied herself to charge around the corner. "So, it's a good thing we're not going to fail."

"Right," Arin said. "Final blessing?"

Rota nodded, and Arin rose on her tiptoes. "Rota Brandrsdottir," she began the intonation, reaching to touch her fingertips to the paladin's temples. "You are keen." Arin shifted to grab her shoulders. "You are mighty." Her arms then slid for a hug, sincere as well as sacred. "You are radiant."

She stepped back to look her in the eye for the last part of the blessing. "No one should have to be everything..."

Rota, looking intense, then joined her in unison for the sealing-line of the blessing. "...But right now, we'd better try."

They each took a breath. "Very good," Arin said, steeling herself, drawing her own knife and sacred mirror, ready to follow after with more prayers on her lips already.

Rota charged around the corner at full speed. She led with her shield, smashing the nearest of the four guards in the face, sending it staggering into another. She caught a second still off-balance and cut cleanly into its neck with the broadsword. Pale light flashed as the blessing interacted with the demonic flesh, and the body fell. She recovered from the shield smash in time to deflect the first counterattack away, as Arin ducked in behind her.

A glance into the room revealed two very surprised-looking humans—though humans should never have such festering welts across their faces. "Cultists," Arin said, loud enough for Rota to hear, making the word sound like the curse it was. Readying her dagger, she rushed into the room.

Rota backed into the gap in the wall, trusting Arin to handle the cultists while the demons closed in around her. She caught an attack on the shield and counterattacked. This slash wasn't as deadly as her first, but still left a deep gash in the demon's side. The light from the blessing wasn't as strong this time, but it still left the wound smoking even after the blade had passed.

The training of Arin's order was heavy on healing and herbalism, light on combat. The Temple of Gold and Brass did, after all, teach of each to their duty. Still, the folk of the Northlands knew that not every rough day was in the past. And thus, every man, woman, and child of the Temple and its environs trained in basic blade work.

Arin had the cultists by surprise, and neither man showed a lot of combat reflexes, staring at her in shock. She took the opportunity to run at them, stabbing the one nearest to her as he was starting to chant. His words cut off as she gave him a cleaner death than the festering would have provided. The other was still casting, however.

Rota blocked an attack from another demon with her shield and knocked the weapon aside. A counter-strike with her broadsword left a deep gash in the creature's leg. As it stumbled, another attack came in low, and this time Rota couldn't get the shield into the way in time. The dark steel bit into her thigh, the metal feeling like it was heating up as it plunged into flesh and bone. The demon's idiotic grin disappeared when she managed to smash it in the face with the pommel of her sword. The blessing seemed to consider any part of the sword fair game, and the brassy light flared again, leaving the demon staggering away, dropping its weapon to claw at its eyes.

A spell fired from the other cultist's fingers, lances of green light lashing out at Arin. She pulled the dying cultist in close, hoping all of her practice using Rota as a living shield would pay off. The body twitched and shook as the lights struck skin, and the smell of burning flesh filled the room. One of the tendrils of magic grazed Arin's shoulder, drawing a muffled scream before she pushed forward, trying to keep the man's body in front of her a few more moments. She shoved the body into the living cultist, sending him toppling with the body on top of him. The dagger found his throat before he could struggle free, and she rushed to Rota's side.

By the time she got there, Rota had managed to inflict a couple more wounds, but three demons still stood, though one was blind, and all were wounded, one badly. The demons got smarter, one feinting, getting her to lift the shield to defend against the attack, as a second drove a short spear into her side. Rota managed to shift enough to keep the wound from being fatal, but it still left a wicked, bleeding gash in her side.

Arin chanted a rapid healing spell to mitigate the wounds and bleeding, then lifted her brass mirror, chanting another quick word. The spell to call for divine light was a thankfully simple one, but it had the desired effect.

The demons shielded their eyes against the sudden flare. Rota took a head off immediately in the moment of surprise. Her wounded leg held up as she drove her shield into the gut of the non-blind one, silencing it before she followed with a disemboweling cut.

Their luck ran out when the demon who'd been blinded by the pommel smash got some sense of its situation and called out an alarm in some twisted, infernal tongue. Rota silenced it as well a moment later, but the damage was done. "Your wounds—" Arin said.

"Will hold up. Your blessings are at work. There'll be more soon. You need to get to work. I'll hold the door for you. No matter what."

Arin smiled. "I have faith you will." She pronounced a couple of brief words of blessing before returning to inspecting the room, the cultists, and their makeshift altar. Rota quickly bound her leg while she had the chance, then stepped into the passageway to stand guard and buy time once again, waiting for the inevitable.

"Oh, Lady of Ensuring the Lessons Are Done Before Supper," Arin prayed as she looked at everything carved and painted on the walls and floors of the chamber. "Grant us all the wisdom to tell the infernal workings of the misguided dead from their simply very disturbing graffiti."

She lifted the brass mirror but couldn't Commune yet. She moved it slowly over the floor, asking for divine aid in determining any wards and traps. This was just the sort of thing they were hoping the guildsman would do while she and the sorcerer focused on the source, but plans had obviously changed. Two symbols shined brightly in their reflection in the mirror, and she worked to undo those first. Every time she wasn't actively chanting Arin could almost swear she heard more noises outside in the hall. Glances verified that Rota wasn't fighting yet and, indeed, was leaning against the side of the short passage, recovering as best she could, and using her own, much more limited blessings and training as a paladin to tend to her wounds.

As she finished the second symbol, Arin caught the sound that, ultimately, was much worse than imaginary footsteps: silence out in the hallways. No more spell strikes, no more screams. Whether the others had fled or fallen, there was no more distraction, and they were running out of time. A few moments later, a different sort of call echoed from elsewhere in the caverns, and this time she was sure the footsteps she was hearing, lots of them, were real. She got back to work with renewed vigor.

The warded marks seemed to spiral out from the altar. That was certainly the key. Once she reached it safely, she tried to determine what sort of ritual the cultists might have done to begin summoning the demons.

The first clash of metal on metal, followed quickly by a demonic scream that cut off with a strangled sound, came from behind her. She forced herself not to look back as she inspected the signs, remembering the lore studied by those who commemorated the rough days.

"You messed up, and badly," she said to the cultists' bodies, looking up from where rough runes fell in curves on the flat surface. "Flawed circle. Checking your work slows you down, but there's no need to rush to death."

Arin knelt, looking into the mirror. Whether anything else succeeded or failed, she couldn't take the risk of leaving those who tried next to stumble in the dark. Especially since, if this botched rite went unchecked for long, those who tried next would need to be an army, not an adventuring party.

She thought of all that, thought of these madmen who'd tried something too big for them, and given something dire a foothold in this world, something for which all the creatures they'd faced so far were just loyal footmen and hunting hounds—something that would make its full entrance soon. She thought of everything she'd seen, everything to hope the next priestess to Commune would know. But it was hard to feel confident that the mirror could take it all in, could connect, when even the air felt sick.

"Faith," she told herself in a quiet breath, before moving on to the objective.

Arin laid one hand on the altar—then hissed and drew it back, feeling the deviant magic radiating. Gritting her teeth, she laid her hand on it again and held up the brass mirror.

"Lady, I ask of you," she prayed. "Look upon this place, upon this wound in the world. I ask your aid and your guidance and call upon the first lesson of the Copybook: that the truly strong acknowledge times of need…as the Golden Child needed succor…as the Gods of the Walls needed the Lady of All Things…as I need your help now."

Another scream almost broke her concentration. This one wasn't demonic. She felt the urge to rush back to the doorway, to respond to the need for healing. They'd done this dozens of times before, Rota Brandrsdottir, the 'Great Wall of the North', standing before her in that distractingly shiny armor designed to draw enemy attention to her, with the shield and sword, and the fierce grin. Always knowing Arin Jardarsdottir would be right there, closing her wounds, blessing her next strike, and guiding their mission. Arin couldn't help thinking that Rota looked so much smaller without her armor. She even seemed to take up less of a doorway. Arin had taken that from her, to buy them time and get them here. The work came first.

And now Rota was buying her time, not for her next healing spell, but to save them both. To save everything. Now that it was necessary again, even without her shiny armor, Rota was fighting defensively, making the enemy focus on her, while Arin, in her drab dress, worked in the back.

Arin calmed herself and resumed praying as she got out the last bottle from the spring water. "Evercleansing Lady guide my hand…" After the long contact with the top of the altar, her fingers felt almost nerveless, but she managed to open the bottle and pour it out onto the altar. It seemed to bubble, then cleared as she forced her fingers to grip her knife again. "…as I draw out the poison."

She began to scratch slowly into the surface of the stone. The ragged infernal circle had indeed poisoned the world. No force could stop the worst it would bring in. She had to mend the wound.

Which meant she had to keep standing even amidst the power of this abomination. "Lady of Labor," she prayed, the old rituals coming to her as she continued to acknowledge the need. "Grant strength for the dependable." All the times she had depended on Rota to hold off the enemy, she'd never been let down. And now, among so many unwitting others, Rota was depending on her. She had to save them all.

Half-rendered runes of control were lengthened into precise runes of cleansing. Scrawled symbols of blood were transformed, with focused grinding, into antidote symbols.

She drowned out more sounds of screams and battle, but when Rota spoke, she heard the words clearly. "The ones with minds are scared of something! Keep going. I'll hold...I promise you, I'll hold!"

Arin believed her. She had to believe her and go on.

Grey mist began to seep from the rune of power in the stone as, scrape by scrape, she softened it into the rune of healing. With her free hand, Arin pulled her scarf to cover her mouth and nose, and kept at it, scratching steadily. She couldn't be sloppy. She had to do it right.

Which soon meant needing that free hand to grasp her own wrist to stop it from shaking.

Out in the cavern the noise level rose, demons howling and snarling. A brief glance revealed more of the marked demons coming to join the fray. One, heavily marked across blood-red scales, managed to push past Rota before she got her footing and drove him back into the hallway, leading with her shield. Two freshly harvested skulls on his belt, standing out amidst older but equally grisly trophies, told Arin just where—whom—they'd come from. And now the host was coming to collect two more.

"Do it!" Rota called, a mass of blood and cuts, still in stance, still holding the passage with shield and blade.

As soon as the last rune was changed, trembling fingers dropped the knife and went for her salve, with its blessing and its bane against poison. "Lady of the One Last Thing, see me now, hear me now, and bless this place, that it may know relief."

Her vision was obscured as black smoke poured from the altar and into the room, then the cavern beyond. She dropped to the floor, struggling to breathe. As it began to dissipate, she heard mostly silence. No more roars, no more clash of steel. Only herself, scratching for hand and footholds to drag herself along the floor, her shoulder and hand aching, and raspy breathing at the doorway.

"The demons?" she asked, before her words faded into a healing chant, down to the last of her rituals, thankful her hand was still coated in some of her salve, hoping that wasn't somehow tainted with contact with the altar.

Rota's breathing eased. "Eighteenth rule, weak connection. Some demons who haven't been here long will be banished if you sever the connection. Unfortunate."

Arin checked the level of the smoke, and helped the paladin sit against the passage wall. She used the last of her salve and last of her healing blessings alike—but was feeling more certain Rota would make it. "How is that unfortunate?"

Rota Brandrsdottir grinned with bloodied teeth. "They dissipated. Look at all of these demon skull bounties we're not going to collect on."

Arin decided to take the dark humor as a good sign and set to binding the numerous wounds. "I suspect people will take you at your word when you tell them how many you killed."

"Oh, that's not the story I want to tell," Rota said, wincing only a little as the worst of her remaining wounds were bound.

Arin gave her a quizzical look, tearing at a little more fabric to fashion bandages as she ran out of her own supply. "You made the Lady to Whom Champions Bow proud today. You should tell the story. You're good at those, too."

"And you made the Lady of Small Feasts proud. To be sure, I do have a story to tell when we get back."

"As well you should. We did great things today."

Rota's playful, bloodied grin remained. "I killed, what, one or two demons, and held the door? No. You did the real work today, destroyed all those demons and stopped the incursion. I just got you here."

OTHER BOOKS FROM CLOCKWORK DRAGON

ANTHOLOGIES

In Unnatural Dragons, four authors present science fiction stories about dragons because fantasy would've been too easy. Rescue the blueprint. Travel to alien worlds. Discover the universe within. Soar over the remnants of humanity.

Writerpunk Press presents Merely This and Nothing More, one of a collection of award-winning anthologies featuring 'punked adaptions of classic works. All profits support PAWS Animal Rescue in Lynnwood, WA.

SPIRIT KNIGHTS

Portland has a ghost problem, and it's up to Claire to solve it. Whether she wants to or not. This young adult urban fantasy searches for family in all the strangest places and faces grief head-on. Comes complete with a sarcastic horse and adorable dragons.

A completed five book series by Lee French, available on all major book platforms

Girls Can't Be Knights
Backyard Dragons
Ethereal Entanglements
Ghost Is the New Normal
Boys Can't Be Witches

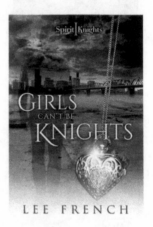

Coming soon, a new novel that takes place after the Spirit Knights series: War of the Rose Covens.

THE FAIR FOLK CHRONICLES

Adventure in a faerie-drenched alternate version of Seattle with a real faerie princess. Unfortunately for Megan, she's the Unseelie kind. A complete four book series, this young adult urban fantasy features real world mythology and folklore from Celtic and Hawaiian traditions.

A completed four book series by Jeffrey Cook & Katherine Perkins, available on Amazon.

Foul Is Fair
Street Fair
A Fair Fight
All's Fair

Also available, a new novel set in the same world as the Fair Folk Chronicles: You're Not a Real Goth Until You Sack Rome.

CLOCKWORK ENTERPRISES

Feisty teenage thief Maeko and her maybe-more-than-friend Chaff have scraped out an existence in Victorian London's gritty streets, but after a near-disastrous heist leads her to a mysterious clockwork cat and two dead bodies, she's thrust into a murder mystery that may cost her everything she holds dear.

A completed young adult steampunk trilogy by Nikki McCormack, available on all major book platforms.

The Girl and the Clockwork Cat
The Girl and the Clockwork Conspiracy
The Girl and the Clockwork Crossfire

MAD SCIENCE INSTITUTE

Sophia "Soap" Lazarcheck is a girl genius with a knack for making robots—and for making robots explode. After her talents earn her admission into a secretive university institute, she is swiftly drawn into a conspiracy more than a century in the making.

A completed young adult teslapunk trilogy by Sechin Tower, available on all major book platforms.

Mad Science Institute
The Non-Zombie Apocalypse
Ghost Storm

Clockwork Dragon offers many more titles, both young adult and grownup. Visit us at www.clockworkdragon.net for a full listing of all our books.

If you enjoyed this volume, please leave a review wherever you purchase your books.

CPSIA information can be obtained
at www.ICGtesting.com
Printed in the USA
BVHW071215050421
604207BV00007B/629

9 781944 334260